Echoes Down the Line

David J. Boulton

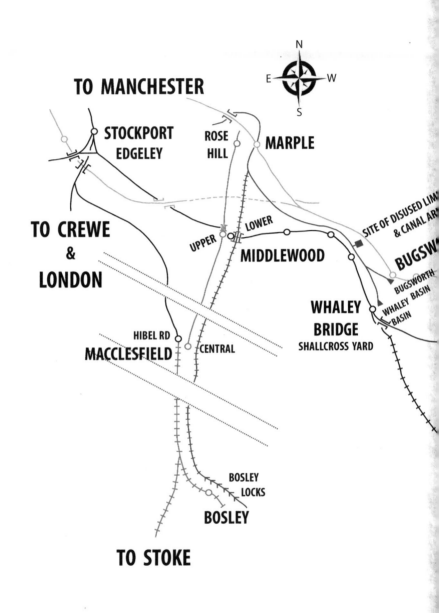

TO MANCHESTER

N
E ✦ W
S

STOCKPORT
EDGELEY

ROSE
HILL

MARPLE

TO CREWE
&
LONDON

UPPER

LOWER

MIDDLEWOOD

SITE OF DISUSED LIM
& CANAL AR

BUGSW

BUGSWORTH
BASIN

WHALEY
BASIN

WHALEY
BRIDGE
SHALLCROSS YARD

HIBEL RD
MACCLESFIELD

CENTRAL

BOSLEY
LOCKS

BOSLEY

TO STOKE

The Principal
Towns, Canals and Railways
in the
White Peak of Derbyshire
and adjoining parts of NE
Cheshire

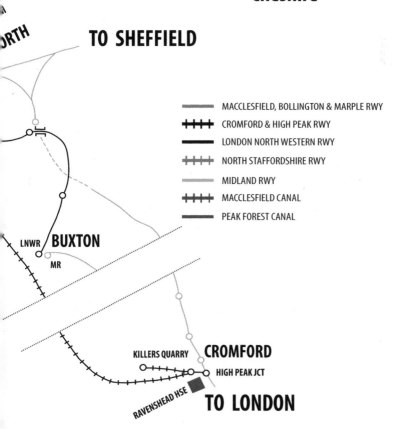

TO SHEFFIELD

	MACCLESFIELD, BOLLINGTON & MARPLE RWY
	CROMFORD & HIGH PEAK RWY
	LONDON NORTH WESTERN RWY
	NORTH STAFFORDSHIRE RWY
	MIDLAND RWY
	MACCLESFIELD CANAL
	PEAK FOREST CANAL

LNWR **BUXTON**

MR

KILLERS QUARRY **CROMFORD**

HIGH PEAK JCT

RAVENSHEAD HSE

TO LONDON

KILN

RTH

A

Published by

MELROSE BOOKS

An Imprint of Melrose Press Limited
St Thomas Place, Ely
Cambridgeshire
CB7 4GG, UK
www.melrosebooks.co.uk

FIRST EDITION

Cover by Hannah Belcher

ISBN   **978-1-912026-53-1**
epub   **978-1-912026-54-8**
Mobi   **978-1-912026-55-5**

Printed and bound in Great Britain by:
Airdrie Print Services Ltd
24-26 Flowerhill Street
Airdrie, North Lanarkshire
Scotland, ML6 6BH

Contents

PART 3

Part 1

Chapter 1

County Waterford, Autumn, 1846

Crack! Crack! Two pistol shots rent the early morning air. And things had gone so well until the horsemen arrived.

—•◦•◦•—

Peat was propped against the wall of the hovel and some of it had been taken inside to feed a smoky fire, the effects of which could be seen in the streaming, reddened eyes of its occupants and heard in the persistent coughing of pretty well every member of the family who lived there. Not that they noticed these small discomforts. It was, after all, the reality of daily life for all of them.

What dominated the thoughts of the more able-bodied present was the lack of food. The oldest and the youngest were past even that, and had sunk into a listlessness that was next to oblivion.

"The pair o' yous ready then?" A voice called from outside and two men – father and son – got up, nodding to each other and went out.

"Right you are, my boy. Where're the others?" Outside, the peat smoke was exchanged for mist; cold and clammy, but suiting their purpose, and not so provoking to the lungs.

"Just along the end of the village – 'cept Aidan, he's keeping an eye on things at the farm." The three of them walked the muddy track that served the little huddle of thatched cottages.

It was early, before first light, and they came upon the

remainder of the group suddenly. Some were equipped with shovels, and nervousness was in the air despite the silence they all maintained. With no leader, the plan, such as it was, had arisen as a distillation of the desperate men's discussions over the past days, of starvation. No-one could remember who had drawn the various suggestions together and voiced them as a coherent whole.

"So, this is it, fellas. We get one of us to keep watch at the farm for when they leave. He legs it across the fields as soon as they're off. We wait under the bridge. The fella up top gets there an' hides. When the last cart's passin', he hoots an' we all rush out an' grab the nags and tip some sacks off the back o' the cart, an' run."

There had been no dissent, no talk of how it might go wrong; not even a careful reconnaissance of the field of battle.

"We all know the bridge, don't we, fellas?"

The first problem emerged as they clambered down the steep bank by the abutment, one at a time. No-one mentioned the difficulty of creating a surprise attack with men emerging in single file. Apart from occasional coughs and a muttered curse as someone slipped into the stream, there was silence.

There was no need for the carters to speak to the paired heavy horses, straining at the traces; they knew the road well enough. The only sound to be heard was the low rumble of slowly turning cart wheels and the clanking of hooves hitting the odd stone projecting from the muddy track. It was this noise which travelled best in the still air of dawn, and it alerted the men under the bridge that the waiting was nearly over. Moments later, the first of the train rumbled over the bridge, the echo below almost unbearable. One young blood had to be forcibly restrained from starting up the bank and upsetting the plan.

"How many's that then?" The whispered question was stifled by a hand quickly clamped over the speaker's mouth. The echoing rumble was coming in waves. No-one knew how many carts there'd be. That was why Aidan was hidden up top ready to signal. Finally, as horses could be heard just setting foot on the bridge, a couple of hoots launched the attack. Given the plan's defects, it all went well to start with.

The two brothers were first up and made it to the horse's heads before they were noticed. "Whoa there, that's it, there now, just yous stand awhile."

Their father was next, jumping onto the footboard to silence the carter. This went badly, and the man fought back, shouting and cursing. Dawn was just breaking but, despite the grey light in the eastern sky ahead, it was still dark. "You bastard you, just stay quiet for a short while."

By now, men were at the back of the cart and having difficulty dropping the tailboard, swearing the while. Finally, it swung free and the first sack of grain dropped onto the track. Their cheers all but drowned out the sound of approaching horsemen, but nothing could mask the gunshot, no, two gunshots, that brought an end to the ambush.

The defence was as inexperienced as the attack. Firing a pistol from horseback was always going to be wildly optimistic. To drop the reins and fire one from each hand at the two struggling figures on the footboard, silhouetted against the weak light of dawn, was madness. They were the only loaded weapons held by the escort, and a determined counterattack might have saved the day for the men on foot. But it was not to be.

"It's th' owd fella, he's down." By some miracle, or mischance, one of the shots had taken their father in the chest, and he fell off the footboard to the track. The other shot had also found a target and the carter, too, was down. He lay wounded where he fell, still on the cart.

At the back, by the tailboard, there was confusion as men ran off the track to get away. In so doing, they startled the two escorts' horses and almost unseated the gunman who was trying to gather up his reins. With the horses under control again, the two riders went forward in single file, taking the cart on the near side; it had come to a stop too close to a low wall on the offside for them to pass. It was in that direction that the stricken attacker had fallen.

"Come on then, let's get th' owd fella out 'o sight." The two brothers dragged their father back down the bank and hoped.

Meanwhile, the two horsemen reached the heads of the heavy horses and one each side, leant over to grab a bridle and urge them to move the laden wagon.

"Gee up, hupp, hupp, get on wi' you, yer lazy nags." Getting the grain to England had to take precedence over an injured carter and retribution for an impertinent rabble.

As the wagon moved off eastward toward the dawn and Waterford, the two brothers took stock. The offloaded sack, lying on the track, was almost irresistible, but they knew their duty.

"We'll have ter get him to the priest. He can't die like this." The sack of grain lay where it had dropped as the two young men dragged and carried their dying father to the nearest church.

The poor community it served looked to it for its sense of self, and the priest for its salvation. He was as poor as his flock, and as they starved he, too, went hungry. He was powerless as he watched grain being shipped out of a starving Ireland against the backdrop of a second year's failure of the potatoes, and mass evictions for rent arrears. In a land where another version of his faith held sway over the ruling minority, he walked a tightrope every day, and on this particular morning his sense of balance was impaired.

The previous evening, he had imbibed rather too much of something that had been slipped through the side curtain of the confessional by a sinner seeking absolution for a misdemeanour involving his neighbour's chicken; or was it his wife? The priest couldn't quite remember.

"Oh God, my head hurts, and the floor's still moving, and I need a drink. And what's that bloody noise?" The priest had a hangover, though none of his parishioners would say such a thing.

"Father's a bit jaded today," was the closest they would get.

The 'bloody noise' that so troubled him was the sound of two young men hammering on his door. When he opened it, his troubles only increased. There they stood, one with a dying man on his shoulder, demanding he give the last rights.

"You've got to do it, Father. He can't die without; he won't go to heaven else."

When 'th' owd fella' had fallen, his coat was open and blood oozed into his shirt. Close to death, there was less bleeding. And more out of propriety than deception, one of his sons pulled the jacket across the red stain as he laid his father on the floor. The priest, in his blurry state, failed to recognise that his parishioner was dying by violence. Had he done so, he might have taken a more precautionary view of the situation.

"*Intróeat, Dómine Jesu Christe, domum hanc sub nostræ humilitátis ingréssu,*" Father Sheehy launched into extreme unction. He mumbled his way through the sacrament, and after what seemed like the eternity to which the body was destined, finally arrived at "*prosperitáte, restítuas. Per Christum Dóminum nostrum*".

Having done his sacramental duty, he retired to his den without a backward glance.

"Amen." The response was automatic. "Thank you, Father, you've made it right for him." The words were spoken as the two brothers headed for the presbytery door. They could do no more here.

"Come on now, there'll be trouble soon enough, an' there's nothing to be done for th' owd fella." Indeed, by the time the two of them were outside, their father was dead. "If we're goin' to do it, we've only one chance and it's now – before they get to Waterford and send the sojers." It was the elder brother who spoke.

With adrenaline still coursing through their veins, the two of them had resolved to set fire to the big house. As before, there was no planning. Perhaps more understandable in the case of this improvised act of revenge, it was anger and resentment drove them forward.

The ancestral home of Lord Sladen was not familiar to the peasants living on his estates. Rents were received by his agent from the hand of a collector, who in turn would employ bully boys to demand the money from the often fractious tenants. Commission would be due, or at least purloined at every stopping off point as it made its way upward to the noble landowner. The Anglo-Irish peer was never seen by the locals and, in truth, he and his family spent little time at the big house, preferring their estate in England and the attractions of London. Nevertheless he gave his name to it and it was universally known, amongst the peasantry at least, as the Sladen place.

"Yous know the best way in?" asked the younger of the two. It was nearing mid-morning by the time they had found their way through the woods and the Sladen place brought into view. The futility of their intention was exposed. Gardeners were to be seen clearing leaves from the vast lawns, and as they moved through the trees to get a view of the tradesman's entrance, servants could be seen making sporadic forays to the outside world.

"Tis no good, we'll never get near enough without being seen." On the verge of defeat, they turned to go, only to see a clearing in the woods in which stood a summer house. In spirit if not in style, it owed something to the late Marie Antoinette. It was large, sported an ornate veranda and best of all, given the objective of the two men, it was made of wood. Furthermore, stacked outside were the makings of a fire in case alfresco evenings were found to be chilly.

"Come on, my boy, the luck is wid us after all." They stacked firewood against the outside walls and, almost by accident, found an unlocked door.

"Let's get somethin' going inside as well." The structure was octagonal, with the roof rising to a central peak supported by a heavy timber from floor to apex. "Would you just look at that? It's perfect."

With firewood taken in and placed around the pillar, the stage was set. Out in the woods, they were oblivious to a commotion back at the main house. The eldest had the honour of setting light inside the building; he was in any case acknowledged as the most competent firelighter in the family, and flames were soon licking hungrily around the small pile.

As they turned and headed for the door, the younger of the two saw a picture hanging on the wall. 'They were owed, weren't they? Th' owd fella was dead, wasn't he? It was the gentry as did it, so they should pay.' He lifted it from the wall as he passed by, quite blind to the danger of being found with it, should he be caught. The door was in the rear of the building, facing the woods. The mounted militia men now milling around the main house escaped their notice.

Inside, the fire was going well, and as the stack outside caught, smoke began to billow up into the surrounding trees. Standing back, admiring their handiwork, the two arsonists finally realised their danger. The smoke, and by now flames, out toward the woodland, had gained the soldiers' attention. At last they had a quarry that suited them; men running through the woods would make for good sport. There was nothing to compare with a manhunt to raise the spirits.

As the cavalry advanced across manicured lawns, the fugitives disappeared deeper into the trees. The result would have been a foregone conclusion had the pursuers been well-led regulars, but as it was, the best that could be mustered were ill-trained militia men. They were commanded by an arrogant amateur who'd learnt nothing from his occasional forays with the hunt, nor had he paid any attention to the drills and stratagems practised by his troop.

As the two brothers tried and failed to retrace their steps, the elder jumped off a bank only to find himself knee-deep in boggy ground. Unable to move his legs, he pitched forward and started to sink. The troopers could be heard nearby, but instead of spreading out to cover the ground, they were proceeding in single file and completely missed the man in the bog – by now almost completely submerged and in danger of drowning. Still on dry ground, the other escapee leapt into an old ash tree, with branches thick enough to make him invisible from below. Stubbornly, he kept hold of the picture; symbol of their defiance.

Chapter 2

Whaley Bridge, Summer, 1876

The old man was dying. He knew it, and those around him knew it. Even his son knew it although he was finding it difficult to accept, so he continued to act as if his father would recover.

"Is that you, son?" The sound of the back door latch had wakened the dozing invalid.

"Aye, it's me, Father." Stephen Thomas had just finished his turn as a railway guard and was home from Shallcross yard. "Just come to see how y'are. Better, I hope?"

Patrick Thomas had spent his day, or the waking parts of it, rehearsing this moment. If he didn't speak up soon, it would be too late.

"Stephen, come and sit by me. It's time we had a talk." The younger man was reluctant, thinking he would be forced to confront the unpalatable truth he'd so far avoided.

"Now listen, son, there's some things you should know before I die. Your mother forbade me talking of it, but she's dead and gone, God rest her soul, and I must speak out."

Unaccountably, a sense of relief crept over Stephen. He'd grown up in a loving, close-knit family, but always there had been this big secret, never alluded to but ever present. So far as he was concerned, his father's life had started the day Stephen was born. He had relatives galore from his late mother's side of the family, but from his father's side? No-one.

"The first thing, son, is your name; my name, too. I'm not Patrick Thomas, I'm Patrick Thomas Lynch, and by rights, you should be Stephen Lynch." The old man paused, whether for effect or to catch his breath wasn't entirely clear. "Ye see, I'm from Waterford, and it all started like this." Patrick had acquired over the years the accent and argot of the Peak District. His family found it entirely authentic, but to outsiders there had always been an indefinable burr. As he told his story, the legacy of his youth began to emerge and his speech, even to his son, betrayed its origins.

"It was the last time I saw Eamon. I fished him out the bog and we went off opposite to the sojers. We couldn't go home, with the man on the cart probably dead and the militia out, we were goin' to get blamed whatever; an' we'd begun to think Aidan must have betrayed us, else why the men wi' the guns?"

Patrick, who had become quite animated about the ambush, was suddenly rather hesitant. The thought of betrayal by one of their own grieved him. Then doubtfully, "There'd been trouble at Dungarvan not long before. I suppose that might have been it." He brightened.

"I set off for Waterford to try an' get t' England. Eamon went off t' his wife an' kiddie to get them from her ma's, an' then he was off to Canada. Never seen him since.

"I made it to Liverpool, but that weren't no good. Irishmen everywhere, wi' no work an' the locals all against us, so I set off walkin' towards the rising sun, eastward. I didn't know where I was goin', but t'other way was into the sea. I'd not heard of Manchester, not until I was on the road anyway, but in the end, I missed it and ended up in Stockport."

Stephen could see his father was tiring, but the old man was clutching something to his chest which was clearly important and hadn't yet been mentioned.

"Are y'all right, Father?" Patrick nodded, but there was a pause whilst the old man regained his strength. "Would you like me to come back later when you're rested?" His son was desperate to hear the rest of the story and was relieved that his offer was refused.

"No, son. No, don't go. If I don't tell y' now, it'll be too late." Another pause, then a heroic effort. "I managed to get by wi' labouring jobs. The work was no worse than back home." Home was said with a catch in his voice. Stephen wondered how long it had been since his father had voiced the word 'home' in connection with Ireland. "But I was lonely. My only comfort was the church. I'd no idea what it all meant, but I was used to it and it eased the sorrow; and then I met your mother there." Now tears filled the old man's eyes. After a while, "She was a wonderful woman, was your mother; she was the making of me." Talk of his wife seemed, once the tears were over, to give him renewed energy.

"Her pa didn't think much of me – well, he wouldn't, would he? What with me being a poor Irish labourer. But Catherine wouldn't give up, and in the end he agreed an' we got married." Stephen remembered his grandparents with affection. Whatever they thought about his father, it didn't stop them loving their grandson.

"The best present your grandfather ever gave me was getting me a job labouring on the line out here from Stockport. 'Twas hard work, building it, but you, me, and your mam were able to get out of the town, and that was a relief. There'd been a heap o' trouble just before, and they nearly brought down our church in Chapel Street."

Stephen couldn't keep his eyes from straying toward the package in his father's hand.

"We're getting there, son, just be patient. The one thing, the only thing, your mother insisted on was that nothing was ever said about the past: my past, that is. I changed my name when we were wed, and nothing more was ever mentioned.

It hurt, but in the end I could see it was for the best. With her family around me, I got no trouble, and in the end I became a Derbyshire man. I only defied her in one particular." The wrapping was coming off, and a picture emerged. "I kept this."

Stephen found himself looking at an imposing country house, with lawns in the foreground and a small family group as the centrepiece. "She never knew, but it mattered to me." The infirm old man sat up with head held high, and for a moment looked defiant, as he had once been. "It was the only time I got anything from the thieving swine and it made me feel…" he searched for words, "feel like a real man." He sank back exhausted onto his pillows. "'Tis the picture I took from the garden house before we burnt it down."

———•••———

Stephen didn't want his father dead; far from it. He loved the old man, but now he had to face the passing, he found it easier to bear than he'd imagined. He hugged the death bed revelations of Patrick's early life to himself like a comforter, and found his heart lighter for them.

Father Murphy was perplexed by the ease of spirit displayed by the nearest living relative of the deceased. Grieving families were part and parcel of his ministry, and they usually seemed singularly unimpressed by his assertion that leaving this life delivered their loved ones into the infinitely superior existence to be found in the hereafter. Stephen, in contrast, bore his loss with fortitude, or so it seemed to the priest, who was glad of it. Making the arrangements was less fraught, not least because Patrick Thomas had left sufficient to fund a respectable funeral. True, he hadn't seen Mary Thomas, Stephen's younger sister, yet. She was in service over near Cromford and could not be spared until the day of the funeral, but a sixteen-year-old girl hardly counted in the grand order of things.

With no Catholic Church in Whaley Bridge, Father Murphy tended his flock from a church in St Mary's Road, New Mills. The two-and-a-half miles between the two places was a regular Sunday walk for the Whaley contingent, and the coffin would be pushed on a handcart from Stephen's front parlour on the day of the funeral. With quite a few communicants in the town, there would be plenty of willing hands to help it along its way.

They were a mixed bunch, the Whaley congregation, with Italian, Irish, and home-grown adherents drawn together by their minority status, but unlike some bigger towns there was no animosity between the faiths. Indeed, so well liked was Patrick Thomas that many from other churches were intending to make the trip to New Mills and then back for the wake. Catholicism may have been reviled by the Protestant majority, but its adherents certainly knew how to give a body a rousing send-off.

So it was, on a fine Saturday afternoon in the middle of July, thirty or so sombrely dressed citizens, along with the body of the late Patrick Thomas in a coffin on a handcart, walked to the Church of the Annuncion to give their friend, neighbour, and relative a dignified send-off. They arrived to find a crowd from New Mills assembling, and in the end the mourners amounted to upward of a hundred people. Many knew each other, fleetingly perhaps, from regular Sunday attendances, but with members of other faiths swelling the numbers, there were strangers in the crowd. Those from Whaley were best placed in this respect, as most of the outsiders were from there, but even so, as Fred Maida looked round, there were one or two faces he didn't recognise

"Who you think that is?" Fred asked his wife. "I not see

him before." The subject of his enquiry was pale and drawn with a shock of black hair, in his early thirties. "He look like I should know him, but I don't." He hadn't run to a black suit, but his dark grey jacket sported a black armband. "You see him before, Elsie?" Too late, the man disappeared into the crowd and his wife couldn't be sure.

As the congregation filed into the church, the chatter subsided to hushed undertones. Some sat in silence, contemplating the spirit of Patrick Thomas winging its way to its just deserts in the afterlife. Others, unfamiliar with the rituals of the Romish Church, wondered what was coming next.

Father Murphy, having exhausted his Latin for the moment, spoke generously and at length on the subject of the deceased's life and virtues, commencing in 1850 when Patrick had married Catherine. Stephen wondered if his father had confided anything of his earlier life to the priest, perhaps in the confessional, but as the eulogy proceeded, he realised that his father had seen no sin in his escapade in Ireland. What he'd done was only an attempt to right the wrongs visited on his community, and bring down justified retribution on the perpetrators. No, there would have been no sins to confess.

"Patrick Thomas was a loving and dutiful husband, and the best father anyone could wish for myself and my sister Mary." Stephen was on his feet now, trying to find some space between Father Murphy's words to insert some of his own. Mary had arrived in New Mills on a train from Cromford that morning. Her brother had hardly had time to speak to her, but as they sat together he could see how upset she was by their father's death. He told himself that if he was doing this for anyone, it was for her.

"He worked hard all his life to give us all the best he could." Their mother had died young, leaving Patrick with five-year-old

Mary and thirteen-year-old Stephen, who had done his best to mother and protect his little sister.

"When our mother died, he kept a home for us children, and we wanted for nothing." Despite himself, Stephen was beginning to enjoy the speechifying. He could see why Father Murphy's sermons were so long. The old humbug enjoyed terrifying his congregation with hellfire and damnation. The priest, with the Holy Book to draw on, had more raw material than Stephen, who soon exhausted his reserve of rhetoric.

"We all loved him very much. Goodbye, Father." Stephen sat down and found his hand in his sister's.

———————

The coffin left the church on the shoulders of half a dozen burly railwaymen, followed by the priest and servers enveloped in the aroma-burning incense, with the rear brought up by the congregation. During the service, sounds from outside had intruded on the quieter moments. Fred was curious, and after the interment left Elsie chatting in the churchyard and went to investigate. As he turned into St Mary's Road, it was clear that the disturbance was just in front of the station.

A noisy group, too small to call it a mob, clustered around a man with a placard. As Fred approached, he caught some of what he was saying. He heard 'Disraeli', or rather heard the prime minister's name drowned out with booing; as he came closer, Gladstone's name evinced cheers. Finally, he was able to see the placard, but the words meant very little. Fred knew the name of the prime minister and had heard of Gladstone, but of Bulgaria and the atrocities being committed there he knew nothing. He was about to leave when The Ottomans were named as the perpetrators. Here was something he did recognise, having fought alongside Turkish soldiers in the Crimea, but it was all too confusing and he set off back to the church.

Walking toward the hubbub, he'd paid little attention to the man in a doorway lighting his pipe, but he was still fiddling with it five minutes later as Fred returned.

"Good afternoon, sir." Fred's greeting was motivated as much by curiosity as civility. The man was nondescript. His jacket was a dull grey, and trousers once green were now a muddy colour. With a workman's cap pulled low over his forehead and hands up to his face holding the pipe, still unlit, he would have been totally unmemorable.

"Afternoon." In making this brief reply, he automatically let his hands drop momentarily and revealed his face.

The mourners started to pour out onto the road. As Fred waited for his wife, the man with the pipe set off ahead of them with surprising alacrity and, reaching the bottom of St Mary's Road, turned left and disappeared as he joined the demonstrators still milling about in front of the station. Meanwhile, the Whaley crowd set off for home in better spirits than earlier. Indeed, judging from the convivial chatter and increasingly raucous laughter, the spirit originated in liquid form. Several from New Mills accompanied this homeward trek. A two-and-a-half mile walk was little enough price to pay for a free tea and a party.

Finally, Stephen could talk to his sister, and they drifted away from the rest.

"Come now, Mary, tell me how you are? It must have been sad for you all on your own in that big house." Her brother's kindness was too much for her, and tears began to flow. She spoke through her sobs.

"I didn't know he was so ill." A brief pause. "I should have come to see him more often." More tears, this time of power-lessness. A young girl in service was not her own mistress. There was also a tinge of guilt over one occasion when something other than her employer had detained her.

She was a beautiful girl, slim and raven-haired with a pale translucent complexion. Her mouth, perhaps a little severe in repose, transformed her face when she smiled. Her radiance was all the more appealing for her total ignorance of it. She was completely unaware of the effect she had on young men. So far, her innocence and her brother had protected her, but it was a fragile thing.

Arm-in-arm they stepped out in companionable silence. Stephen had thought long and hard on whether he should say anything to Mary about their father's early life. Having arrived at no firm conclusion before the funeral, his mind roamed back and forth over the subject as they walked. The decision was made, at least for the moment by their arrival in Whaley Bridge, with nothing having been said.

"Come on in, there's plenty for all." A motherly woman stood outside the door of the cottage which Stephen had shared with his father. It was Mary's home, too, and the welcome was being given by one of their late mother's sisters who had stayed behind to make everything ready.

Brother and sister were first over the threshold, the rest of the party having hung back to ensure it would be so.

"Thank you, auntie, that looks magnificent." The sixteen-year-old girl was easily moved to tears, but her appetite dimmed her grief. Mary was hungry. The house soon filled with people, and stragglers had to make do with whatever was passed through the parlour window by those inside. With an enormous kettle hanging over the fire to keep up with the demand for tea, even the early arrivals soon found their way back outside to cool down.

"Look. It's that man again I said about at church." Fred was indicating to his wife. As he spoke, the stranger stepped toward Stephen and the mystery was unravelled. They were so alike they must be relatives. The party was becoming more boisterous and the two men slipped from view. By now the street was full, not only with the original mourners but neighbours, children, grandchildren and workmates. A hard core of drinkers made the most noise, but a whirl of constant movement was maintained by the youngsters, fortified by the remains of the food, playing tag and running to and fro.

Finally, things calmed down and those with least stamina began to drift away. Stephen walked with Mary to the station. She had to be back at the big house by early tomorrow and the journey was rather more complicated, setting off from Whaley Bridge, than her earlier one to New Mills.

"Will you be alright now?" Stephen was still fussing over his sister. "You get out at Buxton and then walk to the Midland next door and get a train to Cromford." Mary who had made the journey at least once a month, on her day off, since she was fourteen, didn't need the advice, but indulged her brother's concern and thanked him. He cared for her and she was grateful.

Fred and Elsie had gathered up their family and the gaggle of grandparents, children and grandchildren was making its way back home as Stephen was returning from the station.

"Ver' good send off for your pa." It certainly had been. If the quality of the wake was any reflection of the community's regard for the late Patrick Thomas, he must have been a popular man.

"Well, it was what he wished. He'd had a good life and he wanted it celebrated." Stephen walked on toward his now almost empty, but untidy, house. Auntie had worked so hard he'd have to help her clear up. The one remaining guest sat in a corner and waited.

"So, you're Patrick's son." With order restored and auntie off home, the two men sat as the summer evening faded. "I heard he'd come to England." The accent was difficult to place; probably from America, but Stephen wasn't sure.

"And you must be Eamon's boy." Of course, the twang must be Canadian. Hadn't his father told him Eamon had taken his family to Canada?

"Sure, I'm Cathal. We're cousins and we're Irish." Whilst Stephen was happy to agree about the kinship, he wasn't so sure about the ethnicity. Until two weeks ago, if he thought about it at all, he'd seen himself as a Derbyshire man. The Canadian drawl continued.

"We all set off in a coffin ship for Canada to get away from the famine when I was a bab." Cathal took a swig from a flask. "My mam died on the trip. Da' said we were two weeks in the St Lawrence before they'd let us off the boat. That finally did fer her." He spat with disgust at those responsible.

Drinking from hip flasks and spitting on the floor was not at all familiar to Stephen, any more than the history lesson he was being given. He kept his peace.

"First thing I can remember is being trailed round by Da to meetin's an' bein' farmed out to old crones who beat me. In the end, I got to understandin' what the old fella was about." No prompting was needed; Cathal kept on talking.

"It was Irish independence, the Fenians and such like. I never understood the politics and I'm not sure he did, but the principle was clear enough. Get the English out of Ireland, and good riddance." There was a pause in the story. "So, what's this Thomas business? You're a Lynch and should be proud of it."

Three weeks ago, Stephen would have had no idea what he was talking about. Even now, he was unsure about discussing it. He replied with a question.

"How did you hear about Father's death?" It was Cathal's turn to prevaricate.

"Ah well, y'see," he tapped the side of his nose and gave a knowing look. "There's ways an' means." At this point, he resumed his family history. "We ended up in Pittsburgh. Well, Canada wasn't much use. No work and the English in charge, so Da moved us south. He got in wi' a lot of wild men who were getting together t' invade Canada an' push the swine out. I was twenty by then and old enough to please myself, so I went along, too." It seemed to Stephen that it wasn't just a life story he was being given, more a panorama into which he was being drawn and perhaps trapped.

"So, we all ended up in a place called Ridgeway on the border, an' there was a lot of firing and men fell. Da was one of them." For the first time, Cathal was visibly moved. His father had obviously meant a lot to him. "It was a waste. How the devil were a few hundred Irishmen with muskets going to conquer Canada? Anyway, the Americans took our guns away and sent us all back where we'd come from on a train." Another pull at the flask. Stephen was fascinated and repelled in equal measure.

"It was all a mess in America. We weren't troubled by the police, but anything we tried was a fiasco. The only place to get anything done was over here." With a change of tack, Cathal moved onto Stephen's life. "You're on the railway then?" He didn't wait for an answer. "Must get to know a lot about what goes on."

How had Cathal found out about the funeral? Why did he seem to know so much about his uncle's side of the family? And what was he up to now? Stephen was confused and clear at the same time: confused by twists and turns the conversation had taken; clear that it had to stop there. He stood up.

"I think, Cathal, we'd better get this straight. I'm an Englishman, well… a Derbyshire man really. I'm pleased to have met you and what you've told me about the family is interesting, but no more. If you've got battles to fight, you're on your own."

This hadn't been a family get-together; it was a recruitment campaign, and finally Stephen understood he was the target. He knew nothing about Irish politics, and didn't want to. He did know about crime on the railway and wanted nothing to do with it.

Cathal stood up, too, and heading for the door, said, "I'm sorry about that, but it was worth a try." Then he was gone into the warm summer night outside.

Across the road, unseen by either brother, something moved in the shadows.

Chapter 3

Whaley Bridge, September 16th, 1876

Sergeant Sam Spray alighted from his train, right on time, and despite his habitual reserve, was unable to ignore the celebratory atmosphere. It was a glorious early-autumn day, sunny but not hot. Around him, fellow passengers milled about on the platform, gathering up family groups, greeting old friends and all bent on having a good time.

Whaley Bridge is a long string of a place, the main street crossing and re-crossing the river in the bottom of the Goyt Valley. Some houses clung to the steep western side, as did the railway, so that the station overlooked Market Street. The sounds of an outdoor party rose up the valley side and as the new arrivals made their way downhill, they were absorbed into the happy throng.

During the journey, the others in his compartment, if they had bothered to look, would have seen a reserved man sunk in his own thoughts. Clean-shaven, hazel eyes, with greying hair barely visible beneath a black bowler, itself freshly brushed and firmly pushed back into shape, he did not attract attention. From his demeanour, they would have been surprised to know he was bound for an afternoon of celebration. When his invitation to the 'Grand Opening' of a new 'Reading Room and Library' arrived, he had been inclined to ignore it. Grand anything was not much to his taste, and he had worked hard at putting Whaley Bridge and its inhabitants to the back of his mind. The Tarp investigation and the people associated with it were in the past, but he hadn't been able to resist reading the embossed card and turning it over to find the message written on the back.

The hard facts were plain to see. Mrs Elizabeth Oldroyd and her father Isaac had endowed a library and reading room for the town, in the memory of the late Mrs Kezia Bennett, mother and wife respectively. Considerable sums of money must have been involved and could only have come from the estate of the late Arthur Oldroyd, Elizabeth's brother-in-law, which she'd inherited on his death. That the money had been acquired dishonestly was known to both Sam and Mrs Oldroyd.

It had taken some time for the implications of this generosity to sink in, and it was during his musings that Sam reverted to thinking of her as Lizzie, as he had come to do during the Tarp investigation. Lizzie must have had the same scruples about the money as he'd had when he heard of the bequest. All he, Sam, had to do was walk away, as he had done, and his precious integrity remained intact. Lizzie had a more difficult problem, which she had solved with a wisdom and ingenuity that he could only admire.

It was at this point that his feelings for Lizzie had broken out of their little prison in his mind, and he resolved to accept the invitation. Having previously established an equilibrium in which he had felt numb but not unhappy, suddenly his mood started to swing violently between ecstatic and despairing. On the one hand, so his rational detective's mind told him, she must want him there – and what's more, she had made sure he had the first invitation off the pile. He'd examined an indentation at the bottom corner minutely on more occasions than he cared to admit to himself, and every time concluded it was a No 1 in a ring, pencilled in and then erased.

"I would value your attendance. Please come." Sam had taken to reading out loud to himself the handwritten note on the back. But then, in his despairing moods it would seem to be no more than mere politeness. Why else would she write 'It will be Jimmy Allcroft's debut with the band playing cornet alongside his father'? What had Jimmy got to do with anything? Then again, when in optimistic mood, he would admit that mention of Jimmy delicately neutralised any sense of personal pressure from Lizzie.

By the time he had changed trains at Stockport and boarded the Buxton service, it wasn't so much Lizzie's intentions that troubled him, but what he should say when they met. "Good afternoon, Mrs Oldroyd. What good weather for the Grand Opening, don't you think?" No, of course not: he'd never addressed her in those terms, and now was not the time to start. "Such a pleasure to meet you again, Elizabeth. A fine day for the Opening." Oh dear; just as bad. What really troubled him was the possibility of bursting out with, "Lizzie, my darling," arms outstretched, "I've missed you every day since we last met" followed by an embrace that had started to figure in his dreams.

In the event, he needn't have worried. On hearing the train's departing whistle, Lizzie had started up the hill to the station entrance and met Sam on the way down. He carried a small case, sufficient for the overnight stay he had ventured to book when he'd screwed up his resolve and written, accepting the invitation.

Dressed in her best silk dress, its colour complementing her grey eyes, with a lilac bonnet trimmed with a ribbon, she was a picture. Sam, blind to fashion, had no idea why, but knew only that she exceeded his imaginings. Her outstretched hand met his and shook it warmly. "Sam, how lovely to see you again. Have you had a good journey? Come on down and join me in the celebrations." Imperceptibly they slipped back into the

24

easy, intimate relationship that had existed at Christmas, as if it was yesterday.

Market Street was a hive of activity. Apart from the shops, there were stalls laid out with treats for the children, an area for games, and the town band was beginning to congregate. All the pubs were doing good business, and the sounds of revelry which were so enticing from high up the valley side became deafening down in the bottom.

"It will start with a parade through the town by the band." Lizzie was explaining the day's events. "Then there'll be children's sports; that should take a bit of the steam out of them." The couple were walking through the crowd and met Jimmy Allcroft, along with his father, heading toward the band.

"Hello, Jimmy. My, you do look smart." In truth, this was an overstatement. The boy was clean and tidy, but the nearest he'd got to a uniform was a peaked hat, battered and too big for his eleven-year-old head. He looked shyly up at Lizzie and then as he muttered "Hello, missus", they both glanced at his cornet. Polished to within an inch of its life, he cradled it protectively.

"He seems happy enough." And so did Lizzie, thought Sam. Perhaps not all of her legacy had been spent on the Library enterprise. Jimmy must have benefitted, too.

"After that, we all go to the Library. The Mayor – he's not really mayor, just chairman, but stands on his dignity a bit – makes a speech, and Father cuts a ribbon. Then the band play 'God Save the Queen' and we troupe in for tea in the reading room."

The band finally formed up and, with a flourish from the bandmaster, launched into a march. Sam was no musician, but was put in mind of his military service by the first piece. "What's this, Lizzie? I've heard it before."

25

The Huntsman's Chorus blared out, setting a fine pace for the marching musicians. After two more numbers, they came to a halt outside the Railwayman's Arms. *How Much is that Doggy in the Window?* didn't seem to require the full ensemble, and the redundant instrumentalists disappeared, only to re-join refreshed for the next stretch. Jimmy trotted along with the rest and, as third cornet, was not much heard.

"Hello, are you all enjoying it?" Lizzie greeted Fred Maida, who was shepherding two of his young grandchildren. "Do you remember Sergeant Spray?"

Fred certainly did remember. The Tarp arrest had been headlined in the *Derbyshire Times* over several weeks during the previous winter. Apart from a description of an empty mineral wagon in the canal and the alert railwayman who averted anything worse, he'd kept out of the public eye. He attributed this to the discretion of the Railway Constabulary, and was grateful for it. He'd no desire for a reputation as a blower.

"Sergeant, of course I remember." After a handshake, he turned to Lizzie. "We old soldiers fought side by side." They had indeed reminisced about the war in the Crimea at Christmas, although it wasn't clear, to Sam at least, that they had ever fought shoulder to shoulder.

"It ver' good fun. Lots of people I not see before."

The little Italian was right. The Grand Opening had received a lot of publicity in the paper and there were visitors, eager for entertainment, from all over the Peak District. The crowd was thicker now and the two of them struggled to keep up with the band. The finale was to be *The Last Rose of Summer*. By now, the musicians were shuffling rather than marching. Regular pub stops were beginning to take their toll. The playing had lost its crispness with mistimed entries and some cracked notes; except for third cornet, that is. Kept from the inebriating effects of alcohol on account of his age, Jimmy Allcroft's few notes rang out clear and true as the bandmaster brought the parade to an end.

Everyone began to head for the children's games. Jimmy, in his role as bandsman, was rather above such frivolity. To preserve his status, at least until the last notes of *God Save the Queen*, he wandered aimlessly clutching his cornet. Amongst the people just ahead of him was another youngster, perhaps a year or two older than Jimmy, bent on practising rather different skills.

Getting a hand into someone else's pocket and then out again unnoticed, preferably holding a wallet, is the essence of the dipper's art. The young man didn't quite hit his notes as squarely as Jimmy and the mark, realising he was being robbed, grabbed the lad's wrist and with a vicious twist threw him to the ground. As the boy, clutching his shoulder, cried out, his erstwhile victim melted into the throng.

In the ensuing commotion, it was only Jimmy who noticed something white flutter to the pavement. With an attempt at nonchalance, he stooped, picked it up and stuffed it into his pocket. The responsible budding musician had reverted to the streetwise urchin. Well, he couldn't return it to its owner, Jimmy thought; he'd disappeared. Funny that. It certainly didn't belong to the boy on the ground; he'd been caught in the act of stealing it. No, there was no ethical problem in pocketing it. He'd have a look later.

Fred Maida had also seen something of what had happened. As the mark was melting into obscurity amongst the citizens of Whaley Bridge, Fred glimpsed his face. It would have been obscured by the peak of his cap, but the exertion of dislocating the dip's shoulder had displaced it so that Fred, whilst not knowing quite why, had the uncomfortable feeling that he was missing something.

The egg and spoon, the three-legged, and the sack races, along with a myriad of other children's delights, were over and the self-styled mayor was on his feet outside the new library.

"It is with considerable pleasure and no little pride that I stand before you today at the Grand Opening of…" There was nothing for it but to stand and listen. After some minutes, the man was still being pleased with himself and proud to serve the town of his birth, where, as son of a fishmonger, he carried on the family business. Known behind his back as Fishy Firth, he hadn't quite eradicated the aroma attached to his calling.

"The munificence of today's benefactors can only be compared to that of…" The Earl of Shaftsbury got a mention as did Miss Octavia Hill, included no doubt in deference to the gender of the day's principle donor, and several others. "I now call on Mr Isaac Bennett to cut the ribbon on behalf of himself and his daughter, Mrs Elizabeth Oldroyd, and declare this magnificent…"

Finally, with the cutting of the ribbon, the band struck up *God Save the Queen* and the self-important fishmonger was silenced.

"Thank goodness that's over." Lizzie, joined now by her father, clearly didn't relish being in the public eye and was relieved to be ushered into the reading room as guest of honour, along with Isaac, to the celebratory tea.

"I'm afraid you'll have to sit over there." All the places had name cards, and Sam found his seat. The table was arranged with the two principles sitting halfway down one side, flanked by Fishy Firth and other notables of Whaley Bridge. On the opposite side were those of lesser importance, Sam amongst them. He was near enough to the middle to catch Lizzie's eye, provoking a response that almost degenerated into giggles. Not quite the thing in present company; he resolved to behave himself as he and the other guests tucked into slices of cold ham and beef, along with salad and potatoes, bread, and goodness knows what else. There was ale all round for the men and sherry was offered to, and refused by, the few ladies present. Tea was the order of the day for them. It was all topped off with cake and blancmange, wobbling slightly as the table was nudged from time to time.

Before the meal was quite over, there was a disturbance behind Sam, who had his back to the door, and a rather agitated Fred Maida made an entrance in search of the detective.

"Sergeant," he would have whispered, but there was so much chatter that he had to speak up. "You have to come quick. Please, quick. There's a body, dead, murdered, up at Shallcross yard."

Part 2

Chapter 4

With an apologetic glance in Lizzie's direction, Sam followed Fred Maida outside.

"I not see it myself. Boy come an' tell me. He say bit of blood an' hole in head. I send him back to keep watch till you get there."

They arrived at the yard to find it much as the young shunter had described. The body of a man lay hidden by undergrowth at the rear of the yard. There was a gunshot wound in his forehead and he was lying on his back. Judging from the state of the nettles, he'd been dragged from the yard. There was little blood to be found, and in the policeman's judgement he'd died somewhere else and an attempt had been made to hide the body.

Fred had explained the position as the two men hurried to the goods yard. There was no traffic expected routinely on a Saturday afternoon, and in view of the celebrations all the staff had been given permission to be in the town. At the last minute, news of an unscheduled arrival meant that at least one man had to return to work. What arrived was an overdue train consisting mainly of empty mineral wagons returning from somewhere north of Manchester.

"It should be here last night, but engine failed and it had to wait until they get replacement this morning. It arrive 'bout three this afternoon."

The train had set out from Whaley Bridge on Friday morning with a full complement of loaded wagons, and had

31

struggled all day to get to its destination on the northern edge of Manchester. Its diagram was to pick up empties and run them back to Shallcross ready to be sent up the Cromford & High Peak Railway to various quarries in the Peak. Such was the state of the engine's leaking tubes that the driver had failed it. Nothing was available as a replacement until Saturday morning. By the time it set off for home, the only connection the return working had with the original train was the disgruntled crew and a guard's van The three men had spent the night in various degrees of discomfort in the van, all their snap eaten and cans of tea drunk on the outward journey.

"It weren't no problem ter put away, sergeant. The driver just left it here in the siding and set off fer Buxton with the van. Mr Thomas went home straight away."

"Mr Thomas?"

"He's the guard, lives in Whaley." The young shunter was explaining what led up to his discovery. "Light engine don't need no van, yer see." He assumed that the bluebottle would need a tutorial in railway procedure.

"Sergeant know all that. He work for railway." Fred put the youngster right.

Crestfallen, he returned to his story. "Mr Thomas was all in, so I said I'd make sure the train was properly braked, and when I'd finished I came round here for a piss. Didn't see anything at first, but I'd knocked over a couple of nettles and when I'd finished I could see a bit of his boot."

On their way from the town, Sam had asked how Fred came to be the one the lad had called. He'd assumed, mistakenly, that he was the only shunter to be found. In mock indignation, the little Italian drew himself to what height he could muster.

"I foreman shunter now."

Sam looked suitably impressed, privately wondering how it

had come about.

"Riggott head shunter, but he dead."

Perhaps he was mistaken, but the detective thought he detected a note of satisfaction at the murdered man's death.

"Oxspring offer job to Tim Pott, he next in line. You know Tim? He an' I mates, but Tim love horses an' he not want to leave stables an' wharf yard." By now, the two of them were puffing a bit, the hill out of the town was steep. The story continued to tumble out despite their exertions. "So, I get offer. Is good, yes?" There was a moment's pause. "I ver' good at job." This was said without any conceit, just a statement of plain fact.

For some time, Sam had struggled with a problem. Despite a successful conclusion to the Tarp affair, the detective still didn't know how the man had been detained. He'd been there right enough and so had Constable Archer, but there was a blank between jumping off the runaway wagon and staggering to his feet to find Tarp handcuffed to a rail. William Archer was no help; he suffered the same blank spot. Now seemed the moment to find out.

"I'm sure you are; Tarp might have made his escape otherwise." A moment's hesitation. "The trouble is, Fred, I can't remember how it happened."

"Oh that. It nothing. I see Bill in trouble an' I start running to help. Then I see runaway truck coming down incline with you hanging on, so I set road for you get to the fight quick – then I run again. You jump an' knock Tarp over, he drop gun, an' you all on ground. He start getting up first, so I hit him with gun." The Italian's tone was dismissive. "It got no bullets. In case he get better quick, I fix him to rail. Then it time for my tea. My wife worry if I not home in time."

They had reached the yard gates and still Sam hadn't found

a suitable reply. The matter-of-fact manner with which the dramatic events of the arrest were recounted left him little room to respond with the gratitude and admiration he felt for the shunter's action. All he could say in the face of Fred's nonchalant professionalism was, "Oh, I see, so that was it then."

Looking along the line of crushed nettles, Sam made a guess as to where the body had come from. If it had been dragged straight into its hiding place, all he had to do was retrace a line across the yard. By the time his trajectory took him to a row of wagons still with no blood or torn clothing to be found, he was ready to give up.

"This the train just arrive today." Fred was just trying to fill out the picture, and failed to realise the importance of his snippet of information.

"Just stay here, Fred, whilst I go round the end of the train, so I know where we are."

"No need for that." Fred's voice became muffled as he ducked under the buffers and wriggled round the chain coupling. "You come through here with me."

Sam creaked a bit as he followed the shunter and straightened up in the six foot on the other side. 'Darn it!' He'd have to clean up his boots before going back to his lodgings. His irritation evaporated as quickly as it arose. As he looked in distaste at the patch of mud, he could see parallel scrape marks disappearing into the small puddle and out the other side, running to the rail and into the four foot he'd just crossed.

They were certainly following the route the body had taken on its journey to the nettles. Walking further across the yard, the detective began to wonder why it had been dragged so far. They were much nearer to the far side when…

"Sergeant Sam." Fred was uncertain as to the correct mode

of address, but backed his horse both ways, trusting his broken English to excuse any transgressions. "Over here, look at this."

They were on a bit of hard ground where there were no scuff marks, and Fred was slightly ahead and to one side. The patch of blood wasn't large, although smeared in the direction the body had taken. Sam pulled a handkerchief from his pocket to wipe the sticky mess from his finger. The blood wasn't exactly fresh but was still moist to the touch.

"What the dickens is this?" He bent down again and put his fingers back into the little congealing pool. "Yes, I thought so." It looked as if he was the casualty by the time he'd retrieved what he was after. In the palm of his hand, rather misshapen after its passage through the dead man's head and partial burial in the hard core of the yard, was a bullet.

"What d'ye make of this, Fred?" Both men had experience of firearms and came to the same conclusion.

"He lying on ground when he shot." Fred had spoken first.

"Ye...es, but there's something else." Sam was talking to himself rather than his companion. "Darn it, I should have looked a bit closer at the body." Sunk in thought, he retraced his steps.

Seeing the change from the rather hesitant Sam to Sergeant Spray at work, his companion said no more, although he derived some private amusement at the detective's insistence at taking the long route back to the body rather than ducking under the buffers again.

Seeking to avoid any further rebuke, the lad had remained on guard by the body. With the return of the others, all three stood contemplating the consequence of a bullet to the head. The two railwaymen made no further deductions, but Sam wondered why the nettles were trampled down on both sides of the body which had been dragged head-first into its hiding place. He lifted its legs, still easily moveable; rigor mortis hadn't set in yet, and noted the scuff marks on the heels of the boots.

"Lend a hand, you two – let's get him out and have a closer look at the other end." Sam, in the middle of his examination, had no time for social niceties. "Right, let's just roll him over and see what's on the other side." With the body face down, the point of exit of the bullet was surprisingly over to the left of the head. "Well now, that explains it." The detective, oblivious now of his audience, was muttering to himself. The indentation to the skull, opposite to the bullet hole, must have produced most of the blood across the other side of the yard. He'd been struck on the head prior to being shot dead.

"Just stand there, lad." Sam walked behind the young man and symbolically raised his right arm and made a gesture in the direction of his head. "Lie down, head toward me, and roll toward your left side." He did as instructed. "Now, Fred, go over there and approach from his feet end. Do you see? He'd fallen over backward or onto his left side because of the blow to the head from behind, so he was down but not out. He saw you approaching and tried to draw a gun from his waistband. What should have been a knockout blow had failed, and with a gun in his hand the victim could only be dealt with by another gun."

Sam walked round the recumbent railwayman and took a sight line over Fred's shoulder. "Yes, that would do it. In through the middle of his forehead, and as he struggled to raise his gun with his right hand, and lying over toward the left, a shot from here would just come out in the right place."

"Do you want me to stay here?" The lad had scrambled to his feet only to see the back of his erstwhile 'assailant' heading toward the other side of the yard.

"Yes, Roy, you'd—"

"No, no, you come with us," Sam cut across Roy's foreman. "The body's not going anywhere just now and you may know something I don't." Realising he'd been a bit peremptory with the lad, what with the 'assault' and acting the role of corpse, he went on. "So, you're Roy?"

"Yessir, Royston Batty."

"Well, Roy, tell me, did anything else happen in the yard this afternoon?"

"No, sir. Nowt out of th' ordinary, sir. The delayed goods came in, left the empty wagons where I told 'im, did the usual, an 'e were off." There was a pause.

"What's the 'usual'?"

It was time for proper authority to be restored. In Fred's view, the lad should be put in his place.

"It nothing at all. Just bit of shunting." To Fred's chagrin, Roy was invited to expand on the 'bit of shunting'.

"Tell me just what was done." They were in the middle of the yard now and all the roads were visible, along with a line of loaded wagons waiting for a Monday departure.

"'E brought the train to a stop where it is now. It's a loop road so I uncoupled the engine. Whilst I were doin' that, driver got off th' footplate and walked toward the guard's van."

"Hold on, which side of the train was he walking on?"

"This'n, of course – an' Mr Thomas got down from the guards van and walked toward the engine. Same side, o' course."

Fred was exasperated at Roy's increasingly familiar tone and tried to remonstrate, only to be waived aside.

"Do you know the driver's name?"

"No, sir. 'E's from Buxton shed."

That was a bit more like it. Fred approved of the 'sir'. "I see

37

'im a time or two, but I don't know 'im." Here was something the senior man could add to the conversation.

"He's old…" Again, Fred was silenced with a look.

"Alright, it doesn't matter. What happens next?"

"I 'ave ter set points fer engine t' get on't next road."

Sam was puzzled. "The engine has no driver – he's walking back to speak to the guard."

"Ah well, y'see – in't yard, if 'e's any good, the fireman gets ter drive. So anyways, I sets the points an' lets the engine out of the loop an' then back up the next road, an' I hops on the step as 'e goes by. I gotter get t'other end fer 'im ter get back on ter t'loop an' collect the guard's van."

"So, you're running in the next road to the train you've just left?" Roy agreed they were. "Which side of the locomotive were you?"

"Same as the train we've just left. Then we stops when we'm level wi' Mr Thomas an' the driver in the six foot. I get down – the driver gets onto the footplate – I get back on the step an' we're off again."

Sam enquired after Mr Thomas. "'E waits till we'm movin' then walks round our back end, over the four foot an' across the yard."

Sam asked how he knew where the guard had gone? With Roy on the side of the engine away from the yard gates, the man must have been out of sight.

"I 'ad ter change the points at road end, so when we stopped, I hopped off and went round th' loco – the ground frame's on t'other side. I could see 'im then an' 'e were goin' through the gates."

Sam calculated that he'd have to have kept walking to get there in the available time. "You're sure it was him?"

"Course I am. My granda' an' his dad are pals, an' I knowed

'im all my life." He corrected himself. "Were pals – old Mr Thomas died a while back. I were at the funeral. Anyways, he'd a guard's uniform an' he walked just like Mr Thomas, an' 'e turned round to wave as he went through the gates. It were 'im alright."

What happened next was a lesson in the assembling of trains. With the wind in his sails, Roy expounded on the business of establishing the destination of each group of wagons, knowing the layout of the yards involved, and getting everything in the right sequence for easy disposal. His words sounded familiar to Fred, but he thought the lad was pursuing matters to excess.

"You seem to have the hang of that." Sam was impressed.

"I ought to. It were Mr Maida what taught me all I know." He glanced in Fred's direction with something akin to the look of a puppy with its master. All was forgiven.

"So, have I got this right? The train is made up of mineral wagons at the front, three box vans in the middle, and coal wagons with the brake van at the rear?"

"That's right, sir." They were standing close to the little pool of blood. "The box vans were just here before we got 'em into line."

"So, anyone standing here would have been hidden from over there." Sam waved an arm in the general direction of a line of two empty wagons with a brightly coloured box van between them. "What are they doing over there – so far away from anything else?"

At last Fred found an opening. "It's a consignment of explosives. It go up the Cromford & High Peak on Monday for the quarries. It have special locks and truck each end for safety."

Sam, with his military service behind him, wondered if one empty truck between an accidental explosion and the rest of the train was quite enough.

"How do you guard it when it's in the yard?" There was an uncomfortable silence.

"Well, there's the locks...." Sam already knew about the locks "...and we bolt the gates at night. And there always someone about the yard during the day. And it not here for very long. And no-one know it here..." Fred's voice trailed off. "I do what Oxspring say."

"There didn't seem to be anyone in the yard earlier today?"

"No..." The little Italian looked very contrite.

"I asked Mr Maida if I could go down to the town until the goods was due." Roy was doing his best to take his share of the disapproval. Sam took pity on the pair of them.

"It's as well you weren't here, or there might be two bodies in the nettles. Come on – let's have a look." As they walked over to the isolated wagons, Sam asked how long Roy had been in the yard before the goods train had arrived.

There was another awkward pause followed by, "'Bout the same time as the train."

"That was convenient. How'd you manage it?" It was like pulling teeth, slow and painful. Another pause.

"I ... er ... had a word wi' the signalman. 'E stopped train in the station and got the driver ter give a crow on the whistle an' I runs up the hill and climb on the engine. Then we sets off to the yard." Roy turned to his foreman. "I'm ever so sorry, Mr Maida, I knows it's against reg'lations."

Fred dismissed the matter. "We got more to worry 'bout than that, lad."

Passing the recently assembled train, Roy pulled a locking lever shut on the door of one of the box vans; second nature to him after eighteen months in the yard. "The youngster's coming along alright." Fred was watching his efforts to negotiate the plentiful debris strewn about the place – sleepers, piles of ash, the residue of sticky oil where engines were serviced, and a whole lot else, not to mention the running tracks.

Sign-written in white on its red sides, the words 'Danger' and 'Explosives' only added to the sinister air of the low box van. At a distance, it had seemed innocuous, but close to and looking up, the afternoon's grisly events seemed concentrated on the door's padlocked hasp.

"It secure this side, best look round the back." Fred led the way. Beyond the siding, nature had had its way and the undergrowth encroached close to the track.

"Hold on there. Let's have a look first." Sam wanted to see for himself. "Someone's been here before us. See there." He pointed to trampled nettles and a fragment of cloth snagged on a thorn. Taking a clasp knife from his pocket, he hacked away at the bramble and passed the little trophy back down the line. "There you are, Roy, hold onto that and don't lose it."

"This side's shut and padlocked…" As he spoke, he reached up to test the lock. "What the D—"

Watching over Sam's shoulder, Fred saw the heavy lock fall open.

Chapter 5

Sunday Morning, September 17th, 1876

It was the compelling aroma of frying bacon that had brought Constable William Archer downstairs. Breakfast was a mid-morning meal in the house of a master baker, and William – on duty late the previous evening – had slept through the sound of his father's four o'clock rising and the later hubbub as the rest of his family got out of bed. Even the youngest, with whom he shared a room, hadn't disturbed him. But the bacon had managed it.

The pig had made a big contribution to his plateful, and as he tucked into black pudding, sausages and, of course, the bacon, not to mention fried eggs and bread, he ignored the door knocker's rat-a-tat. It'd be for his father.

"Message for Constable Archer." Why was the high-pitched adolescent squeak so annoying? He shared the family home with two brothers of about the same age, and got on perfectly well with them. In his heart of hearts, he knew why and it was nothing to do with the messenger boy.

Messages delivered like this only meant one thing, and today's was no exception.

Report to me immediately at… There followed an address in Crewe Green near the Hall, then *Wayland. Chief Superintendent.* Well, that was a turn-up. He'd never been summoned to the superintendent's home before. No-one at the station knew if the old man was married; not even Sergeant Spray, and those two had known each other for over twenty years.

There was no way of replying. The lad had accepted a tip

William had given him and shot off; anyway, it was an order, leaving no room for discussion. Breakfast was not going to be enjoyed at the leisure its aroma had promised.

"Don't be daft, William, eat up before you go." His mother, practical as ever, wasn't going to let him out on an empty stomach. He wondered, uncharitably, if it was her eldest's welfare or the waste of food which prompted her advice.

By the time he was outside Hall House, he'd repented of his lack of charity. The half hour walk and more time spent locating his superior's home had confirmed his long-held view that nothing should be attempted on an empty stomach.

"Ah, there you are, Archer." Superintendent Wayland opened the door himself. The detective in William, never far from the surface, mused on this singular event. Didn't Wayland keep servants? Perhaps he did and let them have time off for church on Sundays. Yes, that would be it. "Come in here, man." Was this all a bit hurried?

The constable was ushered, propelled, or possibly ordered – it wasn't entirely clear which – into a room whose atmosphere was laden with tobacco smoke. With the door shut, the superintendent relaxed a little.

"Right. You're to go to Whaley Bridge and see what this is all about." A telegram was waved about.

Sergeant Spray had composed the telegram with care, but there was some difficulty in its despatch. Whaley Bridge was in holiday mood, and by the early evening of Saturday much drink had been taken. As the sun slipped over the valley lip, plunging the town into shadow, the sounds of revelry only seemed to get louder.

From this maelstrom, he first identified and then extricated a very excitable postmaster. Fred had been on hand for the first element of this enterprise but stepped smartly aside whilst, assuming his most authoritarian persona, Sam sought to get the man to open up the Post Office and demonstrate his expertise on that most miraculous of inventions, the telegraph machine.

"Gi' it here, I'll send it tomorrow." This was said with a casualness that would not, had he been present, have impressed the District Commissioner for Posts and Telegraphs. Sergeant Spray took a similar view.

"Now see here, my man, I'm an officer of the law." His warrant card was thrust in the man's face. "And this is an urgent constabulary matter."

The official fought it out with the partygoer on the battle-ground of the postmaster's face.

"Oh, er, you'd better come wi' me then." The official had won.

Seeing how things stood, Fred was sent back to the yard. Young Royston had been left behind to keep an eye on things, with instructions to keep out of sight. Probably nothing more would happen, considering what they had discovered, but with at least one gun – and possibly more – in the hands of desperate men, it was better to take no chances.

The response Sam wanted from the telegram's recipient was the urgent despatch of William Archer to Whaley Bridge, and an agreement to launch an investigation into the murder. An aura of approval had surrounded the pair of them in the aftermath of the Tarp affair. It had, after all, been the first murder enquiry undertaken by a young department, and a successful one at that, but nine months later the glow was fading; perhaps more slowly in the eyes of Superintendent Wayland than elsewhere.

Sam was banking on it as he wrote:

**MURDER ON RAILWAY PREMISES WHALEY
BRIDGE STOP HAVE COMMENCED
INVESTIGATION STOP REQUEST PERMISSION
TO PROCEED STOP ASSISTANCE REQUIRED.**

He toyed with the idea of mentioning Archer by name, but
tactfully left some space for his superior to exert his authority.

"See here, Archer, what d'ye think this is all about?" The
telegram stopped waving about just long enough for Archer
to read it.

"Can't really say… Sir."

"No…" There followed some harrumphing, then, "You'd
better get off there and see what he wants."

"Sir."

"And what's more, don't go spending money the department doesn't have." As soon as it was said, Wayland regretted
it. Departmental finance was not a subject for discussion with
a mere constable.

He'd always had a problem with Constable Archer. Plucked
from the works by Spray, he was the only man under his
command without a military background and seemed slovenly.
No, that wasn't it, his manner just lacked the crisp edge of
the ex-soldier. And yet he'd found himself revealing things to
Archer in unguarded moments that he'd rather he hadn't.

"He doesn't say where to find him, but I expect he'll be
about somewhere in Whaley Bridge."

"Sir."

"Yes, tell him I want to know what the devil's going on."
There was the briefest of pauses. "I mean, give him this note."
Wayland, by now at his desk, was scribbling furiously.

———•••——

Sergeant Spray had a busy Sunday morning behind him when
he received the chief superintendent's note. By the time he'd
finished at the murder scene on Saturday night, the official
festivities were over, but many of the revellers were unwilling
to let things end so prematurely and the Whaley Bridge public
houses were still doing a roaring trade. Their customers spilled
out onto the street so that the town was almost as busy as it had
been earlier.

Before he'd found his way to 37 Old Mill End, there was,
amongst other things, the little matter of finding a suitable
resting place for the body. With a contrite Fred insisting that
it was his job to make sure the yard was secure, young Roy
was detailed to help with identifying the undertaker. Finding
him was easier than persuading him into any action. He was
discovered, together with a group of local personages, including Fishy Firth who was attempting to repeat his afternoon's
speech. It was less coherent second time round on account of
the drink that he'd taken in the meantime, and to that extent
was more bearable. And despite him taking longer over it, the
drink taken by his audience rendered them more receptive.

The undertaker showed greater resistance to the sergeant's
demands than the postmaster; he had, after all, had longer
at his cups, Spray's priority having been with the telegram.
Maybe the other man's official position as a representative of
the Royal Mail also played a part in his final capitulation. In
the end, Spray had to drag the mortician bodily from his ale

and rely on Roy to show him where to find the man's premises. Even then, it took a bucket of cold water, thrown in his face, before he would cooperate.

It was only then, with the corpse taken care of, that Sam gave any thought to Lizzie.

His breathing became laboured as he climbed Old Mill End. He slowed perceptibly, but it was not just the incline. What to say to Lizzie preoccupied him on two levels. He had to admit to himself that the afternoon he'd spent in her company had been the happiest few hours he could ever remember. It was not only the pleasure of sharing an outing in fine weather with a congenial companion, but the dawning realisation that Lizzie was enjoying his company as much as he was enjoying hers. Beyond the immediate lay something more profound: the all-pervading dullness of things that had been the best he could achieve for himself in the aftermath of the Tarp investigation had dissolved. In its place, a clarity and energy seemed to have entered his world, and in consequence he felt his head to be held that little bit higher. It was a more risky situation; there was something to lose now, but he felt he had a future, and it was good.

He hadn't resolved his dilemma as he knocked, rather late in the evening, on the door of No 37.

'Sam, come in, you must have been very busy.' No reproach, no demand for explanation. 'I expect you're hungry. Come into the kitchen and I'll find you something to eat.'

In the end, he told her everything. Perhaps he trimmed the details, but when he'd finished she knew there'd been a dead body found up at the yard, and two boxes of dynamite destined for the quarries up in the Peak, had been stolen from a locked wagon.

"There had to be two of them. Dynamite needs careful

handling and the boxes are too heavy for one man. And where's it gone? They must have got it away somehow."

Lizzie was in the scullery doing the washing up. With his belly full and his hand round a mug of tea – no delicate porcelain in the kitchen – he found himself conducting a conversation through the doorway.

"Do you think the dead man was one of the thieves, Sam?"

It was a question that had been on his mind for some time, and he couldn't make it add up. Had two men moved the explosives and then one killed the other? If so, why? Or were two men disturbed by a third, who they killed to silence him? If there were only two of them and one was now dead, how did he dispose of his booty?

"I don't know at the moment." He was going to have to find out in the morning. "I sent a telegram to the superintendent asking for assistance."

"Do you mean Constable Archer will be coming?"

Sam wasn't too sure, but devoutly hoped so. "Will you be able to accommodate us both?"

Sam was away early next day and back at Shallcross Yard by sun up. Though much quieter than last night, the usual hush of a Whaley Sunday morning was disturbed by the groans of men with headaches, whose wives had refused to allow them home until they'd sobered up. Waking up with hangovers in the chill of an autumn morning after a night on a hard bench, they were regretting their excess.

"Cor, that lot must have had a skinful." Royston was on his way to the yard, too. "Said go back for six and let Mr Maida go home for his breakfast. Don't work Sundays regular, but with the…" The lad couldn't quite say murder. "With what's happened, he thought we'd better keep an eye on things."

Not much to watch over now, thought the detective, *what with the body at the undertakers and the dynamite gone.* It was all about the explosives. He'd realised that as soon as they'd found the broken lock on the special wagon. *But how had they got the dynamite away?*

According to Fred, each of the two missing boxes required two men, and careful handling at that.

"You must have a sack trolley or a handcart in the yard, Roy?" As the words left his mouth, Sam knew the question to be ridiculous.

"Yes, sir, we got both, but I don't think Mr Maida would let us move explosives on them. Little bump, big bang, he says."

"You're right, lad. I don't suppose you ever take them out of their special wagon anyway."

"Not regular, no, sir. We did once when it got derailed. Mr Maida had us empty the explosives wagon whilst the break-down gang put things straight. Careful we had to be, too."

They were at the locked gates of the yard by now and, after shouting for Fred, they were let in.

"Nothing's happened here overnight," he said. "I put new lock on the explosives truck. We lucky only two boxes missing."

"Hmm. I suppose so." Sam was thinking of the damage that could be done with that amount of dynamite.

The night before, when the three of them had found the broken lock, Sam's first thought had been that thieves had got away with half the load, whilst Fred had wondered if they'd taken anything at all.

"No, no, the wagon's never full," he'd said. "I get the docket." Inside, there'd been small stacks of wooden crates.

Each group of six was about five foot long and six foot wide by four high, and anchored securely to the floor by ropes through ring bolts. It wasn't immediately apparent that anything had been tampered with. Perhaps the order had been for a number indivisible by six, and the neat stack on its felt underlay by the door had been the last four. It was the lad Roy who'd pointed out the absence of rope ties, and when the van's contents were matched against Fred's docket they were indeed two boxes short.

Back at Shallcross in the cold light of morning, Sam had an uneasy feeling he'd missed something.

"Come on, Roy, let's go through it again."

They started at the point where the body had lain in the undergrowth, now more trampled than before. Apart from its removal, the detective had crawled about to see if anything had been dropped. He got on his hands and knees again, but to no avail. Royston went over the shunting manoeuvres and they re-examined the ground across which the body had been dragged. Sam even followed him under the train where the body had been pulled across the track before Sunday's late arrival.

"We went over there next," Roy said. They were alongside a row of laden trucks that had waited all weekend to make up the first departure on Monday. "And the last thing was getting the guards van out of the head shunt and onto the rear of this lot." The two of them were level with three closed wagons in the middle of the train as he waved his hand in a finalising gesture.

"You did something like that yesterday, what were you doing?" Roy was taken aback by the urgency in Sam's voice.

"Didn't do nothing, we just walked alongside the track."

"Yes, you did, to one of these wagons as you passed. You

moved a lever or a handle or something."

"S'pose, if you say so. Might have fixed a door if the catch weren't done up. Yes, I might have done that." What came so automatically to the railwayman assumed a huge importance to the detective.

"Which one?"

"Dunno, can't remember."

They tried all three, with nothing to show for their effort, it seemed. Output from the Peak went into open trucks, perhaps covered with tarpaulins, not closed wagons; these were going away empty.

"Hold on a minute." Sam stopped the lad from shutting the door on the third one. "Why would there be tarpaulin in this van? No point in covering something up when it's inside, is there?" They clambered up and through the doorway.

———————

Archer made it, just. There was only one fast train to Manchester of a Sunday morning and with its one intermediate stop, Stockport, it was just what was wanted. He hadn't even time to check the timetable, but when he alighted at Edgeley station he found his luck was out. It seemed that the inhabitants of north east Cheshire and Derbyshire were more devout than those of London and Manchester and had no need of travel to Buxton on the morning of the Sabbath.

"Go and speak t' the signalman, he'll know if anything's diagrammed for the Peak." The ticket collector was trying his best to be helpful. "If y' wave that about, you might get a lift to Whaley." The policeman had shown his warrant card.

As he climbed the steps to Edgeley Junction No 2 Signal Box, Archer marvelled at its cleanliness. Even the outside flight was swept, with its handrail shiny and spotless, and once through the door the place positively gleamed. Passage from outside in had taken a little while. There was the matter of bells ringing, the movement of heavy levers, and the chimney blasts from the engine of an interminable goods train slowly regaining the main line from its refuge where it had been waiting patiently for the Manchester Express to clear.

"What do you want?" The man had a long Sunday shift ahead of him. Archer had knocked and waited, watching the intricacies of the signalman's craft through the window. By now, the door was open but the way through was barred by a burly, choleric man who was showing every sign of shutting it again without more ado.

"I am Constable William Archer of the Railway Constabulary…"

"A Bobby, eh! Ain't no call for one of your kind here." The man glared. "Anyway, how do I know what you are, you ain't got no uniform?"

The sight of Archer's warrant card and official rail pass provoked a disapproving sniff just as a single bell caught the signalman's attention. As he stepped inside to reply to the alert, the policeman followed him into the box. There followed a mysterious jangle of bells then the movement of several heavy levers, their handles wrapped with a piece of cotton rag to protect their polished brass from sweaty palms.

"The station porter suggested I came to you." There was peace in the box again. "He said you'd know if there was a working along the line to Whaley Bridge today and that I might hitch a ride."

For all the time William Archer had worked for the LNWR, he'd never ridden the footplate of a locomotive out on the open road. An engine running light to Buxton was not in the regular schedule. It wasn't until the Edgeley signalman, after much sucking of teeth and pursing of lips, had consulted his daily list that he admitted that there was something moving in the direction of Whaley Bridge before the six fifteen; Sundays only; slow.

"Don't s'pose the driver will let you on. It's his call. They're a cantankerous bunch, drivers, an' I should know. You've no idea..." A single bell, one back then a two and a three interrupted the flow. After his response, he said, "This is it, light engine." Levers were pulled, a note made in a ledger, and the monologue resumed. "I could do with a boy to help with the writing when we're busy y'know, but they don't listen..." As he talked, a shiny black locomotive drifted to a standstill outside the signal box; so close was it that the speaker barely changed his tone in conversation with the driver.

"You'll not be wanting a policeman riding wi' you, I'll be bound." The response to this unpromising introduction was surprisingly friendly.

"Why? You got one there?" The driver turned to his mate. Then, "Aye, we'll have him. Where's he for?"

By the time Archer stepped out onto Whaley Bridge platform, it was clear that his lift had been more than an altruistic offer.

"So, what's going off at Whaley?" This, after he'd been parked in a corner of the cab whilst the crew got their monster moving. "We heard there's summat up."

The policeman knew so little that he wondered if he could pay for his ride. "What have you heard?" He played for time.

"Nothing except there's something up. Come on what's to do?"

Archer marvelled at the ability of gossip to spread. An incident on Saturday afternoon in the Peak was circulating in

Crewe by Sunday morning. He pictured in his mind information somehow seeping into the rails at one end and miraculously reforming at the other. More prosaically he supposed the telegraph office leaked like a colander. However, the superintendent had given him one nugget to entertain the crew.

"A dead body has been found at Whaley Bridge."

"Go on, there must be more'n that. I mean, you're Railway Constabulary so it's gotta be on LNWR property."

"Er, yes. I suppose so."

"An' it's gotta be murder, else you bluebottles wouldn't be interested."

Archer nodded. "Yes, that seems likely."

"And there's a bigger fish than you in charge, I'll be bound." Archer was silent. "Go on, it's that Sergeant Spray; him what caught that murderer from Cromford. I read about it in the paper. An' you was there, too. It said there were two of you."

Archer gave the departing enginemen a wave and set off for the town.

Something momentous happened during Saturday's festivities. The murder was still a private matter between the corpse and his assailant, when Jimmy Allcroft became a man. His transformation took place in full view of the public as he marched with the Town Band, playing third cornet in a borrowed suit and oversized peaked hat. No-one else noticed, of course, but by the time the final notes of *God Save the Queen* rang out, he felt bigger, bolder, and older. The hat still sat uncomfortably on his ears, and he didn't fill out the baggy suit, but he knew that manhood was his for the taking.

"Here, son, sup a bit of this." Under strict instruction from

Mrs Allcroft 'not to let the boy take drink', Jimmy's dad had defied orders. There was no harm in a couple of mouthfuls, he'd reasoned, and anyway he was proud of the lad. More problematical was the pint of ale given to their latest recruit by another bandsman on the quiet, behind the Railwayman's Arms. Manhood became an infinitely desirable state until Jimmy's world started revolving like a roundabout. Then he was sick and finally fell asleep in a corner.

In the cool light of Sunday morning, he woke to the real world. Explaining to his mum where he'd been all night and why his suit was such a mess, would take some doing. With a headache like his, it would be impossible. But yesterday hadn't been a complete disaster; he just knew it hadn't, but the reason for this optimism was proving elusive. Slowly, through the blur of returning consciousness, the paper he'd retrieved materialised, and he remembered the manner in which he'd come by it. There was more: later in the day he'd seen the young scoundrel again, accompanied by a man.

Jimmy knew that kind of man. He was not the sort to be giving food to a young criminal. Nor would he be helping a scally cope with the one-handed eating of it. The lad's other arm dangled, immovable, by his side. When he'd put the previous day into some sort of shape, Jimmy knew he had to do the responsible thing. The thing a proper man would do. That finding Sergeant Spray would put off the inevitable encounter with his mother played no part at all in the decision…

William Archer resolved to call at 37 Mill End next. He'd asked around the station in case it was the 'railway premises' mentioned in Wayland's telegram, but drawing a blank, he set off. Shallcross yard and the wharf yard were the obvious places to try, but Lizzie Oldroyd might save him a lot of time.

Would 'Lizzie' be alright, he wondered. It was some months since they had met, and it was back in the early spring they had been on such terms. When he'd written, he'd signed himself William Archer, but as soon as he'd arrived it was 'William' and 'Lizzie'. And what a relief it had been to talk with her. Lizzie had understood perfectly about Sam's depression, and they had discussed her plans to set things to rights.

"Just look after him, William, he's as important to me as he is to you."

Yes, 'Lizzie' it would be.

"Mr Archer." Young legs were taking Jimmy up Mill End faster than the older man. "Mr Archer, I know something important." The two came level. "I was going to see if Mrs Oldroyd could help, but you'll do." In truth, Mr Archer would do very well. It was a last resort on Jimmy's part to enquire at No 37. What he had in mind was man's business, and he didn't want a woman meddling in such things; she might just send him home to his mum.

"You see, there was this man…" The story came tumbling out and the paper produced. "And then I saw the dip with this policeman and…"

"You sure about that, Jimmy?"

"William, how nice to see you," the door of No 37 had opened to his knock, "and Jimmy Allcroft, too. Sergeant Spray was hoping you'd come. He's left a message."

—◦•►◦—

Constable Archer spent the walk to Shallcross yard trying to find some significance in what Jimmy had told him. He didn't say anything of his failure to do so to the youngster. For his part, Jimmy hurried along in the belief that he'd done the responsible thing and his information would help solve the case.

The yard was open when they arrived. Beyond the wooden gates, a knot of three men dissolved as Royston, relieved by his boss, set off for a late breakfast. Eagerly, the other two came forward.

"William – thank goodness. The Whale sent the right man." Away from the office, the superintendent's sobriquet didn't seem out of place. "Am I glad to see you." Spray and Archer shook hands.

"You come. Good." Fred was equally glad to see him, "And you got young Jimmy, too." Fred turned. "You play good yesterday, Jimmy, only one keeping time by the end." Fred raised an imagined tankard toward his mouth. "Band take too much of this."

There was plenty to discuss, what with a murdered man and stolen explosive. Jimmy waited patiently.

"I've got an idea. See what you think, William…"

"It too dangerous, an' we lose dynamite if it go wrong." Spray had already given it an airing and Fred was not convinced. "I responsible for goods in yard." He did his best to stand tall. "I'm head shunter. I can refuse to let it go."

"And I can arrest you for obstructing my investigation."

"Er…" The argument raged over Archer's intervention.

"You can try. This is my yard an' I got friends." Fred wasn't giving up.

"We'll see about—"

"Can I just get a word in?" Archer had never heard his sergeant in this vein. He didn't like it and he wasn't sure Spray would either when he'd calmed down. "We're all friends here and we've been through danger together. We don't want to fight amongst ourselves, do we?"

Jimmy was fascinated, whilst knowing full well that the argument was not for his ears. He made himself small and waited.

The row collapsed like a house of cards.

"You're right, William, of course you're right. Why don't I start at the beginning?"

The whole tale came out detail by detail. Archer listened, Spray talked, Fred chipped in with bits and pieces.

"So you see, William, we don't know who the victim is and we don't know why, and the only place to start is the dynamite."

"But it's been stolen. Hasn't it?"

"Ah, but we found it again. I was just coming to that bit. The thieves stole it and put it into another van that's due to leave in the morning. They must be going to collect it at the train's destination, and when they do, I want to be there."

"And that's your idea? It's hardly a plan. What if they're armed? With one dead already, they'll hardly worry about another body – or two more? I assume you want me with you on this escapade."

"You see, sergeant, Constable Archer thinks you crazy."

Jimmy felt a tickle at the back of his nose and only just stifled a sneeze. *They'll have to notice me soon,* he thought, *but please, not yet.*

"I didn't say that, I was just thinking – and what I think is, we've got to do it."

Two figures walked slowly toward the town centre – one, short for an adult but stocky; the other tall for his age. Fred had the best of it by in inch or so, but Jimmy was still growing. In the end, he'd been unable to suppress his sneeze, and the spell had been broken.

"Good heavens, you still here? I hadn't realised." Spray looked sternly at the youngster. You should…" He paused and changed direction. "This is a very big secret and if we're going to pull it off, you'll have to be careful to keep it."

Jimmy swelled inside his baggy suit. *I'm part of it,* he thought. *I'm really part of something big.* "Yes, sir. Say nuthin' to no-one."

"That's just it, nothing to no-one. Now, from the look of it, you haven't been home since yesterday and Mr Maida here is going to take you back to your mum, and explain you've been helping us." Spray's bit of bribery had been unnecessary; he'd already got the lad's loyalty by the time the two set off.

"Mr Maida, you saw what happened to the dip yesterday, didn't you?" He and Fred Maida were part of the same team now, Jimmy thought. "I didn't see much of the mark, it was the boy I saw mostly, and the paper he dropped."

Fred had caught a good look at the victim and he'd been curious ever since. The man had just melted away when most upright citizens would have been noisily indignant. More troubling, he had an uncomfortable feeling he knew the face.

"You see where he went, that man? Cos' I saw the dip later with his arm in a sling with a man – a different man, I reckon." The other was listening. "An' he was a bluebottle; I'm certain sure of it."

Fred trusted the lad's judgement on this last point. *You can tell a policeman a mile off, everyone can,* he thought. "The man I saw wasn't one, that's for sure."

They walked on in silence, Jimmy desperate to prolong his time in the grown-up world. He had a question.

"You saw the body, what was it like, Mr Maida?" Death was commonplace in Jimmy's world. He'd seen many a corpse laid out in the front parlours of his neighbours and relatives, not to mention his own when his Nan had died. None of them had had the added glamour of being murdered, though. "The sergeant said he'd been shot. Was there a lot of blood?"

To the old soldier, a veteran of the Crimean campaign, this interest wasn't in the least bit ghoulish; more an appraisal of how things stood. "Not much, Jimmy, but he not shot where we found him; much more blood in middle of yard. Sergeant Spray found bullet there, too. It go in here," he pointed to the middle of Jimmy's forehead, "and out through the side."

"Mr Maida, could we go and see the body? Sergeant Spray said the undertaker's looking after it until Monday. Please... could we?"

Fred wasn't at all sure this was something he should be doing, but yesterday, in the yard, so much had been happening that he hadn't had a good look at the body himself, and it worried him. He wrestled with the problem as they walked, aware of the pleading eyes of the lad.

"We'll go and have a look."

It would be more accurate to describe the man as a carpenter, some of whose business was making coffins. Of necessity, he had somewhere to house their occupants whilst he measured them up. But for the inhabitants of Whaley Bridge, a day or two in the front parlour followed by a short trip to the House of their favourite version of the afterlife and a tip for the gravedigger sufficed. In a town of working people there were thin pickings for an undertaker.

On any normal Sunday, the man would have been only too

happy to come down from his living quarters above the work-shop in the hope that the summons would bring him work. But the day after the Grand Opening wasn't normal. Along with most of the men of the town, he'd drunk too much yesterday and didn't feel quite up to facing today. He rather assumed that Fred Maida's knocking originated in his head rather than from his door downstairs until the shouting started.

"Halloo… Halloo… Anyone there?" Rat-a-tat-tat. "Anyone at home?"

The dishevelled man who opened the door was not happy. "What'd you two want?" He glared evilly in Jimmy's direction. "Him in particular?"

"We want to see a body."

"Why in God's name would you want to do that?"

"We're working with Sergeant Spray and—"

"Oh, 'im." Dimly, the man remembered being taken to task the previous night by the policeman. "You'd best come in."

It seemed an unlikely place to provide dignified repose for the dead. A scattering of tools lay amongst shavings and sawdust. The gap between the bench on which the debris lay, and a trestle, was bridged by a plank on which a bloodstained piece of calico shrouded the corpse. The body from Shallcross yard had been preceded by a paying customer who lay more decorously in a completed coffin. It was this, and the prospect of the ceremony of which it would shortly be the centre of attention, that unlocked the logjam in Fred's power of recall.

Old Mr Thomas's funeral was the last one Fred had attended, and at that moment the memory of it floated into his mind. The walk to New Mills pushing Patrick Thomas in his coffin on a handcart, the noisy demonstration outside, all figured in his mind. He never did understand what the crowd by the station were shouting about, but it was on the way back that he'd caught sight of the stranger's face. The man had slipped away as soon as Fred had greeted him, only to reappear in Whaley Bridge yesterday.

One hidden memory out in the open had dragged another with it. The young man at the funeral that he'd almost mistaken for old Patrick's son; he, too, had been in Whaley Bridge yesterday.

Chapter 6

Monday, September 18th, 1876

The van's interior was becoming stuffy as the September sun rose through the morning, its potbellied stove unlit for now. Nonetheless, Spray and Archer stayed out of sight; only the guard rode outside in the cool. From time to time, one man or the other risked a peek through the ducket, but there'd be no need for action until they reached Stockport. The dynamite would be safe until then.

"What's happening now?" Spray called to the guard.

With a crow on the whistle and much clanking and bumping, the long line of waggons bunched up as the train slowed. The guard started winding his brake wheel to assist the engine in halting its heavy load on the steeply descending track.

"Signal's agin us at Middlewood. The shunt mustn't have cleared the mainline. Lazy buggers probably started late."

With the train at rest, the detective took another look through the ducket's slitted windows. On the right, it gave a view of truck sides disappearing round a long, slow curve, but on the left he could see them passing below a bridge and just reaching daylight on the other side before the abutment cut off his line of sight. In the distance, their engine would be simmering quietly, unseen at the head of the train. Nothing could be heard of protesting trucks being chivvied into position by an officious shunter; the sidings must be some way ahead.

All that Spray could see, apart from the train, was a peaceful strip of pasture with an embankment beyond. Even by shifting his head from side to side, the scene was much the same. A twitch of movement on the skyline caught his eye. A horse's head was just visible appearing at intervals atop the straight edge of the bank.

Ten minutes later, two pops on the whistle warned the guard of his duty. He released his brake, the train struggled into life, and they were on the move again. As the brake van rumbled under the canal, the horse, still plodding sedately along the towpath, disappeared from view above them. Overhead, narrowboats moved silently on. Despite the might of the modern railway system, the canals were not quite dead yet.

Three hours ago, their train had arrived at Edgeley yard and since then, nothing of note had happened. Both the guard and their engine had departed for other duties, and the abandoned train stood like a stranded whale awaiting its fate. From their vantage point in the guard's van, the two policemen watched and waited.

Suddenly, there was shouting and then the sound of foot-steps approaching.

Archer sounded nervous as he asked, "Do you think this is it?"

Spray patted a comfortingly hard lump in his coat pocket. Back at Shallcross yard, Fred Maida had only agreed to coop-erate in their risky undertaking if Sam accepted the loaded revolver which had been thrust into his hand. Where it had come from was never disclosed, but it looked suspiciously like the one last seen several months ago being waved about by the miscreant Tarp as the detective had careered on a runaway truck into the wharf yard at Whaley.

There had been nothing unusual to see through the narrow windows of the duckets, other than trucks extending in both directions, but now a portly, red-faced man in LNWR uniform came into view. Though not quite running, he was certainly hurrying and, as he approached, the two watchers recognised their erstwhile guard. The man didn't call out as he scrambled onto the outside platform and almost fell through the door.

"I ain't told no one you're 'ere," he gasped, "cos you said how secret it was, but I think you ought to come and see what's happened."

"What's going off?" Spray wondered if there could be a connection with their operation. Although dynamite hadn't been mentioned, he'd explained to the guard why he'd had two passengers in his van that morning.

"All I know is the line's been blocked up both ways. We were the last to get through from the Buxton end. They'll have to send someone to investigate why all the signals are set at danger."

There was no dawning realisation; his understanding of what must have happened arrived fully formed like a blow to Spray's head.

"Come on, quick as you like." Archer was following down the van steps, his sergeant calling over his shoulder as he ran. "Check the van first."

By the time they arrived, the constable, younger and fitter, had caught up. Spray put his finger to his lips and pulled the revolver out of his pocket.

"Unlatch the van door and step back behind it as it swings open," he whispered, "but wait until I'm ready."

He clambered up onto the top of a loaded truck across the six foot from the van, one foot on the plank top and the other on its load of limestone. The door swung open. He leaped through to the darkness inside.

Afterwards, he understood what a foolhardy thing he'd done, but with his blood up he'd made the distance and landed squarely on his feet. He stood peering into the gloom. Nothing moved, no shot was fired, no desperate assailant shouted… and no boxes of dynamite lurked in the corner of the van.

———•••—

"Keep an eye out for anything that looks out of place." The two of them walked single file down the narrow path, and Spray was speaking over his shoulder.

After the anti-climax in the covered wagon, he and Archer had made their way toward a small knot of men whose discussion was just on the civil side of an argument.

"Can't take anything else in the yard." The shunter was adamant.

"This'll play havoc with my book-keeping." A clerk was viewing several intruders that had been given refuge from the main line in a vain attempt to keep control of the congestion. He'd have to account for the loaded trains somehow.

"Right, I've worked out where the stoppage is. By now, there must be a train standing in every section, and with the number that've gone through it has to be at Middlewood." The signal supervisor was talking as the two detectives arrived. "And who the devil are you two?" He glared at them. "Are you responsible for this mess?" Two warrant cards didn't do much to mollify him, and Spray's explanation of their presence only confirmed their culpability.

"You've been chasing after thieves on my railway, and I didn't know, and then you get it stopped up like a cork in a bottle…" His indignation was beyond words and Spray ventured into the silence.

"Something serious has happened, and I'm sure you're right about Middlewood. What's the quickest way to return there?"

Now, back on his own ground, the signalman calmed down.

"Nothing has come through from Buxton since this all started. We'll take a light engine and run down on the up line. It'll mean getting a wrong line order signed at every box, but it's quicker than walking."

It was a very crowded footplate. The Webb goods had been the easiest locomotive to release from the congested yard. A brake van would have been ideal, but the shunting required to extricate one would have taken an age, so the disgruntled fireman had to manhandle his shovels full of coal around three extra bodies to keep his boiler pressure up to the mark.

At each box, a signalman – puzzled, angry or resigned, according to his temperament – told the same story. Three bells repeated from the man ahead had meant his section was blocked and nothing had moved from then on. Up ahead, a short tunnel came into view and, as they came to rest outside Middlewood Box, a heavy horse plodded sedately above the railway, its silhouette clear against the sky. Behind it would be a laden narrowboat, unseen from below.

From the lineside nothing looked amiss; even as they climbed the steps, a dog's bark, disturbed at the sound of their boots, didn't seem that unusual.

"What the devil…" The signal supervisor had insisted it was his domain, and he was first through the door. "Good God, what's happened to you?" A groggy man sat unmoving on a chair. His hands were still behind his back, tied with sisal string. A smear of blood oozed from an injury to his forehead, and a nasty black bruise had started to make an appearance.

With all three newcomers inside, the dog beat a retreat and hid. Spray noticed, as he went to untie the bonds, that they were already loose and some were already severed. The man, still recovering from his ordeal, was mute. The detective was in charge now.

"You get things moving on the line," he told the supervisor, "and we'll deal with this." They helped the victim out into the fresh air and down the steps. "Archer, go back and get his chair, then leave him to me."

———•••••———

"You do all the work here?" They were looking over a half-dug row of potatoes. "And the pigs?"

The man nodded. "We're not busy all the time and..." he fingered a bruise on his forehead, "...this sort of thing don't happen every day."

"Are you up to telling me about it all?" Spray had done his best to gentle him, but time was racing by.

"I'd opened the box, let 'em know along the line that I'm here, then I went to feed the pigs."

"Notice anything odd, out of place, that sort of thing?"

"Not until I'd gone back to the box. I weren't looking at anything much, but when I got up the steps, there were this gun pointing at me from inside. Well, a man was holding it, but the gun was what I noticed first."

"Bit of a shock."

"Y're right there. He didn't say much, just waved it toward the levers, as much as to say, just get on with it."

"He knew about the timetable then?"

"Not him, the other one."

"So, there were two of them?"

"S'right, one with the gun, he didn't hardly speak. T'other one did the talking." The signalman was getting into his stride. "He sounded like he was a Scouser. I know what they talk like; I worked a box over there a while ago. Anyway, nothing happened for a while. I accepted the early Manchester fast, then the Buxton early freight."

"How long did this go on?" Spray was eager to move the story forward.

"He kept looking at a bit of paper. Next bell were for a down train. 'This the Whaley goods?' he wanted to know."

"So, he didn't understand which bell was which?"

"No, he didn't. He knew what he wanted but he hadn't much idea how to get it. He wasn't no railwayman, that's for sure."

Spray nodded. "And then?"

"'This got t'be the Whaley early goods,' he said. He was looking at his bit of paper again when I got the next bell from Newtown, and he was right. I accepted it but, once it was in my section, he told me to stop it leaving. The other man was waving his gun at me, so I did. They tied me up, sitting on this chair, then they disappeared."

"Where'd they go?"

"Only one way they could go." The other waved in the direction of a footpath. "It's the way I get to work, along the towpath to the bridge and then I come up that track."

"So, they headed for the canal?"

"Must have."

"What then?"

"'Bout ten minutes later, the man with the gun came back and untied me and waved at the levers."

"How did you know what he wanted?"

"He went to the window and sort of waved the gun along the line."

"You pulled the signal off for the train to proceed?"

"S'right. I'd had the acceptance from High Lane before the other man told me to stop it; the signalman there must have been a bit surprised at time it took to get to him."

"Then?"

"He said, 'shut down the box'…"

"But you said the man with the gun didn't speak."

"Well, he did just that once. But I fooled him."

Spray saw a gleam in the signalman's eye. "I gave six bells up and six bells down the line."

"What does that mean?"

"*Obstruction, Danger.* Nothing could get into this block from either end. I could see what they wanted. If I closed out the box like he said, trains would run straight through my section, things'd return to near normal, and then they'd tie me up again. The first person to think about what had happened to me would be my missus when I didn't get home after work."

"So, this way you'd alert the authorities that something bad had happened."

A nondescript dog clattered down the steps from the signal box and nuzzled up to its master. It limped, and blood seeped down its neck from a wound on the side of its head.

"They kicked him; they kicked my Willy-Webb."

For the first time since they'd met, the policeman saw uncontrolled emotion in the man. Tears rolled down his cheeks as he fondled his pet. "He nearly set me free, did Willy. He's a great one for chewing string. Loves what postmen tie their bundles up with. When I came round, he'd gnawed through what was round my wrists, but then you lot turned up."

"Come round? What from?"

"What do you think? This!" Indignantly, he pointed to his forehead. "After I'd deceived him with the bells, he hit me and I don't remember anything till just now."

Chapter 7

There's only one thing to do when your tail's between your legs, thought Spray, *keep trying and hope it doesn't trip you up.*

Whether catching the first train of Wednesday morning to Manchester would help him to avoid being tripped up, remained to be seen. He and Constable Archer would have to suffer the discomfort of a Parliamentary amongst a crowd of labourers travelling to work. There'd been little time on Monday afternoon to worry about the ruination of his plan. The loss of the dynamite would take some explaining, but after investigating the goings on in Middlewood signal box, he and Archer had spent their time on the canal. Once he'd seen where the train had been halted, the absence of the bait was easily explained.

What a fool he'd been not to think of it. Even before he and Archer had discussed the loss, both of them had come to the same conclusion, that the dynamite had been unloaded when the train was held at Middlewood home signal. It wasn't until they had returned with the relief signalman that Spray realised the significance of the Macclesfield Canal. With its connections to a countrywide network, it was an obvious route to transport the stuff.

They had both clambered up the embankment and started asking questions. Things moved at a leisurely pace along the cut, but they moved nonetheless. And the boatmen had little time to spare for a couple of nosey policemen who called to them from the towpath. Nothing was moored close to the bridge, and Spray found himself dodging horse droppings as he walked alongside moving boats, trying to find out if anything unusual had been seen earlier.

"No, ain't seen nuthin' unusual."

"Nowt out of line t'day – never is on the Macc. Cut, tha' knows."

It was hopeless. Of course it was. No-one had seen anything, because there'd been little to see, and what there was had taken place hours before these boats had come by. A lock keeper would have been their best informant, but the Bosley flight was thirteen miles away, with no change of level in between. Three miles the other way there was a single lock giving access to another canal.

Two more boats came into view, approaching from opposite directions. In an attempt to question both skippers, Spray and Archer separated and walked alongside each one as they closed. One of the heavily laden craft steered toward the opposite bank and drew level with its horse, standing well clear of the towpath, a lad at its head.

The second horse plodded on, its boat unchecked as it floated over the submerged tow line of the other, by now well below the surface. Two lines, two horses, a boy and two men not looking where they were going, met. The resulting chaos could have provided the basis for a farcical routine on the Halls, had anyone been present to record it. As it was, the best view was to be had from the boats. Their skippers were not inclined to laugh.

"Why don't you two bugger off back to the railway?"

"That's where y' belong an' that's where y' should stay."

"An' good riddance." This last from the boy as he tried to disentangle his horse.

It was the final straw. Without saying a word, the two

embarrassed detectives set off for the bridge. They climbed, skidding and tripping down the embankment, to familiar territory. Then, walking side by side along the cess, Archer spoke.

"There's Jimmy's find, of course, Sam."

"I've been thinking about that. He called it a paper, but it's a letter."

"It doesn't say much, just WBGY 15, 2 30. Means nothing, must be a code."

The camaraderie of shared disappointment had moved the two detectives into a more intimate connection.

"There's an address in Manchester on the other side, William. It's the only thing we've got and not much at that."

Tired now, the two detectives had regained Middlewood box. The injured man had disappeared with his dog; both of them off home to lick their wounds, leaving the box in charge of the signalman they'd travelled with earlier. He'd been busy. The business of clearing the congested main line had taken him and his colleagues up and down the track the rest of the day, but now, with the light starting to fail, longer gaps were opening up between successive trains; things were almost back to normal.

Sam knocked. "May we come in?" In his own box, a signalman ruled. Politeness on the verge of brow-knuckling was the order of the day.

"S'pose so." With a final heave, the Middlewood home signal clanked on and, giving the shiny brass a wipe, he turned from his bank of levers. "Come on in."

The autumn evening was cooling rapidly. At the door, they were surprised by a waft of warm air. Inside, a kettle sang. Beneath, coals glowed in the grate of a shiny black stove. "I was just hoping for a brew-up before the next train. You'd best join me."

Well stewed tea in chipped mugs was handed round. "Not exactly class, but it's hot and the milk ain't gone off yet." With the tea had come a thaw in relations. "Don't s'pose it was your fault. So, what's up then?"

The man was owed an explanation. Sam kept it as brief as he could.

"So, you got a body with no name, an' y' lost the dynamite. That it?"

"That's about it." Sam hadn't gone into the injured pick-pocket and the dropped letter. As he talked, he realised how little attention he'd given Jimmy, and now with nothing else to go on his guilt began to grow. "Could you stop the next up train and help us get a ride back to Whaley Bridge?"

———⚫✦⚫———

Monday had been a long day and it was over at last. The door opened without the need to raise its brass knocker, gleaming in the moonlight.

"Come on in. I heard you on the path."

How she'd done it, the two men could only guess, but by the time they'd washed and taken off their coats, they were sitting down to plates loaded with stewed beef, dumplings and boiled carrots. Lizzie's shiny black stove-enamelled range radiated a warmth at variance with the chill autumn night outside.

"You two look done in." By now, their plates were almost empty and Lizzie was back with a tray. "I'd prescribe an early night, except it's almost midnight already." She poured two mugs of tea. "Milk, both of you...? Oh, I nearly forgot, Mr Maida was round earlier wanting a word with you. I think he needed to know you were back safely, but he said he'd something to tell you. It'll have to do tomorrow now."

It was raining on Tuesday morning as the two men walked out to find Fred Maida, the kind of mizzle that passed for "a bit damp, tha knows" from men on their way to work. Perhaps it was the onset of autumn, or maybe the residual effects of Saturday's over-indulgence, but anticlimax was in the air, catching the sergeant's mood to perfection. William was in an altogether different frame of mind.

"Come on, Sam. We've got that address to investigate, and it sounds like Fred has something for us."

"You don't have to write a report for The Whale explaining how we mislaid the dynamite."

William tried to recall exactly what the superintendent had said on the subject of reports. "He wanted to know 'what the devil was going on'. Those were his exact words. Just now, we aren't exactly clear about what's going on, so there's no need to send anything."

Sam, harrumphing, found no comfort in this exchange.

"Come on, Sam, you send something to …" as a constable in the presence of a senior officer, he hadn't the nerve to call his superintendent by his nickname, "to Mr Wayland when you're good and ready, and I'll do the worrying for now." Together in silence, they continued uphill towards Shallcross.

By seven o'clock of a Tuesday morning, a busy goods yard would be a hive of activity and Shallcross was no exception. Sudden loud puffs from a locomotive would result in clanking from a line of trucks; after the movement, it would rest quietly, only to jerk into life again, called up for a fresh task. Standing high on the footplate, the crew looked to be in charge of everything, but the new arrivals could see that control rested with a man on the ground who gave orders to others carrying long poles and flags, midgets beside the rolling stock, engaged in running, summoning, halting and attending to couplings. Standing at the gate, it was difficult to distinguish between them, but the two detectives knew it must be Fred Maida directing the busy shunters.

"Best wait until things have quietened down, if they ever do." Archer recalled a near miss. "Nearly got myself killed last year in the Wharf yard."

At last, the locomotive headed onto the main line, straining noisily at its heavy load. The beats of its exhaust were fading into the distance before the guards van finally disappeared. Later, with hindsight, Sam regretted its prompt departure, but as he and William crossed the yard toward Fred, he was heartily glad to see its tail lamp disappear towards Stockport.

"You get my message?" Hands had been shaken and the three of them were heading toward the yard office. "I remember things. I tell you; you tell me if they're important." Fred saw himself as part of the team, and expected to be kept informed.

"First, I see dead man before." Patrick Thomas's funeral was described in more detail than Sam felt was entirely necessary, but it was worth the wait. "I see the stranger and Patrick's son, Stephen, together. It stand out big; they look the same, like they brothers, 'cept I know old Patrick only had one son. Family anyway."

"And this was at the funeral?" Sam wanted the details.

"First at church, but I not understand then, they not together." Fred explained he saw them talking to each other as he was leaving the wake. "Then I see. They look just the same. Gotta be family."

"Ever see him again?"

"Not until he dead over there, but I see Stephen this

morning." Fred waived a hand in the direction of the recent departure. "Freight guard on that train."

"Why the devil didn't you stop him? Don't you see how...?" Even as he spoke, Sam knew he was being unreasonable.

"Stephen on roster, I can't change it. I try to get message to you as soon as I know things."

"And we didn't get back until late. Yes, you're right, you did all you could."

"There's something else." Sam's irritable outburst was forgiven. "The pickpocket man, I see him the same day."

"You mean the man who you and Jimmy saw twisting the dip's arm and then disappearing?" Fred nodded. "At the funeral?"

"Not in church; in the street outside. There was a lot of noise, I go to see." Fred explained there was a mob shouting about Turks and Bulgars outside New Mills station. "On my way down to find out what's happening, I see a man in doorway. All that noise don't mean nothing, so I come back and say good afternoon when I pass him. His hat was pulled down before, but he jumps when I speak and it slips so I see his face. Off he goes like a frightened rabbit."

"What was he watching? The demonstration?" Having fought with the Turks in the Crimea, Sam suffered twinges of conscience whenever their Balkan excesses reached the newspapers.

"No no, he was looking towards the church." Fred was certain.

"So, he was interested in Patrick Thomas's funeral, or at least, someone in the congregation."

Long stewed, a thick brown infusion oozed out of a teapot into the motley assortment of mugs held out by the assembled company. It was time for a wet and as head shunter, Fred had to be there so his constabulary companions were, too.

"Here, mister, have this." One of the men handed Sam a mug. "Make y'hair curl, it will." Whatever they thought of sharing breakfast with the two policemen, the locals were friendly enough. "Tha must be here about that body. D'ye know who he is?"

A tricky question just then, without confirmation of Fred's guess at its identity.

"Can you think why anyone would dump a body in the yard?" The best Sam could do was counter one question with another. At least the news about the missing dynamite hadn't leaked out yet.

Another engine whistled as it drew into the yard, and the break was over.

"One thing I don't understand." The men were back at work and the three could talk freely again. "Why didn't you tell us all this earlier?" It was nearly three days since the body had been found and Sam was curious.

"It was Jimmy, on Sunday morning. He asked to see the body on his way home."

"And you took him, Fred?" William could only think of protecting his younger brothers from such a sight.

"He's a good boy, and I couldn't see the harm."

Sam had no such scruples. "So, what happened?"

"We get to the body. Jimmy's not so keen by then, but I get a good look." Fred explained that he'd not really examined it in the yard on Saturday. "First it in the nettles, I see face upside down, then we turn it over to look where the bullet come out, then all the trouble about dynamite…"

The second body laid out in a proper coffin had been the trigger. It had put Fred in mind of the last funeral he'd attended. "Old Patrick Thomas's, then I remember."

———•••••———

"That boy's always getting into mischief. He needs an eye keeping on him." They were walking back to the town, confounded by a diagram that would not bring Stephen Thomas and his brake van back to Whaley Bridge before evening. Jimmy was a convenient outlet for Sam's frustration.

"That's a bit hard; his mischief, as you call it, has brought us our only useful lead."

"Hmm." Sam didn't want to let go of his whipping boy.

"We could do worse than see him again. He may have something else up his sleeve."

"In his imagination, more like." Despite his scepticism, Sam found himself sitting on a low stone wall at the bottom of Mill End.

"This is where he turned up first time I came across him."

One or two passers-by looked askance at two grown men of employable age sitting on a wall in the middle of the day, eyeing the school gates. The sound of a bell from within signaled the end of morning lessons, and the road filled with children off home for dinner. William looked anxiously for Jimmy; Sam, still in need of an excuse for his irritation, was quietly pleased by his absence.

"Lookin' fer me, Mr Archer?" The lad appeared as if from nowhere; not at all the same one as last December. This Jimmy was a member of the silver band, a junior detective, someone with a position to maintain. "Want some more help wi' yer investigation?" He climbed onto the wall, completely at ease with his older companions.

Sam had nothing to say. "Just wondered if you'd remembered anything else?" William was asking the questions.

"Mr Maida told us he'd gone with you to see the dead body on Sunday." There was a silence.

"Didn't see nuthin' there." Another silence. "Did I tell yer I'd seen that dip wi' a bluebottle?"

"Yes you did, that's not new." Sam spoke at last.

"But I saw them again later on."

"Go on."

"He'd had something done to his badly arm, a bandage hanging from his neck holding it up."

"You sure he was with a policeman? He didn't have a uniform, did he?" Sam should have known better.

"Course he was. Y' can tell a Jack a mile off. First time I saw him I knew what Mr Archer was. Mind you, he is a bit different to most. But you all look…" Jimmy couldn't quite describe what it was that gave the game away.

Constable Archer took this last as a compliment. It wasn't at all clear that his sergeant saw it the same way.

"They were up by the station."

"What time was this?" Sam wanted detail.

"Not sure. Evening, still a bit light, anyway." Things had become a bit hazy after Jimmy's first sup of ale."

"Did they go into the station?"

"Must have done, the crossing gates was shut and they just disappeared."

"So, you saw a train go through the crossing. Which way did it go?"

"Dunno, not sure I saw a train. Heard one, though, puffin' away."

"Come on, we'll go and have a look." Sam's sulk was over. He marched off toward the Railway Hotel. By the time he'd turned the corner and started up the steep road to the station, the other two were trailing. "Where do you think you were standing when you saw the... the man and the pickpocket?" Sam called over his shoulder.

"S'pose it was about here." Jimmy waved carelessly at the considerable gap that had opened up between himself and the front runner. "Not sure."

Sam's irritation, still close to the surface, began to bubble up. "You're not sure of much boy, are you? What were you doing up here, anyway?"

After an embarrassed silence, "Came for a piddle." Jimmy pointed to a quiet spot in an angle between two walls.

"He must have seen the crossing gates on the way up." Sam was talking over the youngster's head now. "Probably saw them go into the station, had his piss, turned round and saw nothing else."

"I were bustin', mister, took a long time." Even now, two days later, the relief of it was clear in Jimmy's mind. "Then I looked round for a bit, then I heard the train."

"So, how is it that you can remember this all of a sudden?"

"Cos I'm bustin' right now, and it brought it all back."

———

Sergeant and constable were making enquiries about Saturday evening train times. There had been one down working, an all-stations stopper to Manchester, SO, arriving Whaley Bridge at a quarter past nine. There were two up trains; one an hour earlier and the other an hour later. If the lad's account was to be believed, it had to be a down train. It would have passed through the level crossing first and then disappeared out of sight behind the station buildings, just before he arrived. If the signalman was a bit laggardly with the gates, they could well have been set against the road traffic for a minute or two after the train's passing.

"I'm not sure. The lad must have been more concerned with his bladder than the railway." Sam was still sceptical. "He certainly took his time over it today."

Whilst Jimmy had gone off to his quiet corner to attend to his call of nature, they had discussed plans.

"By the time Stephen Thomas and his guards van return, it'll be too late for anything else today."

Sam agreed. "First train tomorrow, the Parliamentary with the workmen, it goes through to Manchester. We'll investigate that address."

Jimmy had returned unnoticed and stood listening. It couldn't last.

"Right, be off with you."

"Ain't had no dinner."

William remembered the boy's mam worked at the mill and there was no-one at home in the middle of the day. "I could get him a bite to eat." The baker's where he'd treated the lad the day they first met, beckoned invitingly.

"We've got enquiries to make." Sam, still not reconciled, set off up the station approach. William followed, but not before handing over the price of a pie.

—•••••—

The timetable had offered up useful information, but now, back at the station, the staff were less forthcoming.

"Lot of passengers Saturday evening, goin' home after the gala." The ticket clerk couldn't remember a policeman with a boy. "Fair amount of pushing and shoving out there, been drinking all day most of them."

Sam wondered if there'd been some drinking behind the

ticket window as well. They moved onto the platform.

"A boy with his arm in a sling, you say, and a Jack? Can't say I saw them." Only one porter had been on duty that evening. "But the platforms were empty after the Manchester train departed."

It had been outside the modest establishment of Theophilus Brimple, behind whose shop window jars of Mrs Winslow's Soothing Syrup vied for attention with Parker's Tonic, Quaker Bitters and St Jacob's oil, that enlightenment had struck.

"Sam. Listen, Sam, the boy must have had his arm seen to somewhere. Why not an apothecary, like this?"

A bit ahead of his companion, the sergeant turned back. The display was certainly arresting. He caught sight of Mugwump Specific, but preferred not to dwell on its purpose. "It's worth a try. We'll go in and ask."

"Right, what do you two want?" With moustache bristling, the truculent figure standing four square behind the counter was quite unlike any medical man the policemen had come across before.

"Don't get Jacks in here as a rule. Usually bad news, you are." Mr Brimple limped into the middle of the shop.

"Don't get too many old soldiers in this business either." Sam eyed the apothecary's wooden leg. "Where'd you lose it?"

"Africa, the bloody Ashanti got me, with an Enfield rifle. Who sold it to 'em, that's what I'd like to know?"

"You did well to survive; most died of disease, I heard."

"Bloody army sawbones was no good. Had to look after myself mostly. Then he died an' I looked after the others, too."

"So, that's where this all started?" Sam looked round the shelves. "I don't suppose a lad with a poorly arm would be much of a problem then?"

"So that's it, is it? I knew there'd be something. Y' never

sees a Provost's man without he's on someone's tail."

"So, you know who I'm talking about?" Brimple knew alright and, appeased by Sam's interest in his army service, was happy enough to talk.

"Two of 'em came in here late Saturday afternoon. Well, I knew it wasn't straight up as soon as I saw them: him a Jack, and the youngster a scally. Said the lad had fallen, but it weren't true. He'd got bruising all round his wrist and a bad shoulder. That wrist had been grabbed and twisted. But the Jack looked after the boy, and paid up like a good-un."

"Expensive?"

Brimple looked evasive. "Charged him a fair fee, yes. I can't afford to put a dislocated shoulder back for nothing."

———•◦•———

It had been a trying turn. Stephen was in trouble from the start. The brake control in his van was so stiff that his shoulders ached from slowing and releasing the rear of his train over the changing gradients. He knew the undulations of the Buxton route as well as he knew the staircase in his own home. There, at least he only had to use his legs to get up and down stairs.

Perhaps his father had felt the same way about the stairs in his dying months. Certainly, Patrick had put up less resistance to moving his bed downstairs than his family had expected. Mary had cajoled him into agreement with the gentle grace she carried so carelessly. Since his father's death, Stephen had found comfort in the few hours a month he and Mary spent together. The house was as much hers as his, but as she was away in service his sister only had one half day a fortnight when she could come home. Lately, their meetings had become irregular and it was Stephen's intention to find out why.

As if he hadn't enough on his mind, he'd arrived back at Shallcross yard to find these two policemen lying in wait for him. However, they'd been friendly enough.

"Mr Thomas, I would much appreciate it if you would give us some help," That was Sergeant Spray. Fred Maida had introduced him as soon as the brake van had come to rest. "To do with the unfortunate death here on Saturday last."

"You can't think I had anything to do with it." Stephen spoke with assurance, safe in the knowledge he'd been on his way home from Manchester when the man had died.

"No, no, of course not, sir. We saw you arrive here, much as you've done just now."

Stephen had climbed off his van, and they were walking toward the yard gates. "It's just a matter of identification. We don't know who the victim is and we think you might know him."

"Have I got to do this? Now?"

"We could get it done on your way home, sir." The younger policeman hadn't spoken until now. Fred had introduced him as Constable Archer.

"And I've got to look at a dead body?" Saying it out loud in so many words brought to mind the last corpse Stephen had seen; his dead father lying in the parlour before the funeral.

"It really would be the greatest help to us, sir." Archer sounded very persuasive.

Flitting through Stephen's mind were fragments from the funeral. It had been, despite the sadness of losing his father, a rather jolly affair... and enlightening. That was it; if the murdered man was local, they'd know who he was by now. And as they obviously didn't, they must think he was...

By now, the three men were on their way downhill into the town.

Spray pushed open a door and walked into the carpenter's workshop. It wouldn't do to look intimidated, Stephen had concluded during their walk together, so he stepped boldly after him. He'd been disciplining himself not to think of the two policemen as officials – just ordinary mortals who could be treated like any normal person.

"See here," said Spray officiously, "we've come to look at the body." Its proprietor was both manual worker and respectable man of business. Stephen knew he prided himself on the latter, from their dealings at the time of Patrick's death, but Spray assumed the former.

"Over here, Mr Thomas." Then, to the carpenter, "Get this off will you?"

The man obeyed without protest. *Those two have clashed already*, thought Stephen, and the policeman had won out. Stephen squared his shoulders, determined not to go the same way.

September had been mild, despite the mizzle, and when the shroud was removed, what had been a background odour of putrefaction intensified as the body was exposed. It was still lying, as it had when it had arrived, on a plank. At the time rigor mortis had rendered it rigid and manageable, and wrapped tightly it had remained there. But over two days had passed and an arm, freed from constraint, fell limply towards the floor. It would have brought the body with it had not Stephen, with the reflexes of a young man, stepped forward smartly, and saved the situation. In so doing, he found himself staring into the discolored face of his recently acquired cousin.

"Have you seen this man before?" Sergeant Spray wasn't giving Stephen any thinking time.

"Yes, I met him for the first time at the funeral."

"Your father's funeral?" They were replacing the shroud;

Stephen had lifted Cathal's arm and was still preventing the body from rolling off the plank whilst Archer and the carpenter were fixing things more securely. He was grateful for the distraction.

"Do you know his name?"

"He told me he was Cathal Lynch." Keep to the truth and say as little as possible, Stephen told himself. "I had no reason to doubt him."

"And no reason to believe him either?"

"As you say." Stephen was relieved. He had no wish to be associated with the victim.

"Do you know where he was from?"

"I couldn't place his speech, but he said he'd been in Canada." By now, the three men were walking together towards Stephen's house. Perhaps it would be over soon. So far, he'd told no lies and kept a distance between himself and the dead man.

"Do you know why he was at your father's funeral? Do you think your father had known him?"

During that last, revealing conversation, Patrick had said he'd not seen any member of his Irish family since the day his brother had gone off to collect his young wife and baby son on their way to Canada. On the spur of the moment, Stephen decided that the infant Cathal and Patrick had never met.

"Not to my knowledge."

"Could there be a family connection? A likeness between you and the dead man has been noted."

All at once, Stephen was out of his depth. The policeman had barely glanced at Cathal since they'd arrived, and anyway his body hardly looked at its best after nearly three days of putrefaction. He knows, thought Stephen.

"He... he said he was my cousin. Son of my father's

brother." There was no hiding from the truth now, Stephen told himself, but still, say as little as possible.

"And you believed him?"

"I… I suppose…" Stephen floundered.

"Your family names are different, aren't they?"

"My father changed his name. When he and my mother married, she wanted it that way. The Irish aren't held in high regard round here."

"No-one has said anything about an Irish connection in the town."

"I only learnt of it just before Father died. I haven't told anyone, not even Mary." At the thought of his sister, Stephen's resolve hardened. Whatever this was all about, he must protect her. "You won't need to speak to her, will you? I have to tell her myself when the time is right."

It was over. They had arrived at the Thomas family home.

"Thank you for your co-operation, sir. I hope we don't have to trouble you again."

Was there menace in the policeman's words? As he made his escape, Stephen wasn't sure.

Chapter 8

Wednesday, September 19th, 1876

William Archer doubted whether catching the Parliamentary at quarter to six in the morning was strictly necessary. Sam had insisted they got on with things early.

"Pretty easy day, William." That was Tuesday he was talking about. "We haven't got much yet. Got to keep The Whale happy, y'know."

None of this was true, thought William. They'd covered a lot of ground, established some important facts, and The Whale would not be any happier because he knew nothing of the case's progress.

It had even been too early for Lizzie. She'd left some food to take with them in lieu of breakfast. "Will you be back for an evening meal tomorrow, the two of you?"

"We're only going to do a bit digging in Manchester, we'll be back."

In the gloom of early morning, a throng of workmen converged on the station. They were an assorted bunch, but most were heading for the bleaching and finishing mills of the next stop along the line. They could have walked the three miles or so to New Mills, as the mourners at Patrick Thomas's funeral had done, but the Parliamentary was so cheap that they caught the workmen's train. It would call at every station on the way to its destination, with men riding one or two stops and being replaced, as they got off, by new passengers.

"It'll be the slowest train of the day," was the best William could manage in opposition to Sam's plan. He might also have added "and the most uncomfortable". Forced by the government to provide one cheap journey a day, the Railway companies saw no reason to waste money on rolling stock. As it drew into Whaley Bridge, the five forty-five stopper was an unappealing sight. Made up of elderly third-class coaches with wooden benches, it rattled and clanked much like a freight train. In amongst the motley collection were some even older carriages of a more distinguished pedigree, but now too decrepit for the full fare public. They sported luggage racks in some compartments, and here and there an unlit gas lamp.

There was a good deal of pushing and shoving as the crowd on the platform surged toward the places opposite the doors. Such was the press that the two detectives lost sight of each other and were separated. Doors had slammed, the guard had shown green, and the locomotive whistled, when the door opened again for a late arrival. Stephen, across the other side from the platform, felt the crush as the extra passenger tried to find space.

"He's only a lad, hoist 'im up on the rack. He'll fit there." The men nearest the door lifted the late arrival as if he was a piece of luggage.

The third stair from the top would creak if he stepped on it. Jimmy knew it well from trips to the privy. Everybody in the household tried to avoid it at this time in the morning. Not that going downstairs of itself was the problem. When nature called, what else could he do if his brothers had filled the pisspot? But Jimmy was fully clothed, and on his way through the lobby he would grab his cap and his father's muffler. No, it was his failure to return that would alert the household. Best if no-one heard him go.

His decision had been made yesterday. After finishing his piddle near the foot of the station approach, he'd edged slowly back toward the two Jacks. He'd told them all he knew and they weren't very grateful, particularly the sergeant. Mr Spray was tetchy and didn't seem to believe him.

They owe me, thought Jimmy, as he strained to hear what they were saying; *I'll show them*. In the end, Mr Archer had given him a tanner, but what he'd overheard was better than any money.

They were going to Manchester to do some detective work with the piece of paper he'd retrieved on the day of the gala; that much was clear. So was the day – Wednesday. He knew when the first train departed, and the sergeant told Mr Archer they had to start early. Better start there, he thought. He was alright really, Constable Archer. The tanner was still in Jimmy's pocket, for emergencies.

He had a plan. The first bit was to wait till he was sure the two detectives were catching the train, then...

A slow trickle soon turned into a crowd of those who'd cut it fine and hurried past Jimmy, tucked away in the corner where he'd lurked the day before. It stank; he wasn't the only person to use it as a urinal, but that was the least of its disadvantages. With a narrow field of vision and the sudden rush, he was having difficulty in checking all the passengers. Then, in amongst the sea of caps, he caught sight of a bowler with enough of the face below to be almost certain. It was the best he could do, a probable sighting of the sergeant.

In the distance a whistle, then up above clanking, and with the squealing of brakes the train drew into the station. Still he waited. There were only a scattering of latecomers, running now. Timing would be all. Finally, the last one passed his refuge and Jimmy set off. What he lacked in length of leg and bulk, he had in energy. He was certainly out of breath by the time he made the top of the station approach, but he'd timed it to perfection.

For the early workmen's train, the Company only provided a skeleton staff. As the guard whistled for the off, the ticket clerk was shutting his window. The man at the barrier was a porter who, at the sight of a green flag, had set off along the platform to attend to other duties. Jimmy shot through the booking hall, onto the platform, and ran in the opposite direction. The guard saw him and shouted, but with slow, powerful beats the engine was already getting the train underway. Hearing the shout, the porter turned, only to see a carriage door hanging open and Jimmy being dragged aboard by the other passengers. The point of boarding drew level with him, but by then Jimmy was up on the luggage rack and out of sight. Anyway, with the door shut by the men inside, the porter wasn't at all sure which compartment the lad was in.

There was no comfort to be found in a luggage rack. It was made up of a net suspended between the coach panelling at the back and a rail at the front. At intervals, curved brackets supported the rail and ran under the netting. These brackets pressed hard into sensitive parts of his anatomy, and he was sharing the space with a variety of items belonging to the passengers below. Jimmy could see a row of caps and knees belonging to the men on the bench directly below him. There must be another row facing, but his view was interrupted by standing passengers. Their heads, on the other side of the net, were level with his. He found himself staring at a familiar profile.

They were moving anyway. It was no satisfaction at all to William, pressed against the far door by all those who'd followed him in from the other side, to know he'd been right about the early train. He hoped Sam was similarly placed. Serve him right if he, too, was jammed up tight like the unfortunates who died in the black hole of Calcutta. Not that he thought dying was likely.

As things settled, each person found just enough space to stand and breathe, but at the time of the latecomer's arrival, William was facing the other way and only heard what was said. Now, with enough space to turn a few degrees, he tried to satisfy his curiosity about the occupant of the rack, but all he could see was a cap, obscuring his view.

The train stopped at every station on its way down the Goyt valley to drop some and pick up other passengers. In amongst these rearrangements, William found himself a seat. Still on the same side of the carriage, when they arrived at London Road he was last in the queue to leave. He was the only one, apart from the occupant of the rack, to have boarded at Whaley Bridge. The compartment emptied slowly, departing passengers paying no attention to the stranded lad.

"Want a hand down?" William, only trying to help.

"No." A muffled voice from above spoke through the cap still covering his face. In the presence of a policeman, the lad remembered his manners. "Thank you, Mr Archer."

His secret was out.

———

"You took your time." William had been one of the last off the platform. "What kept you?" Sam had been waiting impatiently by Smith's.

He's getting more like The Whale every day, thought William. "Just got myself jammed at the back."

"You spent a long time at the barrier."

"The ticket collector was asking about my pass. Not a lot of Police Department issue seen this far from Crewe."

"He let me through straight away."

"That must have been it, two on the same train."

It was not mentioned that Jimmy, released from his luggage rack, had been shielded by the policeman from the ticket barrier and the station concourse beyond as they walked.

"What the devil are you up to? Shouldn't you be at school?"

"Yes, sir." Jimmy, very contrite.

"And you got on without a ticket." This could have been a question, but they both knew it to be fact. "What were you going to do once you'd arrived?"

"Have a look round, see how to work it… sir."

"Now look here, Jimmy." William was feeling in his pocket for coins. "If I get you through the barrier, you take this," money changed hands, "and buy a ticket for Whaley Bridge."

They were at the barrier.

"Railway Police pass, eh? Second today." The ticket collector looked at Jimmy. "What you got there?"

"Fare dodger. I'll deal with him." The policeman tightened his grip on the miscreant's arm.

"You sure?" The man wavered. "Oh, alright. You give 'im what for. Little varmint."

They were through.

Jimmy was nowhere to be seen as the two detectives made their way down the station approach.

"Have you any idea where we're going. Sam?"

The sergeant, half a step in the lead, was striding ahead with purpose.

"I asked whilst I was waiting for you. The man at Smith's seemed to know." William caught up a pace. "We had plenty of time to talk. He said that in his dad's day, no-one respectable dared go there. Said he's surprised any of its left."

"Why? Have they tried to burn the rats out of it?"

"You're about right. It was known as Little Ireland, up by Oxford Road Station."

"You mean we could get there on the train?"

"Had enough of being packed like salt fish in a barrel – and you can wipe that smirk off your face." William's expression didn't change. "So, we're walking."

Finding Oxford Road was easy. A southern walk across the centre of Manchester was bound to end up somewhere along its length. New Warwick Street was a different matter. The two men walked past acres of dereliction. The Irish had certainly been driven out but the rats remained, as did an army of street urchins and derelicts hunting through the rubble. Sam wondered what there was to find in amid such desolation, but he too was hunting – for evidence of surviving habitation.

Hearing the familiar sounds of a railway only made it worse. The man at Smith's had been adamant. If the street Sam wanted still existed, it would lead off the main road south of the station.

"You sure you know where we are?"

Sam, scowling, was silent. Some distance ahead, a freight train rattled its leisurely way across a bridge, raised above the road. Walking on, the rubble gave way to derelict houses and factories, still standing but forlorn and abandoned. The destruction of Little Ireland was not so far advanced, and here the remnants of streets suggested how the area had been in its heyday. Then, in the lee of the railway embankment, signs of habitation. A street, parallel to the track, led to others where dishevelled men and women, downtrodden and half starved, moved about without apparent purpose. Some of the women carried listless babies. Older children with more energy than their elders ran about playing in the mud.

"This New Warwick Street?" William enquired of a woman standing on the step outside her front door.

"Hello, mister, you looking for something? A good time? I got lovely girls inside, just suit a punter like you." Innocent that he was, he had no reply.

"You can keep your whores, woman. We just want New Warwick Street. Is this it?" Sam was doing his best to save the embarrassed William's blushes.

"'Tis today, won't be tomorrow." She waved in the direction of the advancing devastation.

"What number are you? We want thirty-six."

"Oh, you do, do you? Well, you won't get much joy there." She pointed to next door. "Very hoity-toity they are. Keep themselves to themselves."

"See here, if I give you the price of a Judy, I want you to let my constable stand hidden in your doorway for a while, and don't you go tempting him whilst I'm next door."

Jimmy's day was turning out better than he'd hoped. When he disappeared with the price of a ticket home in his pocket, he had not gone straight to the booking office. For one thing, it was on the route the two detectives had to take to leave the station. For another, the policeman hadn't said when he was to go home. Anyway, he hadn't come this far to be fobbed off by Mr Archer. So, he watched and followed.

After setting off down the station approach, they almost

gave him the slip at the bottom. For a moment, it wasn't busy and he'd hung well back. A hansom overtook him and the cab horse slipped on the cobbles. It didn't fall, but in recovering was pushed faster and faster down the hill, and only narrowly avoided a collision with a dray that was making the sharp turn off London Road to come up to the station. For a moment, Jimmy's view had been obscured and he lost sight of his quarry.

He ran, bumping into someone. With his case knocked to the pavement, the irate man shouted at the boy to stop, but too late. Jimmy had reached the main road. He'd never seen so much traffic. The road was filled with carts and vans, and dodging about in between, handcarts and pedestrians. It wasn't that he hadn't seen a heavy dray before, or a baker's van, but here they were in an unimaginable profusion. And the pavement was full of people hurrying in all directions. It was this crush that saved the situation.

The two detectives had reached the junction as a crowd arrived, blocking their way to cross. The two roads ran almost parallel so that they had to almost double back on themselves to avoid the onrush. They were hidden from the station approach and, as Jimmy looked round the corner, he found himself only a few feet from them.

"Come on, we can make it now, Sam." The two men, intent on crossing, had been concentrating on the traffic and – half walking, half running – made it safely to the west side of London Road. Jimmy had to follow suit, but it wasn't so easy. Those he was following could choose their moment, but if he wasn't to lose them again he had to take his chance.

It was simpler now there were fewer people and he had to hang back, but his quarry kept straight on for quite a distance. Jimmy could see a green space coming up beyond them when they suddenly turned to the west. This time, he was on to it and even caught sight of the street name as he followed them into Rusholme Road.

"Better try and remember where I'm going, just in case," he said to himself. He'd given little thought to the matter until now. The excitement of the chase had kept any consideration of its final outcome at bay. However, there was nothing for it but pressing on.

Now he was passing a cemetery bearing the same name as the road, but it was the last sign he saw. The streets became meaner and dirtier, rows of dilapidated houses were mixed in with factories, and the people looked poorer. Still the detectives kept on, so Jimmy had to follow.

When at last they turned northward, the road was bigger, busier, but even more desolate. Across the other side was nothing but rubble where once had been a community. He could see its last remnants, destitute people picking over the remains of their houses. *What do those two want with a place like this?* he wondered. But they kept on and so did he. In the distance, up ahead, he heard the regular pulse of a locomotive as it blasted smoke into the already polluted air. Jimmy could see it crossing a bridge over the road. By now he had left the rubble behind, and things were more difficult. The two men could turn down any one of the side roads that were coming up in quick succession. He risked closing up on his quarry for fear of losing them, although he couldn't see why they'd go into streets where no-one was living.

Finally, just short of the bridge, they turned and Jimmy, running, found himself in a living community again as he followed them round the corner. Terraced houses lined both sides of the road. Between every second one, a communal arched entrance led into a ginnel with back yards beyond. *Perhaps Mr Spray wasn't so daft after all*, he thought, as he watched from across the muddy street.

Mr Archer spoke to a woman on her step, but then Mr Spray took over. As he watched, a furtive looking man emerged from the alley as another pushed past the three people standing on the step. What did the detectives want with a brothel? he wondered. He knew about brothels; a friend's big brother had told them. Men visited women and paid money, and it wasn't very nice. He was a bit hazy about what actually went on inside, but he'd seen the consequence of bitches on heat loose in the street and thought it must be rather like that. He wasn't at all clear why it went on, but there were a lot of unexplained mysteries in the adult world. Just now, he was trying to understand why Sergeant Spray had gone next door whilst Constable Archer was hiding in the entrance to a bawdy house.

An old crone came to the door when the sergeant knocked. Jimmy would have liked to hear what was said, but even from across the road it was clear that he'd got a flea in his ear. He went back to Mr Archer and they both tried to look as if they weren't there. As Jimmy watched, he could see a steady stream of men pushing past them and then reappearing a few minutes later out of the alley. The lad was surprised at how little time they spent inside. Dogs in the street took much longer; perhaps he'd got that bit wrong, he thought.

Out in the road, some boys were kicking what looked like a human head from one to the other. Occasionally it strayed in Jimmy's direction and he kicked the inflated pig's bladder back to them. Imperceptibly, he was drawn into their game and became part of the gang. It was useful cover, he knew, but made the watching more difficult. The old crone reappeared and looked up and down the street. Before the door closed, a man came out. At a distance Jimmy didn't know why, but he seemed familiar. There was no time to think about it; suddenly a lot was happening all at once.

Sergeant Spray emerged from the brothel and set off after the man from next door. Two customers were eager to get in and almost prevented him leaving.

"Nebuchadnezzar not up to the job today?" They laughed. "And here's another one." Standing in the doorway, they prevented Constable Archer stepping forward to see what was happening.

Jimmy wasn't sure what they were talking about, but it was obviously something his mother wouldn't want him to know. Just for now, there was too much going on. He tucked it to the back of his mind and watched as another man emerged from next door. Did the sergeant know he was being followed in his turn?

Two men came out from the alley. Jimmy immediately knew they were different from the others. For a start, he'd not seen them go in and none of the others had spent more than ten minutes inside; and they looked hard and purposeful, not furtive. By now, a red-faced Constable Archer had escaped his tormentors and emerged to see one of the men from the alley going in the same direction as the sergeant. The other loitered as Archer walked past him, and then stepped out to follow in his turn.

Jimmy grabbed the pig's bladder and gave it a good kick toward the main road. Without shoes, the local boys were no match for someone in boots. He raced after the ball and in so doing overtook the last stalker and Archer. Turning, he kicked it straight at the constable whose attention was on the back of the first man from the alley. Just in time, he saw it coming and caught it, only to find Jimmy in front of him apparently asking for it back.

"Sir, sir, you've got to know, there's two men ahead of you

after Mr Spray, and a man following you." He held out his hands for the ball.

Where Constable Archer and his tail went, Jimmy followed. As he walked, he did a little sum in his head. First up was the man from next door to the brothel that Mr Spray went after, so that made two. Then came another man from the same place behind the sergeant to make three. The two men from the alleyway had split up, one in front and one behind Mr Archer, so that was another three. Should he count himself? He didn't know, but he was sure there were six in a line up ahead.

———•••——

His mother had warned him. "You'll get mixed with all sorts of dreadful people if you take that job." Sergeant Spray had brought a special message from Superintendent Wayland, and that had won her round. Archer's Bakery delivered bread to Crewe Hall and Wayland had connections there. It was enough to earn her blessing, though it was doubtful if she ever imagined her eldest son standing furtively in the entrance of a brothel. The same sergeant was next door making enquiries while his constable was keeping watch.

"Nothing's going to happen when I knock, William. It'll be afterwards." And nothing had happened.

"Told me she'd no idea what I was talking about, to mind my own business, and to be off." Sam was in remarkably good spirits for a man with nothing to show for his efforts.

It was awkward, the waiting. The two of them had decided in advance that if Sam could flush someone out from the address on Jimmy's bit of paper, he would follow, and William would go after anyone else who took an interest in what was going on. Initially, next door's entrance had seemed an ideal spot for keeping watch. The customers turned out to be the problem. Men – some furtive, others loud and rude – kept pushing past, blocking the entrance at crucial moments.

Sam had just managed to slip out and follow the first man to emerge from next door, but a particularly obnoxious individual had got in William's way. By the time he had a good view along the street, Sam was turning into Oxford Street. There were others milling about and some youngsters playing in the roadway, but one person seemed to be moving with more purpose, heading for the main road.

William set off in pursuit. He was leaving the street urchins behind, when their game overtook him. Out of the corner of his eye, he saw movement in the air. More in self-defence than any wish to participate, he caught the pig's bladder, and found himself face to face with Jimmy Allcroft.

What else could he do? he told himself afterwards. He was on official constabulary work. He had to keep the man up ahead in sight, Jimmy wasn't his responsibility… At least the lad had the means to get home… but that rather implicated himself, since he'd given money to him.

He gave the ball back without a word and walked on. It certainly complicated things. He and Sam must be in the middle of something much bigger than their own investigation, he thought. By now, they were round the corner and under the railway bridge. William had a desperate urge to look round, but he knew enough to keep looking straight ahead. As jam in a sandwich, the only advantage he had over the man behind was the knowledge that he was being followed.

They were heading toward the centre now. Oxford Road Station gave an irrational boost to his confidence. As part of the LNWR, it suggested a place of refuge, but the man in front walked on and the station receded. They turned into a much grander street. It was busier here and William closed up on his man, but it was more difficult to be sure he had the right one. Great Portland Street was a step up the respectability scale from Oxford Road and the remnants of Little Ireland. There were no threadbare coats here, and the stone pavers underfoot allowed shoes to keep their shine. The man up ahead stumbled as another overtook him, and a few words were exchanged before another sharp turn.

Much quieter now, it felt more exposed and he fell back a little. And then, in a trice the man disappeared. Curious, William walked on, thinking the man must have turned into… Minshull Street Police Station. It said so in big letters, over the door. Two uniformed men came out.

"Now then, sir, what do you think you're doing here?" No answer was expected. With one each side of him, William was forcibly propelled through the door and inside. A sergeant behind the counter in the entrance lobby looked up.

"Cell No 3, and put the cuffs on 'im. Don't know what he might get up to."

"But I haven't done anything."

"We'll see about that, sir."

The grill clanged shut.

What The Whale would think of him sitting in a Public House in the middle of a working day, ale to hand and a copy of the *Manchester Guardian* opened up as if to read, he didn't care to contemplate. His superior officer wouldn't appreciate that the required discrete watchfulness could only be achieved with the paper at an awkward angle and that he'd read the same report over and over again.

Positioned by the door, he was jostled by the comings and goings of other customers, and the draught meant he was constantly readjusting pages as they flapped about. Not that the sergeant had found his man difficult to follow; he'd turned north into Oxford Street, under the bridge, across the road and into Great Portland Street, his bowler hat bobbing along amongst the throng. He wasn't tall, but his manner of walking caused his head to move in an easily recognisable manner. Spray missed the name of the side street he'd turned into when Bowler Hat entered a tobacconist shop. Another man followed him in, obscuring the view, but Bowler Hat reappeared and walked on without a backward glance. He'd stopped at a newsvendor and bought a paper, so Spray followed suit. A *Times* reader when he got the chance, he could only get the Manchester paper.

Now, as he peered over its top edge, the man, having extracted a hunter from his waistcoat, started readying himself for departure. The hunter lid was flipped shut, the last drops of beer supped, and the newspaper folded. Instead of heading toward Spray and the way out, he turned on his heel and, after a quick word with the publican, headed through a door at the back.

The jakes was Sam's first thought, a subject that had been much on his mind for the last hour or more, but then what about a back way out? He asked mine host, and was only partly reassured to be told that beer deliveries came that way, but it was locked the rest of the time. "You can have a piss, there's a privy out there; he'll be back in a minute."

He was, too, and went straight out onto the street. Bowler Hat was more difficult to follow now. He showed greater purpose, pushing through knots of people with a determination that his follower had to emulate if he was to keep his quarry in sight. To Sam's relief, he regained his bearings when they entered Corporation Street. It was shortly after that Bowler Hat's destination became clear – Victoria Station.

The constant movement was mesmerising. A good place to hide, for both stalker and prey, but Bowler Hat bobbed along without any attempt at shaking off his follower. He joined a queue in the Left Luggage Office. Sam watched as he re-emerged with a Gladstone bag and joined another line of people at a ticket window. If only... but he didn't dare get close enough to hear the man's destination.

Snaking into the jostling crowd was a static line, rather like a breakwater dissipating the power of waves on a beach. Mostly men, down-at-heel men at that, they stood guarding their cases and bags; a few had sacks tied at the neck with string. Porters were nowhere to be seen. There were no pickings to be had from these passengers. At its head was a board, four square and fixed to a moveable stand. Its blackness was much faded by constant writing and re-writing notices of un-timetabled departures. This one was a boat train, 'Afternoon Sailing, Liverpool to Drogheda, Today.' Bowler Hat added one more traveller to the end of the line.

Could he risk it, or perhaps, could he not risk it? If Bowler Hat was waiting for the boat train, he must be going to Ireland, mustn't he? Sam was thinking furiously. If I don't follow, I've lost him for good. If I let him out of my sight to get a ticket then I might lose him, but if he's still here when I get back I'm still in the game. He took a chance on it.

Something else had become even more pressing than the matter of a ticket. Sam dived into a stinking cavern beneath the station forecourt that constituted the Gentleman's Convenience. He took some while over the matter in hand, that half pint of ale had only added to the required time. Hurrying up the steps, he was relieved to see that Bowler Hat was still in the queue; he'd unfolded his paper and was reading as he waited. Not only that, he'd moved several places up from the end. The train was going to be crowded.

"Liverpool; single." On the other side of the glass, the clerk nodded as he reached for a blank ticket. "That gets me on the boat train, does it?"

"If you've got an advance ticket for the crossing, sir."

"If not?"

"You won't get through the barrier. I can sell you one, sir."

Inside the sergeant's jacket, in a pocket secured by a buttoned tab, was a sealed packet. It had been there for some time and had only seen the light of day when brought out for inspection by Superintendent Wayland. It was, after all, the property of the L&NWR and they had every right to check on the five pounds it contained. 'For emergency use only' he'd been told, and 'I shall expect a receipt if you have to use it.'

A queue was building up behind him. It was no time for sober contemplation, although at the back of Sam's mind there were doubts.

"Ticket for the crossing then," he called as he pulled out the packet.

"That'll be four shillings."

"That all?" He'd got four shillings in his pocket. Hastily replacing his reserve fund, he exposed its bold constabulary stamp.

"Wouldn't show that over the water." Money changed hands. "Can't stand the English, and an English policeman... I wish you luck, sir." The clerk handed his tickets through the window cut out and, looking over Sam's shoulder, "Next please."

It was quiet. No drunks shouting, no pickpockets protesting their innocence, no-one else at all in the row of cages. An occasional voice from beyond the lockup echoed round the police cells, that was all. The solitary occupant sat on the one piece of furniture available to him – a narrow bench, fixed to the wall. Not quite long enough to accommodate his full height and not quite wide enough to lie safely without rolling onto the floor.

In his discomfort, William Archer took to talking to himself. Sometimes out loud, but mostly inside his head. He'd been hungry, but the pangs had passed. A police officer had brought a pitcher of water, but hadn't spoken. Drinking was almost impossible with handcuffs on.

"Question one, why have they locked me up? Answer, they don't know who I am. Question two, why haven't they asked me? Answer, they're trying to soften me up. Well… possibly, but maybe the right man is busy. Big question, when they ask, do I tell them why I'm here in their city or not? Answer, it depends on what they know already.

"That's the key; if I know something they don't, maybe I can bargain with them."

"Right, let's see what we've got 'ere." The time for talking to himself had passed, now he would have to talk to the uniformed sergeant who was unlocking the gate to his cell.

"You…" He pointed accusingly at his prisoner. "You are in a lot of trouble."

Archer said nothing.

"First, causing a disturbance at a respectable house in New Wakefield Street – I might go as far as to call it an affray.

Made it very difficult for gentlemen trying to gain entry, you did." The man spoke as if he was reading from a charge sheet. "Second, intimidating behaviour towards a police officer. If we hadn't arrested you, who knows what you might have done to the man."

"I can't be under arrest; you haven't gone through the procedure."

"Don't you get clever with me, sonny." Then, over his shoulder, "Alf, we've got a right one here, thinks he knows it all."

Boots clattered on the flags beyond the cage.

"We'd better show him he's wrong." Menace filtered through the grill before Alf was through the door. A police officer, yes, from his uniform and truncheon, but inside the blue serge lurked a thug. What had been a pantomime was turning into something else entirely. So far, Archer's problem had been suppressing laughter at the ridiculous accusations; now he was frightened.

"Says we haven't arrested him yet."

"Looks to me as if he's resisting arrest at this very moment." The truncheon, unhooked now, was on its way through a back-swing when...

"Just a minute, lads, let's find out who he is before you beat him to a pulp."

A man in plain clothes had materialised. The truncheon slowly descended to a less threatening position.

"You got a name, sonny?" the first policeman demanded.

"William Archer."

"Well, William Archer, what line of business leads you to cause all this trouble on our patch?"

"I'm a police officer."

For a moment, there was silence.

"You got any proof of that?" The plain clothes man spoke.

"A warrant card."

"Show me."

Archer raised his hands. "Bit difficult with these."

"Get 'em off him. He can't do much harm with three of us here." The plain clothes man was clearly the senior.

They repaired to a shabby office. Papers were scattered about, a half empty mug of tea vied for space with a pot of ink, and the blotter hadn't had its paper changed in months.

"Right, go and get us a brew, and then make yourselves scarce." The uniforms were being dispensed with. "Now, Constable Archer of the Railway Constabulary, just explain to me what you were doing in a brothel in New Warwick Street?"

"Your man said it was a respectable house."

"Don't come all clever dick with me. Whatever you were doing, you were doing it on my patch."

"I was investigating a crime."

"Bawdy houses your usual line in the Railway Constabulary? My bawdy house, I might say. Come on, stop wasting my time."

"We…" Archer realised he was revealing more than he intended. "I, am investigating a murder."

"Ain't been no murders hereabouts for a while. I'd have heard of them, else."

To Archer's relief, his slip was ignored. "In Whaley Bridge, Saturday last."

"And where might Whaley Bridge be?" The sarcasm didn't ring true.

An idea erupted like a starburst in Archer's mind. "You know perfectly well where it is, you were seen there on the day of the murder." There was a startled silence. The gamble had paid off. "Along with your tame dip. How's his shoulder, by the way?" For the first time since he'd been dragged into the station, Archer was enjoying himself.

The plain clothes man stood up and paced about his room. From the back, he looked exactly like the man Archer had followed earlier. "Also, I could ask you why you were at an address that's material to my enquiries?"

The man sat down. "I'm Inspector Downes, attached to the City police here in Manchester."

"Attached from where?"

Downes seemed to be about to quibble, then, "The Metropolitan Police. Now, you tell me something I don't know."

Two mugs of tea arrived, after which the conversation proceeded incrementally. The man who'd had his pocket picked had been under surveillance by the inspector. That he'd been seen in Whaley Bridge at Patrick Thomas's funeral some months before certainly interested Downes. Scotland Yard being worried about a Fenian plot made sense to Archer, who said the dead man was of Irish descent. And so it went on.

Some things remained unsaid until the end.

"Do you think your man would kill, and if so why and who is he anyway?" Downes thought he'd kill to protect himself.

"What were they doing in Shallcross yard?" Archer explained about the Dynamite.

"Who was the dead man?" Downes asked.

"You didn't tell me who your man is."

They sipped the tea. The inspector sighed. "Makes a lousy cuppa, does Alf."

When he'd brought the tea in, Archer wondered what Alf had done with his menace. Perhaps he only produced it on demand. "It's no better at our office in Crewe."

Whilst they sat contemplating the unappealing brown

liquid, Alf returned with a telegram. After glancing at it, Downes looked up.

"Right, one of us has got to go first. It had better be me; I can always get Alf back if you don't play fair. Our man calls himself Slade. We believe he's Irish but he has an English accent. He might be an out and out Fenian. So, what about the dead man?"

"We believe he was Cathal Lynch. Brought up in Canada, of Irish parentage. Looks like he first turned up in Derbyshire when his uncle died a few months ago. Has two cousins who didn't know of his existence; one of them still doesn't."

"How old did he look?"

"Thirties, late probably."

"That fits. Must have escaped from the potato famine as a little'un and then picked the violence up from his dad. Very angry that lot." Downes looked pensive. "S'pose I would have been if I'd seen my family starve to death." He looked at the telegram again.

"That mate of yours, what's his name? He's just boarded an Irish ferry."

"He's my sergeant, Sam Spray. Now tell me, what did you mean, Slade 'might be an out and out Fenian'. Either he's an Irish revolutionary, or he isn't. Don't you know?"

Downes wasn't to be drawn on the subject. "That sergeant of yours, hope he can look after himself. We don't venture across the water."

"You've been following him?"

"You didn't know? I expect the lad who's been hanging around outside does. Best take him home to his mam before he learns how to pick pockets."

Silence prevailed in the bleak, cold room; it reeked of neglect and despair. It was the silence of abandonment.

On the floor lay the body of a man, dropped carelessly, and left where he fell in an untidy heap. How long he'd lain unconscious and bleeding, he didn't know, when finally he stirred. To begin with, he didn't know anything except that his head throbbed unbearably.

Something green moved lazily, revealing a white mark. He'd seen that before, but searching his mind made his headache worse so its meaning remained unexplained as he drifted away, back into oblivion. Later it reappeared, attached to a stick with muffin on top. He concentrated on the muffin. This time he was making progress, and somehow his headache became more bearable. The stick and muffin evolved into a flagpole flying a green flag with a white star on it. Memories were stirred of battles and sea voyages and a railway into the hills.

Time passed, and with the Crimean War almost accounted for, Drogheda slipped – like the last piece of a jigsaw – into place. The Drogheda Steam Packet Co: he'd seen one of their ships moored at Balaklava, men pouring down her gangplank… just like the *PS Athulmney*, with men carrying their bags and sacks onto the quay at Drogheda. Ireland, that was it; he'd boarded a ship for Ireland. The stench: how the old paddle steamer stank. He couldn't get rid of it. Whatever floated into his mind, it was suffused with the stench of manure. That's it, cattle manure. She carried cattle down below and passengers on the deck. His four shilling ticket had seemed cheap when he'd bought it; unbelievably cheap. Not any more.

Yes, he remembered now, Victoria Station, then Liverpool Exchange, then boarding the *Athulmney* with all those passengers, Irish to a man. But why was he doing it? He hated sea voyages, he… He was following a man in a bowler hat.

Where was he now? Not Drogheda; he remembered boarding a train. He was wherever the train had taken him.

Chapter 9

Thursday, September 20th, 1876

They arrived together: the older ones a little out of breath on account of the hill. The women varied in age, and in other ways, but they had all known each other for as long as any of them could remember. The group had evolved over the years. One of its founding members had died some time ago, but she was still present in the person of her daughter. Some, once regulars, were no less part of things despite their circumstances making attendance more difficult of late.

Mrs Allcroft worked at the mill now, but when her children were younger she'd been a regular. Indeed, she was here today, and no doubt would tell them why. Mrs Maida, along with two of the others, had never worked since her marriage. Perhaps the least likely member of the group was hostess for the day. Alone amongst the gathering, she owned her own house, but Lizzie Oldroyd had been known to them all her life and her late mother had started the whole thing. So, the little knot of women converged this Thursday on 37 Mill End for afternoon tea. If anything was common to them all, it was their respectability.

Lizzie Oldroyd was most at risk in this respect. After all, she made a business of accommodating strangers – many of them men – on her premises, but the young widow's reputation was never questioned. In this connection, it was fortunate that the others had no insight into the state of her heart. Ever since the previous Saturday when she had met Sam Spray walking down to the Gala Celebrations, something had changed. A carefully tended glow, kept alight but under control over the last months, had burst into flame with an intensity that she could hardly contain. On the surface, there was little to see. A lifetime of urbanity was not thrown off so easily, but inside she burned.

Ever since William's news, brought to her late last evening, she had been in torment. That morning, they'd left together, but William had arrived back from Manchester on his own, saying he believed Sam to be in Ireland chasing the shadows that constituted their present investigation.

"Tea, Mary?" Lizzie was going through the afternoon ritual. "And you, Emmeline?" The women were all on given name terms. "Help yourselves to cake." From the kitchen, a singing kettle called her away, to Lizzie's relief. On her own, she could agonise about the danger Sam must be in. It had to be danger-ous, with one man dead already and the theft of explosives.

"I really don't know how to manage him." Emmeline Allcroft turned to Lizzie as she came back with the hot water. "Do you know, he missed school and went on a train, all on his own. Said he was helping an investigation." The teapot was being topped up. "It was that Constable Archer who brought him home – all the way from Manchester. You know him, don't you? He lodges here sometimes."

Trying to avoid a spill, there was no reply for a moment.

"He… he is alright, isn't he?" It wasn't spelt out, but all the mothers present knew what she meant.

"He's a very honest and reliable young man. He has younger brothers of his own. I expect that's how he gets on so well with your Jimmy." Lizzie found it easier to calm other people's worries than her own.

She and William had discussed things over his late supper. Each had been grateful in their own way to have a confi-dante. For the young policeman, about to make his first big decision without his sergeant behind him, it helped relieve his uncertainty. For Lizzie, overwhelmed by emotions she had never felt during her marriage, a source of comfort was welcome. They'd decided to give Sam two days to find his way back, then if they'd heard nothing, William would have to confront his superintendent with the situation. It would mean searching him out at his home, on a Sunday, but only a week ago William had been ordered to do just that.

The ladies were readying themselves for departure as the last crumbs of cake were being bunched up and popped into mouths followed by the last drops of tea.

"Your Madeira was particularly good today, Lizzie." Elsie Maida, a plump, comfortable woman enjoyed her food. "I don't suppose I'll match it next week." Lizzie thought if only she could get to next week with news of Sam, she wouldn't care what the cake was like.

The midday post had been late and the only letter to arrive was addressed in an unfamiliar hand. Even though Lizzie was busy with preparations for the tea party, she would have opened it had it borne an Irish, or even a Manchester postmark, just on the off-chance of it bearing some news of Sam. As it was, the Penny Red had been stamped in Cromford and she'd put it to one side.

―◦•◦―

With her guests departed and the tea things cleared and washed, she sat in her now deserted parlour and slit open the envelope.

Dear Mrs Oldroyd,
I need to see you. It is a matter I find it difficult to talk
about and you are the only person I can think of. I shall
be in Whaley Bridge on Saturday. Would you mind if I
paid you a call?

Yours sincerely,
Mary Thomas

She sat for a while contemplating the letter, puzzled by its
formality and concerned by the desperation it suggested. She
and Mary had been close in the past, like sisters really. During
Mrs Thomas's long last illness, it had fallen to the ten-year-
old Mary to care for her invalid mother. Lizzie had become
friend, comforter and advisor to the girl. Indeed, toward the
end, when Lizzie's own mother started to ail, helping Mary
had become a welcome distraction from her own worries.
Between them was a bond of shared suffering that Lizzie had
thought would endure. But now, this stilted little letter asking
for permission to call?

It was true that the two of them had seen little of each other
lately, but with Mary in service it was inevitable. Even so,
Lizzie would have expected the girl to come to the door unannounced and the friendship to resume from exactly where it
had been left at their last meeting. Of course she was welcome,
and Lizzie replied straight away.

Dearest Mary,
Certainly you must come. You know you don't have to
ask, you'll always be welcome here. I'm sure we can sort
out whatever is troubling you. I look forward to seeing
you on Saturday.

Much love,
Lizzie

Not for the first time, helping Mary Thomas was offering a diversion from worries of her own.

———•··•———

The imprisoned man, who could remember nothing after boarding a train at Drogheda, had at last worked out that he was a policeman. At least, it seemed that a policeman was involved and the thinking was being done by a man on the outside, looking on. Why this policeman was following a man with a bowler hat had remained a mystery for a while longer, but slowly, bit by bit, he pieced things together. Not knowing who he was remained a big problem, but most worrying of all was how long ago it had all happened? What day was it? Come to that, was it day or was it night? It had certainly been night time when he boarded the train.

The untidy pile of humanity that had lain on the prison floor when it first regained consciousness had managed to rearrange itself so that it now sat, legs outstretched, propped against a wall, recognisably alive and human. There was a slops bucket in the corner and another containing water. He didn't remember them from when he'd first come to. Suddenly, both became supremely important. He rolled and managed to get onto all fours. Standing was an impossibility, so he crawled to the empty pitcher and, using it as a prop, managed to kneel. He wondered how long he'd gone without emptying his bladder; he certainly hadn't wet himself. As relief came, he concluded that he couldn't have been there much more than a day.

His watch! If it was still ticking, he could have only been here for a short time. He wound it regularly at bed time, and if he missed it would only run on for a few hours beyond the twenty-four. He felt for the familiar bulge in his waistcoat pocket. Nothing. It occurred to him that if this man who'd lost his watch was a policeman, he must have a warrant card, and on that card would be a name. He was really pleased with himself for thinking of that until he found it, too, was missing from its usual pocket.

Water; that was the next priority. His mouth was dry and he had a raging thirst. The last thing he could remember drinking was that meagre half pint in the public house in Manchester. A pannikin had been left by the fresh water, and as he dipped it he thought he heard movement behind him. He looked just in time to see a spy hole in the door snap shut. It was the first sound he could remember hearing since he'd arrived. Even if he didn't know this policeman's name, someone must do.

The analytical part of his mind was functioning better than his memory. It worked at garnering such bits of information that the memory let drop and feverishly tried to make sense of what had been released. It considered why, if Bowler Hat was on the wrong side of the law, he hadn't made it more difficult to be followed. Memory had let it be known that Bowler Hat had stood for some time queuing in full view, when making a last-minute dash for the boat train from a place of conceal-ment would have been more difficult for anyone on his tail. The man could undoubtedly have made a clandestine exit from the rear of the public house, but had chosen to walk out of the front door.

The policeman, relieved, with thirst slaked and now returned to propping himself against the wall of his prison, had to accept that he'd walked headlong into a trap. But whose trap? And where was he? Where did trains go to from Drogheda? Had he ever known where they went? He'd bought a ticket but could only recall saying "single to the terminus" in his urgent need to keep Bowler Hat in sight. Did he look at the ticket after he'd bought it? It was no good; memory was hanging onto that bit of information for a while longer.

Chapter 10

Friday, September 21st, 1876

Bosley Station was a faint echo of the local half-timbered tradition. True, it had white panels surrounded by black painted timbers, but the paint was greying, the timbers were spindly, and the whole structure had a meanness about it. If he'd only come to admire the architecture, it would hardly have been worth the trip.

A complicated journey it had proved, too; a couple of changes and three tickets, each issued by a different railway to travel the twenty-five miles from Whaley Bridge. What with the climb between the Lower and Upper stations at Middlewood, and a walk between Central and Hibel Road stations in Macclesfield, William felt he'd had enough exercise for one morning, but with the first of Bosley locks in view the day's work was only just starting. Here, he hoped to unearth information from amongst the canalside community that might help to explain how Monday's coup had been achieved.

To reach the Macclesfield Canal, he'd walked in the cess alongside the track to the point where the railway passed over the cut. He stood watching the scene below. To the policeman, with the speed and urgency of railways as a backdrop to his working day, the slowly moving boats had an air of tranquillity in the September sunshine. He started counting, a boat every few minutes in each direction, dextrously crossing with each other without checking their speed, the only impediment to progress being the locks. In one day, many boats must pass in this constant flow. His quest was not going to be easy.

He clambered down the embankment to gain the towpath. On Tuesday, it had been exactly the reverse. At Middlewood, he'd had to climb to reach the cut. The steep track was well worn and would have been slippery, except for a recent dry spell. William set off to the south beneath the rail bridge. Behind him was lock No.1 and beyond that a clear run of sixteen miles to a stop lock, allowing access to the Peak Forest canal at Marple junction. Ahead, the cut disappeared to the left, leaving a pool of brown, polluted water, wide enough to turn a boat in. He walked round the slow curve to find a cottage alongside the pound, with an area of mown grass between it and the towpath. To a man used to the dirt and disorder associated with railway property, the scene had a civilised, almost genteel, air.

Beside the cottage, a bent figure tended her vegetable patch. A row of green fronds waved in the breeze, possibly carrots, thought William; certainly potatoes where the woman was digging. He could see some on the surface, with their tops cast aside.

"Good day to you, missus," he called.

The woman stood up, not much straighter than when she worked. She glared in his direction. "What d'you want?"

Back home in his family's shop, they'd call her a 'scratchy old besom'. As customers in a bakery, they were ten a penny, but not so common in his present employment.

"I'd like to speak to the lock keeper."

"So would I, and I'm married to 'im."

"So, he lives here?"

"He do an' he don't. Who's askin'?"

"Constable Archer, Railway Police."

"Y'er not from the Company then? He spends so little time here I wouldn't put it past 'em to throw me out."

"So where does he spend his time then?" The conversation

was getting nowhere and William wanted to get on.

"On the cut during the day, seeing to the locks and that. There's a woman down the flight 'as sells drink. He goes there after work – not all she sells either. Not that I care. If he's getting it there, he's not troublin' me. I'd just like 'im to bring his pay packet home once in a while."

William carried on, picking his way carefully. The edge of the towpath was crumbling here and there, but a more likely accident was tripping over a pile of horse droppings. It was busy, too, what with the powerful animals plodding along sedately, their taut towlines a constant danger to the walker, and children too, running free, oblivious of the risks. Some of the youngsters were already at work, leading the horses and helping move the heavy lock gates.

It was comforting to hear the occasional train. Canal and railway ran almost parallel, and William could have taken a road straight to the cut from Bosley Station when he'd arrived, but he'd have missed his conversation with the lock keeper's wife. Here at lock No.5, he found boats waiting to move in both directions. The pound each end of the lock contained three each, waiting their turn. Old-fashioned it might be, to a man from the modern world of rail, but William could only marvel at the neatness of the manoeuvres. One into the near empty lock; the gate closing as soon as it would clear the boat's stern; paddles opening immediately; and the rushing water bringing thirty tons of coal up to the next level. Immediately, a line passed from horse to boat and as the gate opened, the massive animal leaned into its collar and the heavy craft was on the move. At the same time a line was passed round the strapping post, and with much heaving on the free end another boat slipped into the lock to commence its descent to gain the lower level.

In amongst this hive of activity, one man was a constant. Calling a laggardly boat forward whilst catching a strap from another and looping it over the snubbing post and then leaning into a balance beam to move a gate, he was on the move all the time. Finally, the last boat was on its way and William stepped forward.

"You're a busy man, I see. I wonder if I might have a word."

"You from the Company?" William assured the man he had no connection with the canal owners. "I'm from the railway."

"All right, but it'll cost you a sup of ale." The lock keeper nodded toward a shant by the road to the station. "So, what's yer business, mister?"

Inside the drinking den, it was hot. The small room was packed, and every man must have brought stale sweat, tobacco smoke, and the smell of horse to the party, to join the stale beer and vomit already there. All William could think of when the ale was brought was 'comely wench', despite the baby she was suckling. Holding a guzzling infant on one arm, the woman delivered their drinks with the other hand, and took William's money with practised ease. There was nowhere to sit and it was unclear whether the occasional stumble by a customer was due to alcohol or one of the other children wriggling between the legs of the crowd. As the eldest in his family, William was familiar with young children, and he calculated there must have been a new arrival every eighteen months or so.

"Ay, she's a good lass that 'un." They were sitting on a log outside now. "Keeps them little 'uns looking well."

"On her own?" asked William.

"Her fella pushed off when the first one turned up. Ain't been seen since."

"So the others…" William's indiscretion was saved by the lock keeper.

"Now, mister, let's start with you telling me what you do on the railway?" This wasn't quite how the policeman had imagined the conversation.

"I'm Constable Archer, LNW Railway Police."

"You'll be a bit lost here." He nodded toward the nearby station. "What with the Knotty over there and the cut; that warrant card don't mean a thing."

"I was only hoping for a bit of help from someone who knows what goes on here. You must be the most knowledge-able man on the canal."

The grizzled, muscular man with tattooed arms didn't smirk, but he calculated that this was the moment for a second pint. William thought it could wait.

"After you've given me something."

"Right you are. What d'ye want, Mr Policeman?"

"We had a bit of trouble at Middlewood on Monday. Did you see anything unusual in the few days before or after?"

"Oh aye. I heard summat nasty went off, a signalman, weren't it? But what've we got to do wi' it here on the cut?"

William explained that they thought that stolen goods had been transferred onto a narrowboat where canal and rail crossed. "We think the boat might have come through here, and you might have noticed something out of place."

"Big and heavy, were it? Sort of thing you couldn't just carry away in yer pocket then?"

William agreed and waited. In the silence, the other man finished his ale.

"What sort of thing would that be, I wonder?" The mug was turned upside down and then placed on the ground. More silence.

"Tommy Cubbin were a bit odd, I s'pose. Well, not 'im, his boat. Old Tom's always been odd. He's a bachelor, see;

never had a woman an' no kids neither. Y' needs a family to work a boat proper and he has any old layabout t' give him a hand – always has. No, what was odd was he went through without a load."

"Was that odd?" William asked. "At least one of the boats that has just passed had no load. I could see into the hold."

"Tommy Cubbin might be a queer bugger, but he knows where to find a load better'n any of 'em. I can't remember the last time he went through without one. An' what's more, his boat weren't quite right. Very fussy 'e is about the old *Kingfisher*, allus has the tarpaulin roped up right and everything shipshape, but on Sunday he set off for the Peak Forest with a corner flapping and his straps all over the place."

"Could you see in?"

"No, not into the hold; it were only loose, not folded back."

"How did you know he hadn't a cargo then?"

A pitying look came over the man's face. "Don't you know nuthin'? Look, if the boat has a cargo, it sits low in the water. Depends on the load o'course, but generally there's only an inch or two of freeboard. When she's empty, she'll sit much higher, like *Kingfisher* did. Oh aye, there was something else; his lurchers."

"What about his dogs?"

"He didn't have two of 'em. Ever since I've known Tommy he's had a terrier on his boat, and a couple of lurchers that trot along the towpath mostly. They'm friendly as y' like, the lurchers that is – well, not to the rabbits, if you get my drift. But there weren't no sign of one of 'm on Sunday. An' is bloody little terrier weren't on the boat barkin' and snapping like it usually does. Odd that."

"One last thing," William, busy scribbling in his notebook, nearly forgot to ask, "what time Sunday did she come through?"

"How about another before I tell you that?" The lock keeper had retrieved his mug and it was right way up now. William reckoned he'd earned it.

"Bout mid-morning, just give him time to get to Middlewood by dark."

———

The guard's roster hadn't been kind to Stephen. He'd arrived back dog-tired on Thursday night and only just made it back for an early start at Shallcross yard on Friday morning. Stumbling over the threshold in the dark, he'd not noticed the letter. Addressed to Mr Stephen Thomas, it bore a Cromford postmark. Had he seen it, he would have recognised the hand and opened it immediately.

As it was, Mary's letter lay pushed to one side by the door until her brother had done another day's work. Not so late on Friday, it was still daylight when he arrived home and this time he noticed his mail.

> *Dear Stephen,*
> *I have a little time off on Saturday. I shall be home*
> *for a while in the afternoon and hope to see you*
> *then. If you're still at work, I'll miss you as I have*
> *to be back by nightfall.*
> *From your loving sister,*
> *Mary.*

It was too late to do anything about it; he was rostered for work on Saturday and no-one would change with him now. It was the first time he'd have seen Mary in a while. When their father started ailing, she'd been back regular as clockwork every other Sunday in time to cook for them all and comfort the old man. As he'd become more infirm, she'd even inveigled the big house to let her come a little more often, but since the funeral it had been different.

Stephen had his suspicions. On one occasion when his train had taken him to Buxton, he'd seen her in the distance, or someone very like her, talking to a young man. 'Very like her' that was the problem; he couldn't be sure, and it worried him. What's more, the railwayman was from the other side; even that far away, there was no mistaking the Midland uniform.

Two companies ran trains into Buxton and Stephen knew very well that the L&NWR was the superior. It styled itself as the Premier Line, and a cut above the others was how its employees saw themselves. The MR men weren't at all convinced. They had to accept that theirs was the smaller company, but its network was more universally spread throughout the country and it had an unrivalled reputation for comfort. A boundary ran between the two and woe betide anyone who strayed across it. Stephen just had to know what was going on, and he resolved to do just that on Saturday.

———•◦•———

The policeman who didn't know his name was beginning to see the world with a bit more clarity now, despite his aching head. Earlier, in his befuddled state, he'd found it impossible to separate night from day. Being unable to see a window, he'd thought himself isolated from the diurnal rhythms, but now with a clearer mind he recognised that day was following night and turning into day again. He tried to count back how many times the change had occurred, but the recent past was a confusing place. Nonetheless, he resolved to keep track from now on.

Such daylight as made its way into the cell came through a grill high up on the wall, opposite the door with the spyhole. There was no sky to be seen, only the reveals of a very thick wall beyond the grill. The handle of the pannikin made a poor chisel, but he was doing his best to make scratches on the wall with it, one for each day, when the door opened.

"Stay where you are." He was facing the wall opposite the door and he did what the disembodied voice told him. Footsteps behind him; he wondered if he was going to die there and then, but as a blindfold was put over his eyes he reasoned that, since dead men tell no tales, he would be alive at the end of whatever was about to happen.

"Turn round to face the door." A chair scraped on the floor and then caught him behind the knees. His legs crumpled and he found himself sitting. Immediately, his wrists were grasped and he was immobilised, hands tied behind to the back of the chair.

The steps receded, but the door remained open. It wasn't clear to the prisoner whether he was alone or not, but he'd gained a crumb of information. The man was Irish. The prisoner on the chair knew his Irish accents and this one was from Dublin. Dublin, Dublin; in his mind, he caressed and polished the name. It was more than a brogue, it was a place. It was the place on the other end of the line from Drogheda. He was in Dublin.

"He's ready, sorr." The Dublin voice again. Different feet now, not boots this time, taking their owner round to a position in front of him.

He'd known this moment would come. The moment when he would be arraigned by his captors, and he had prepared for it as best he could. Nothing. He'd resolved to tell them nothing. At the beginning, it had seemed an easy option. He could remember nothing, but now it would be more difficult, he would have to pretend… nothing.

"Who are you?" No Irish tones in this voice. The Quality was taking an interest in him. No answer. No pretence here; he still couldn't remember.

"What are you doing here?" He found it difficult to suppress a laugh. *A pity*, he thought, *it would have been the first one since his incarceration*. But a laugh wasn't nothing. He remained silent.

"Do you know what you've got yourself into?" There was menace in the voice now and the interrogator was in his face. The seated man could feel his breath. "We know all about you, of course. There's no point in being difficult."

Silence.

"Now let us see." The voice was further away. "Not you, of course, you aren't going to see anything. We could have put your eyes out; it would have saved all the business with the blindfold, but I'm not a savage – that's more than I can say for my man here."

Silence.

"I've got an invitation to a celebration in some obscure place in Derbyshire. It has a name on it, and a little message on the back. I suppose we could find out who Lizzie is. I expect it would loosen your tongue if we brought her here. We might even take the blindfold off so you could see what was happening."

Silence. A more fraught silence this time. The man behind the blindfold hadn't considered endangering others with his obduracy. Nonetheless, silence.

"Then there's this official-looking card. Could be counterfeit, probably has a false name on it. This Sergeant Samuel Spray must be an imposter."

Silence, but a jubilant silence this time. I know who I am, thought Sam. And with that knowledge, the muddle of the last few days suddenly found order in his mind.

"The Railway Constabulary. Never heard of it; nothing very important, I'll be bound."

Silence. However, this silence was of the voice's making. Sam pictured its owner poring over the warrant card.

"Superintendent Wayland, hmm." The voice was a whisper now, speaking to itself. "Wayland countersigned this... I wonder.

Chapter 11

Saturday, September 22nd, 1876

Impotence did not sit comfortably with either of them. If only there was something they could do! Activity of some sort gave a semblance of progress, and in this, William was best placed. At least he'd spent yesterday travelling, walking, asking questions, and just possibly pushing the case a step forward. Today, he planned a foray to the other end of the Macclesfield Canal.

Lizzie could find no such relief. What she wanted was to catch a train to Crewe and confront the superintendent with the loss of his sergeant. But as William pointed out, even if he was fit and well, Sam couldn't get back from Ireland in time to reach Whaley Bridge before Saturday evening. Despite her anxiety, she accepted the logic of this, though a nagging little voice in the back of her head kept asking, why hadn't he sent a telegram? Perhaps she'd mistaken his intentions, and his appearance at the gala was only a matter of politeness; black thoughts like these momentarily chased out the anxiety, but were even worse than worry about Sam's safety. She upbraided herself for the selfishness of preferring him being at risk than being indifferent to her, but that was how she felt. So she returned to worrying about his wellbeing.

Mary and her problems would have to provide her only diversion for today.

Mary Thomas had left school when she was twelve years old. This was a matter of regret to her teacher, who thought her an eminently teachable child, but her mother was dying and she was needed at home – first to nurse the invalid, and then to care for the men of the household. No-one thought of asking Mary what she wanted, but if they had, she would have turned the question round to 'what do you want of me?'.

Patrick, her father, retired from the railway when she was fourteen. With only Stephen's wage coming into the household, Mary was transformed from a necessity into an unaffordable luxury. Under the circumstances, she had left home for a position in service. Another transformation had turned her into an attractive young woman, her physical maturity all the more appealing as she was quite unconscious of it.

Pretty, intelligent and innocent was the picture she had presented to the housekeeper at the big house, and – above all – honest, when, accompanied by her father, they had travelled to Cromford for an interview. The testimonial Mary had brought with her was read with approval. Perhaps the only reservation was the stress her teacher had laid on the young woman's intelligence. In the housekeeper's view, an enquiring mind often spelt trouble, but she was reassured by the demure young woman, and Mary had started at Ravenhead House the next week.

Perhaps her father should have asked more questions when he accompanied her to the interview. He might have asked what had happened to the girl who had relinquished the position his daughter was to occupy, or whose house it was, and how many of the 'Quality' lived there; but he didn't. When the sour-faced housekeeper had offered his daughter the post, he was just grateful that she would have her keep and thus relieve him of the expense.

The scullery maid was a big, lumpy girl, older than Mary, with a perpetual smell of onions about her. The two shared a garret, but the incumbent spoke very little. In particular, she had said nothing about that part of the house which was the exclusive domain of the housekeeper. The girls' most intimate connection with each other was the sharing of a pisspot, which it was the newcomer's job to empty each morning.

The older girl had appeared not to notice anything amiss the day the awful thing happened. Over in a few minutes, but far outside Mary's understanding, it had left her so shocked that a numbness came over her and she couldn't cry. Talking about it had been beyond her. How could an innocent convent girl speak of such a thing? The shame would not allow it, even if she had the words. No, she hadn't shared her experience, but the comfort of someone seeing her distress and offering solace might have helped.

The garret had been empty by the time Mary had dragged herself up the rickety stairs to bed. The moon was full and a little of its cold light crept through her draughty window. It flickered, the frayed net – serving as a curtain – rippling as the wind found the cracks. She had to make do with its ghostly effect; servants didn't rate candles, or even tapers. She had struggled with her nightdress, and finally, disappearing into its interior darkness, sought protection for her shivering body against the chill night.

She had emerged into a more frightening darkness as a cloud, racing the wind, passed over the moon. All around were noises, as the old building settled for the night. *The other girl must be up soon,* she'd thought. *Perhaps that's her*? The stairs outside creaked slightly. The light scraping sound, as if a foot, lightly drawn across a step, was unfamiliar. It was nothing like the heavy clunks with which the scullery maid climbed her way to bed.

Mary had knelt, her hands together in prayer. *It's him,* she thought, *here to hurt me again.* The garret door swung open and the girl, eyes tight shut and paralysed with fear, prayed as she waited for what was to come.

"Help me," the voice was tremulous. "Where am I?"

Mary dared to look. With the cloud's passing, there was light again. In the doorway was an old man, bent and unsteady, his nightcap skewed at an unlikely angle, and gown trailing.

"Please help, I've lost my room. I don't know where I am."

———⚫•⚫———

It was from Ravenhead House that she had written the letters to her brother and her friend. With a little time to herself on Wednesday afternoon, she had taken her mail down into Cromford to make sure it caught the late collection. These journeys into the village had once been a pleasure, but now she had to pick her moments carefully. Today, though still watchful, she thought herself safe enough. She'd not seen Mister Henry since the awful thing, although his comings and goings were very unpredictable, and she knew Ben only came to visit his mother on Sunday afternoons.

It had been a Sunday afternoon in Buxton when they had first met: she, passing his booking office on her way to her connection in the adjacent station; he, coming out of its side door on his way to catch a train to Cromford. They had almost collided. In the ensuing "So sorry, Miss" and "Not at all, I'm quite alright, really", Ben had picked up Mary's parcel and found his offer to "Carry it round to the other station for you" gratefully accepted. By the time she was aboard her train for Whaley Bridge, they'd known enough about each other for 'chance meetings' to happen frequently. Later, nothing was left to chance, and the meetings had become eagerly anticipated trysts.

Today, things would be trickier. She couldn't possibly face Ben; it had been bad enough last time, with her body wanting nothing more than to fall on his neck and weep her heart out, whilst her voice was telling him that it was all over.

"But, Mary, I don't understand. I thought we loved each other... I still love—"

"Well, just don't, Ben." It took a superhuman effort to say it. "You will be a much happier man if you walk away now and forget me. I'm not worthy."

It was not until Benjamin Pepperell was well out of sight that the distraught girl had allowed the tears to flow. And they had flowed often in the ensuing weeks, overwhelming her until she could face them no more, which was why she was on her way to see Lizzie Oldroyd this September Saturday. But she still had to negotiate the Midland booking office where Ben would be at work selling tickets.

The large man between her and the booking window was ideal cover until, just on the point of buying his ticket, he remembered his luggage and veered away, leaving Mary and Ben with nothing separating them other than a glass panel and the girl's obduracy.

"Mary..." Ben called her name but she walked on, containing her tears until out of his narrow line of vision. It was the first time she had wept that day, but it would not be the last.

It was back to Middlewood Lower for William, then the steps to the Upper station and a train to Marple Rose Hill, in the opposite direction to yesterday's journey. There, the low brick station did nothing to enhance the reputation of railway architecture, but then not many people lived in the vicinity to see it. Named after a lonely house, it had spawned a Railway Inn and that was all. William took advice from a solitary porter and set off for the long walk to Peak Forest Junction and its stop lock.

This inconvenient impediment to the easy flow of traffic was guarded jealously by a lock keeper in the pay of the older cut.

"I'm not here to answer y'r daft questions. They pay me to see the tolls are paid and we don't lose no water to that lot."

William was puzzled. "Lose water? It's just there, isn't it?" He recognised the pitying look in the other's eye from yesterday.

"You men off the railway, you act so high and mighty, but you don't know nothing. Look here." The man pointed to his stop lock. "It's the boundary between two companies. That water there at the lower level belongs to the Peak Forest Company, and they was here first so they make sure the Macclesfield Company don't get any of it. Valuable stuff water: no water, no boats; no boats, no tolls; no tolls, no company."

"But doesn't it just stay there?" William still hadn't got the point.

"Every time a boat goes through, a lock full of water goes downhill. So, at the top we have to find enough water t'fill it up again. It's got to come from somewhere. T'ain't no good pissing in it, not even a big wet streak like you could keep it full, so we has to have reservoirs."

"I'm indebted to you for enlightenment on the matter." William had no option other than polite interest. "But there's something else you could help me with."

"You're a Jack, aren't you? That's what you said." The man glowered. "Don't hold wi' policemen."

"It's only the Railway Police." It grieved William to underplay his Service, but needs must, he thought.

"What d'ye want t' know?"

"It's Tommy Cubbin and the *Kingfisher*. Have they been—?"

"I'm not bloody well talking to you no more." The subject of Cubbin and his boat seemed to have frightened the lock keeper. "You just bugger off and leave me alone." He perked up a bit. "You ain't got no jurisdiction here anyways."

So that was it. His principal informant had clammed up on him and the rest of the day seemed pointless. William was at a loose end. It'd been a long shot, he knew, but action of some sort had seemed preferable to mooning about. He had to keep his anxieties about Sam's disappearance at bay somehow, so he set off to walk the six miles along the cut back to Whaley Bridge.

None of the skippers of the passing boats had been much help. Some were polite, "Sorry, mister, ain't seen Tommy for days." Others less so. William was keeping pace with one.

"Don't you gawpers have nuthin' better t'do?"

"I was hoping you might have seen Tommy Cubbin and the *K*—"

"Ain't seen no-one." This was patently untrue. His boat was about to cross with another as William watched. The skipper of the other boat nodded to the policeman as the manoeuvre was completed.

"Heard you askin' 'bout Tommy." William had turned and was retracing his steps to keep pace with the second boat. "Ain't seen 'im, but I saw a horse very like his at Bugsworth."

"What about the *Kingfisher*?"

"Nah. Didn't see the boat. Odd that, though, it were a good 'oss and old Tommy thought well of it."

"You sure it was his. What'd it look like?"

"Pretty common, heavy bay mare, bit of a white blaze." The man let go the tiller and made a shape with his hands. "Like this." William was none the wiser. "It was being led out of the basin so I didn't see it proper. Must have sold it off the cut."

The canal was thoroughfare, rubbish dump, and sewer for those who worked and lived on it. The boat's stem cut into detritus of all sorts, pushing it aside to brush along its length. As a bedraggled corpse, its grey curls matted with a dark stain, floated in the water between the two men, William called to the skipper. "Could you fish that out for me, mister?"

It must have been the urgency in his voice that galvanised the man at the tiller. A boat hook appeared as if by magic, and with one deft flick the unfortunate dog was on the towpath.

"What d'ye want wi' that?" His voice was fading as the boat moved on. Despite the grime and the smell, William picked up the rotting remains and called after him.

"Tommy Cubbin had a couple of lurchers." Holding the body by the scruff of its neck and tail, the animal hung with legs dangling. "Anything like this?"

Dirty water dripped from the creature and, as his aching arms sagged, filth from the canal smeared onto his clothing. There was blood in the stain, and William saw that the animal's throat had been cut.

"Mebbe, mebbe not. That'un don't bark and come lookin' fer scraps the way Tommy's did.

"It's dead, for goodness sake. What do you expect?"

"Aye, happen it is Tommy's right enough."

With the dead lurcher left behind by the towpath, William

asked, "If one of Tommy's dogs is dead and his horse is gone, what do you think has happened to Tommy, and the *Kingfisher*, come to that?"

The implication hung in the ensuing silence. The skipper hunched his shoulders. "Ain't got no more to say."

Life had become mired in gloom since it happened. Mary had found that the only way she could negotiate the grey mass of her misery was to treat it as a large Bakewell tart, cut into manageable portions and served one slice at a time. That way, the awfulness was corralled into manageable pieces, and what fleeting moments of pleasure she could find had only to compete with small portions of misery. Thinking this way also contained the spasms of fear that frequently overtook her.

Her journey to Whaley Bridge was being divided up in the same way. The first leg had taken her to Buxton, and on it she had confined herself to worrying about avoiding Ben. Now aboard her connection to Whaley Bridge, she had to think about what to say to Lizzie. Mary knew her letter had not reflected the closeness they shared, but she couldn't help herself. Somehow, if she wrote in formal terms, she felt it would distance the writer from the girl so the shame and fear that engulfed her might somehow belong to someone else.

At the outset, she had succumbed to an overwhelming desire to impart information about what had happened, and had given no thought to how that might be achieved. Now she needed words and Mary had none. How was she to say she had been inveigled into a secluded part of Ravenhead House, and been seized roughly and forced to the floor and...? She had struggled at first and even lashed out, but when she couldn't breathe because of the throttling, she had let herself go limp.

What occurred between loving couples was a mystery. But whatever it was, Mary knew it took place willingly inside marriage. She had supposed that some blinding revelation would come to her on her wedding night. This innocence prevented her from fully understanding what had been inflicted on her. It had hurt, dear God it had hurt, and as she discovered afterwards – because they lay beside her on the floor – it had required the removal of her underclothes. But, as it was happening, the whole thing was a blur, suffused with shame and fear. To try and hide from the reality, she had kept her eyes closed.

Like a rag doll, he'd left her lying on the floor when he'd finished. Mary had made the mistake of stealing a look at this point, and was shocked at what she saw. The large pink thing was above her face, moistly shiny with a drop of something at its tip. For a brief moment, the rational part of her mind pierced her overwhelming emotions and she wondered how such a thing could be returned to the trousers from which it protruded, and when it was, where did it go? She squeezed her eyes shut again and the moment receded.

His voice…"Get up, girl, put your things on. Nothing's happened." He was walking away and spoke over his shoulder. "Do as you're told and be about your duties."

Fear had gripped Sam since the interrogation. Fear for himself, yes, but more overwhelming, fear for Lizzie. The throwaway allusion to 'somewhere obscure in Derbyshire' disturbed him most of all. It was the remark of a man who knew, but didn't care. Such a man could put pressure on his prisoner through

Lizzie, and Sam would not be able to resist.

The surprising thing was his interrogator's abrupt departure before making any further threats. With the blindfold removed and his wits restored, Sam had struggled back to the surface of life. With a more perceptive eye now, he re-examined the details of his prison. The stone walls, if the depth of the reveals behind the grill were anything to go by, were several feet thick. A substantial building then, with a purpose-made cell; perhaps several such, but probably empty at present. Apart from the interrogator and his assistant with a Dublin accent, Sam had heard no voices... until now.

He knew he was under surveillance; from time to time he'd heard a snap as the tiny spyhole in the blank door closed. That door, with no handle on his side of it, was the most intimidating thing about being confined, but this time he could hear something. They had failed to slide the shutter over, and sounds of human activity sneaked through the aperture to feed the prisoner's curiosity.

Sam stood, still unsteady on his feet, by the door and listened. Heavy boots clattered on stone, and the sound, attenuated by its passage through the narrow gap, arrived on the other side for the listener's consideration. Regular, even steps, heavy and stamping when the boots came to rest. Voices, their words unable to make the journey intact, at first casual, and then an abrupt change, to a clipped delivery. Another voice, more refined perhaps, followed by the stamping of boots again and a barely audible "Yes, sorr, right away, sorr."

The boots came closer, then, loud and clear from just outside the door, "Close that spyhole, Corporal, we don't want him looking out. He'll know more than we do." The beginning of a laugh was cut short as, too late, the shutter slid across. Sam knew; he knew he was being detained at the pleasure of the Lord Lieutenant of Ireland, and his gaolers were serving soldiers. He was imprisoned in Dublin Castle.

But why had the man with the questions given up so easily? With roles reversed, Sam would have probed further and used what knowledge he had in an attempt to prise out more information from his captive. It was as if, partway through, the questioner had realised that there was no need for the interrogation.

All this thinking was making his headache worse, and Sam slid off into an uneasy doze.

———

"Mary, my dear, how lovely to see you." The front door at 37 Mill End had opened the moment she'd dropped the knocker. "I was so pleased when I got your note." Lizzie embraced her visitor and found it difficult to disengage herself from the now weeping girl. "Come inside and I'll take your coat."

With tears held back, at least for the moment, and a pot of tea brewing, the two of them were beside the parlour fire. It was early in the year for such a luxury, but Lizzie had anticipated that its friendly warmth would do something to comfort the distress lying behind Mary's formal little note. They sat in silence: the one not knowing how to begin; the other willing her to do so.

"I had a young man; at least, I think I had." Mary found it easier to start with Ben. "We met in Buxton and saw each other from time to time, and I was so happy."

"Did you love him?"

"Yes, of course, and I think he loved me; at least he said he did, and still says he does."

"But?" Lizzie broke the silence that had descended on them both.

"That's the problem; he can't love me now, not after... after... So I broke it off."

Amid tears and further silences, Lizzie gathered what had happened. The word rape wasn't mentioned; such language didn't come easily in the respectable parlour.

"But, Lizzie, I feel so guilty. I keep thinking that somehow I'm responsible. If only I'd refused to go there, or hadn't smiled back at him, or screamed. I was so frightened; I thought I was going to die. I just lay there and let it happen. I... I couldn't stop it, but I still feel it was my fault. I feel so dirty."

"Oh Mary, Mary my love." The girl was weeping again, in Lizzie's arms. "It's not your fault, you've been abused terribly."

Two young men waited anxiously at Buxton Midland. Both were on the lookout for the same passenger and, though their intentions were very different, they both had Mary Thomas in mind.

Stephen, in his LNWR uniform, felt awkward. He'd been shielded by a stack of trunks, hatboxes, and the impedimenta necessary to the comfort of wealthy travellers. It belonged to a party recently arrived from London to take the waters. They had spilled out from the station and provided him with cover until a growler, sign written with 'Palace Hotel', had borne them away to their sojourn of luxury. Their servants had remained guarding the luggage, but now it was being loaded piece by piece onto a waggonette and his refuge was being dismantled.

His early turn had deposited him back at Shallcross yard late in the afternoon. Even if he'd hurried home, it was doubtful if time would have allowed more than a brief word with Mary. She would have to be catching her train back to Ravenhead House shortly. Anyway, Stephen was bent on a different mission.

The footplate crew had welcomed him aboard for their run, light engine, from Shallcross to Buxton. Their turn didn't finish until they'd returned to the shed and disposed of the locomotive. It was the only way he could be sure of arriving in time to see who she was meeting on her journeys between home and Cromford.

Behind his ticket window, Ben's problem was not of concealment. He had every reason to be on Mary's route to Ravenhead House. It was, after all, how they had first met. "A Single to Cromford, please," then a fumble with the change, followed by smiles exchanged through the plate glass. But since the day of their 'words', she had taken to buying a Return and had no need of the Buxton ticket office.

Mary was on the way to the departure platform, so she would have to pass close to it, but Ben's field of vision was narrow and she would be easy to miss. Her connection was tight, too, so he wouldn't have much time either. As he waited, he tried to work out what to say. His diffident manner was part of his attractiveness, but behind it was sufficient self-belief to give him the courage to try and speak with her again. And there she was, just failing to keep an ample matron between herself and the ticket office.

Mary had caught her train from Whaley Bridge with a minute or two to spare; Lizzie had seen to that. Lizzie had seen to everything since the desperate girl had knocked on the door of 37 Mill End earlier in the day. She had coaxed, she had listened, she had comforted, and finally accompanied her back to the house Mary shared with her brother.

"Don't worry. If he's in, I'll say we met each other on the way." The upright Lizzie was quite comfortable with a little white lie. There was more on her mind than a tactful evasion. It had been a difficult subject to tackle and, even after the embarrassed Mary had admitted to missing her 'monthlies, in her innocence she had made no connection with the awfulness of her earlier experience.

The prospect of motherhood was clearly more than the poor girl could bear at the moment, and Lizzie's priority had been to get Mary out of her position at Ravenhead House with a character. One day she would need another job.

"Tell them your brother needs you at home now." This lie wasn't quite so little, but needs must.

"But, Lizzie, what about Stephen, does he have to know about…?"

"We'll see about him afterwards. You'll have to work a week's notice and then come and live with me." Time enough to talk about pregnancy then, thought Lizzie.

On their way, Mary had said, "I want you to stay with me, even if he is there."

In the event, Stephen had left a note on the kitchen table. He would be working, and was sorry to miss his sister. He'd written, 'A bit more notice would make things easier.'

"Where's this from?" Lizzie was looking round whilst Mary was putting a few things together. The print of an imposing country seat was remarkably detailed. Stephen must have had it out of its brown paper wrapping and tried to put it back in a hurry, leaving much of the picture exposed.

"It's something Father gave him before he died." Mary was

looking over Lizzie's shoulder. "He kept saying he'd show it to me, but we never..." In the uncertain pause, the girl took the picture and stared intently. "I didn't see it here, but..."

The fragile gossamer of comfort, woven so gently by Lizzie, was torn away in an instant.

"It's the same, Lizzie, the same." Mary burst into tears. With an arm round the troubled girl's shoulder, her comforter looked more carefully at the inscription below the print.

Sladen Castle
In the County of Waterford

"The same as what, my dear?"

"At Ravenhead House. There's one just like it, with the same name underneath. It must mean something... something awful."

Mary's train was running into Buxton LNW station before she had her tears under control.

———•••———

The luggage had trundled off to The Palace Hotel and left Stephen exposed. He'd gone someway from the MR station entrance and found himself with the same problem as Ben. The two termini stood side by side, with their entrances opposite each other and a narrow roadway in between. Standing well back, he too had a narrow field of vision.

The sound of a train drawing gently into the platform alerted him and he walked forward. The Manchester, all stations to Buxton service was doing good business for a late Saturday afternoon. As passengers squeezed past the barrier, burst into the road and spread out, he struggled against the advancing tide. Mary, if she'd been on the train, would not be in the crowd. She would walk straight across and into the other station. Stephen, with people still ahead of him, couldn't see if anyone made the crossing, and by the time he drew level the rush was over.

In the MR booking hall, two figures were in animated conversation. As he stood by the doorway, Stephen heard something of what was being said.

"I will not do it, Ben." That was clearly Mary's voice. Was there a crack in it? Stephen wasn't sure.

"But, Mary, I…" The man's voice was lost in the crying of a babe in the arms of a woman waiting for her ticket.

"Leave me alone." She was on the verge of tears, her brother was sure of it now. "I do not want to see you again."

"Mr Pepperell." Authority exerted itself. The Chief Clerk had taken in the scene at a glance. "Mr Pepperell, what do you think you're doing? Your place is behind the window providing this lady with a ticket."

The powerful tone had intimidated the bawling infant, and Stephen heard the young man's name clearly. Ben Pepperell, he'd remember that.

Chapter 12

Sunday, September 23rd, 1876

The truth was everything; he'd learnt that much from working with Sam. If he couldn't face the superintendent with the truth, he'd be failing his sergeant. Worse still, he'd be letting down his friend. Even so, William wasn't looking forward to telling The Whale about the manifest failure of their investigation so far.

The aroma of dead dog and the fetid water of the Peak Forest Canal had followed him back to his lodgings. He was embarrassed to present himself in such a state, but Lizzie, apologising for only just arriving home herself, arranged for hot water and pointed him in the direction of a bathtub. William thought her rather distracted, but put it down to the smell he'd brought with him. Then, all cleaned up and presentable, he'd found her in much the same mood whilst she served supper. Perhaps it was the worry about Sam, he thought: she certainly became more animated when she and William discussed his plans for the next day.

"So, will you be back on Sunday evening? I'd like to know…" Lizzie's voice tailed off uncertainly.

William was in a quandary. Once he'd reported to the superintendent, he would no longer be his own master. But knowing more about her feelings than she did herself, he promised either to return that evening, or explain what he knew in a letter to arrive the next morning.

"Perhaps we could keep the rooms?"

Lizzie had brightened at this. "Of course, the two of you

are always welcome." William thanked her. *It must be the possibility of Sam's return that lifted her mood*, he thought.

As he sat in solitary splendour, William pondered the likelihood of that happy event. The first train out of Whaley Bridge didn't attract much custom of a Sunday morning, and he had a compartment to himself; he could worry in private. The longer Sam was absent, the greater the chance that something awful had happened to him. If he was alive and free, he must have attempted to make contact, mustn't he? That he hadn't done so implied that he couldn't, and that meant he was...

These thoughts preoccupied him for the whole journey. He'd changed trains at Stockport, but had no recollection of it later and had been surprised when, through the carriage window, he heard a porter shout, "Crewe, Crewe Junction."

On foot now, he found his way to Hall House, giving no thought to his own family at the Bakery.

"Archer? What the devil are you doing here? I didn't send for you."

The superintendent had opened the door himself as he had a week ago.

"I have something important to report, sir, and it won't wait..."

"What d'ye mean? Haven't you told your sergeant? He'd keep it until Monday."

"Err... that's the problem, sir. He's missing."

"He's what?" The question was rhetorical. Wayland clearly wasn't expecting an answer as he propelled the lowly constable across the hallway and into his gentleman's den. The pipe smoke, hanging in the air, seemed to have remained undisturbed since last week's visit.

"Now." The superintendent sank into a chair. "Now, tell me what's happened?"

A change had come over the senior man since he'd opened the front door. He seemed to have shed his military bearing and weakened; no, that wasn't right, softened, perhaps, thought William, as, for the first time ever, he was invited to sit in such august company.

Wayland listened without interruption until the matter of the dead lurcher cropped up.

"Why on earth did you bother with that?" The old authority had crept into his voice, but it died when the connection with the disappearance of Cubbin, his horse, and the *Kingfisher* was pointed out.

The two men sat in silence for a while – the one with relief at having passed on responsibility; the other pondering what to do now he'd assumed it.

"So, this Inspector Downes has no authority beyond the mainland, you say."

"That's what he said, sir. It seems we blundered into a scheme of his by accident. There must have been more of them than we realised. The man I was following looked as if he was following Sergeant Spray, but then led me to Minshull Street, whilst someone else must have kept up with the sergeant."

"This Ireland business; it could be a lot of poppycock, made up to fool you."

William didn't believe this for one moment. To him, Downes had seemed straightforward, but he thought it better not to say so.

Sam scratched a fourth mark into the forbidding stone wall. He still wasn't sure he'd started the calendar on his first day of imprisonment. His head had been in such a muddle back then, but he'd only be one day out at most, he thought. He pondered how best to mark the weeks passing, but gave up. He'd be let out in a day or two, he told himself without much conviction. If he wasn't, he'd have to find another tool to etch the days with; the handle of the pannikin was showing signs of wear.

Things had improved in that a palliasse had arrived the previous day. They were still ordering him to face the wall when anyone came in, but it didn't matter; he amused himself visualizing their movements from the sound of footsteps. He hugged his secret knowledge to himself. Now he knew they were soldiers. Their crisp, military manner was obvious.

The spyhole snapped open.

"Face the wall." A different voice this time. "Hands behind your back." After the click of the cuffs locking up, a hood was pulled over his head. *Hessian, probably an old potato sack*, he thought, judging from the smell and the bits of mud that went down his neck. "Walk backwards."

All at once he heard the scrape of a chair, and collapsed onto it as he was caught behind the knees.

"Now, no more nonsense. You're going to tell us what you were doing at a whore house in New Warwick Street."

No response.

"You could have gone in and exercised your dick. Saved yourself all of this, if you had."

For a moment, Sam imagined his interrogator waving a hand expansively around the cell. He was mistaken. The chair was kicked from under him and he fell, his hip and shoulder jarring as he hit the floor. A military boot got him in the stomach.

"That's just a start." The chair legs scraped again. "Get up."

The same procedure as before. He found himself sitting again, only this time he didn't know which way he was facing. Such detail was hugely important to Sam. If he was to endure the torture with his mind intact, he needed to concentrate on fragments of normality.

"You were in the whore house, keeping an eye on next door. What led you to that address?"

No response.

"It'll do you no favours, keeping quiet, we know everything anyway. We found it written on a paper in your pocket."

No response. It seemed to Sam that no answer was required, but he found himself on the floor again. This time the boot was aimed at his head. The sacking softened the blow, but as he got to his feet he could feel something dribbling down his upper lip. At least the blood wouldn't have to be washed out of a moustache. He didn't have one.

"Where did you get that piece of paper from?" Sam had regained the chair but didn't expect to be sitting on it for long. "It's a serious matter interfering with one of our people. Some would say it was treason. You put Mr Slade... that is, our man, to a lot of inconvenience." The voice was louder now, more menacing. "Where... did... you... get..."

The sound of footsteps, distant at first, but closing steadily, seeped through the hessian. *He must have left the door ajar*, thought Sam.

"Get... that... paper... with—" There was a crash, as someone in a hurry threw back the door.

"Got anything from him, sergeant?" A momentary pause. "No, you can leave him to me now."

Chapter 13

Wednesday, September 26th, 1876

What does the man want with Wayland? Richard Moon Esq., didn't know the police superintendent; such appointments were beneath his notice. The previous day he'd had to get his assistant to find out who the devil Wayland was.

"Policeman, sir, in charge of the Crewe office. I could send a telegram."

At mention of the northern branch, something stirred in Moon's memory. *A murder, somewhere in Derbyshire, wasn't it?*

"Shall I send for him, sir?"

Moon was still thinking. *All in the papers, made a great fuss for a day or two. A lot of damn nonsense.*

"A telegram, sir, to the policeman?"

"Very well, anything as long as he's here first thing."

But that doesn't explain why this obscure Peer wants to see him. Moon took a poor view of the aristocracy, mostly nincompoops, all of them arrogant, and hardly a man amongst them with an understanding of industry.

Earlier, a note had arrived 'For the personal attention of Richard Moon Esq., Chairman, London & North Western Railway'. It had been delivered by hand. Moon hadn't seen the man, of course, but his assistant had questioned the doorman and there was no doubt about it – he was in the uniform of a Home Office messenger.

"You got my note?"

Inside, there had been a plain sheet without heading. If Moon hadn't enquired the day before, he'd have had no knowledge of its place of origin.

"I did, my Lord."

"And?"

The communication had been abrupt, on the verge of offensive. 'Have Charles Wayland available for interview 11.30am tomorrow at your offices.' Signed 'Fancourt'. Had they been in possession of antlers, both men would have been engaged like stags in the rut, but as it was words had to suffice.

"May I enquire the nature of your business with my employee?"

"You may not." Fancourt glared menacingly. Moon didn't flinch. He'd never heard of the man before yesterday. Most probably an Irish Peerage, he'd thought. That would explain his obscurity.

"Perhaps you would be good enough to enlighten me as to your position at the Home Office?"

"How dare you, sir."

"Not on the political staff, I think. The Home Secretary has an interest in the country's rail network. Only a month ago, I attended Mr Cross and his junior ministers. I don't recall your Lordship's presence."

"Damn your impudence, sir."

Moon continued, "So I take it that you are a member of the civil service."

"Have you got the man Wayland here or not?"

As a captain of industry, Moon was quite up to taking on a bureaucrat, even a First Secretary, but his Peerage gave Fancourt the edge.

"Of course, your Lordship. He's waiting next door in the antechamber."

Superintendent Wayland was not a man of a nervous disposition, but as he sat in First Class comfort on the early London Express he did allow himself a little latitude. He was definitely concerned at the disappearance of his sergeant and, even with his limited imagination, the possibility of a connection between this unusual event and the telegram could not be ignored.

> URGENT   STOP   ATTEND   CHAIRMAN
> 11 30 AM   EUSTON   BOARDROOM
> WEDNESDAY NEXT STOP

Richard Moon Esq. was known to the superintendent only by reputation. It seemed that men of such elevated status did not soil their hands with the disreputable business of crime on their railway. The most senior figure with whom the superintendent had any contact was the head of the Railway Police Department, a mere Commander; and today he did not appear to be involved.

"If you would take a seat here, sir, you will be informed when your presence is required."

If this was the antechamber, who knows what magnificence may lie on the other side of the boardroom door? Wayland looked round at the portraits of admirals, generals, and peers – in some cases, with more than one attribute attaching – previous chairmen all, and had only just sat down when a short, stocky man burst through the double doors.

He bristled with self-importance and, without offering his

hand, said, "Wayland?" No answer was expected as he went on, "There's a very important personage who wishes to speak to you. Through here."

Moon's Railway accepted, as of right, the unofficial title, The Premier Line, and as the largest single commercial undertaking in the country such pride could not be gainsaid. As such, there were appearances to be kept up. An oak-panelled room with an enormous oval table and twinkling chandelier above shouldered its share of this burden as it looked out through enormous swagged and draped windows toward Euston Road.

The superintendent had wondered how a mere commoner, and one without a military background at that, coped with the assorted nabobs who populated the higher echelons of the business world, as he perused their portraits outside.

"My Lord, this is the man Wayland. He is police superintendent of our Northern division, based at Crewe."

"Very well, Moon, you may…" The Peer was turning as he spoke, but lapsed into a momentary silence. "By God, it's 'The Whale'. Charles, old man, I should have known. It's been a long time and the name didn't ring any bells."

It must have been all of thirty years since 'Charlie the Whale' and 'Perky Boy' had wielded polo mallets together in an Indian Cavalry Regiment, and the memory of it made Wayland less sure of himself than the other man. Back then, officialdom had the Peer as The Hon. Percy Fancourt, but in the mess his sobriquet was all but universal. Here, in these august surroundings, and with the Hon. Percy having succeeded to his Peerage, the proprieties had to be observed.

"Good to meet you again, my Lord."

A dismissive gesture of the hand waved away the formalities.

"Really, Charles, no need for flummery between old comrades in arms; Percy, please."

The acquisition of a Commission in a Regiment of Cavalry, even one in the Indian Army, required influence, and a kinsman of the young Wayland had provided it. Indeed, the man positively insisted that his nephew join his old regiment, and such was his prestige that he had obtained for him a Cornetcy without purchase. The Commission may have come without cost, but the mess expenses attendant upon taking it up had been a problem to the young Officer, and the bills connected with keeping a stable of ponies quite beyond him.

Percy Fancourt had been bent on glory, but with a dearth of enemies just then, was devoting himself to winning the All India Polo Championship. As instigator of this competition and tireless promoter of the developing sport among the Cavalry, he'd seen himself in a paternal role, but had needed a midwife to help him deliver the trophy to the Regiment.

The impecunious Whale had been just the chap. He'd turned out to be a consummate horseman with a good eye for a moving object, and was by far the best polo player in the mess. The Hon. Percy Fancourt, heir to a peerage and in possession of ample private means, had found it expedient to provide for the deficiencies in his protégé's income and the trophy had been brought home, to Perky Boy's gratification.

As the euphoria subsided and his fellow officers lapsed back into a spiteful boredom, Charles Wayland had overheard a reference to himself along the lines of:

"Charlie the Whale's only Perky Boy's little fish, don't you know. Hasn't a penny to his name. Perky pays all his bills."

"Ah, Moon." Lord Fancourt's attention reverted momentarily to the Company Chairman. "I can manage perfectly well now."

As this captain of industry was being dismissed, much as a gentleman would his butler, long dormant memories of his time in the Cavalry came flooding into Wayland's mind, and he did not find them congenial. Notwithstanding, he found himself being treated with a bonhomie that was both flattering and disturbing in equal measure.

"This is no place for a reunion of old friends. Come along, we'll go to my club."

The cabbie was given his destination, but with his old wound making for difficulties in climbing aboard, the superintendent missed hearing it.

"That leg still giving you trouble? Must have been a dangerous business, your railway in the Crimea."

The superintendent wondered how the other man knew about his Crimean service. As far as he was aware, Indian Cavalry Regiments had never fought there.

"I would hazard a guess it put paid to your polo."

Damn the man, he knows perfectly well why I gave up polo; and why I left the Cavalry.

"Pity, really, you had a gift for it. I never did understand why you went for an engineer."

The hansom jerked to a halt.

"Careful, man, you've got one of the walking wounded on board. Don't want to make it any worse."

The deep leather armchair, one of a pair in a quiet corner of the club's smoking room, had its attractions, but for Wayland, with his defective leg, getting out of it would be a daunting prospect. Despite a tumbler – rather over-full by his usual standards – of an extremely good Cognac, he felt himself a prisoner. He'd been drawn into a trap, ambushed, humiliated, and was only now beginning to understand why he was here; wherever here was.

The hansom, despite the intervention – or because of it – by his host, had set off as precipitately as it had stopped, before its least able passenger was securely down from the step and it was only prompt action on the part of a helpful passer-by that had saved him from falling in the street. By the time matters had been put to rights, he'd been assisted up a broad flight of steps by a pair of uniformed flunkeys who ushered him through an ornate portico and deposited him in his upholstered prison; and he still didn't know where he was.

"You alright, old chap? The man ought to be horsewhipped; worse than careless, I'd say."

Wayland rather agreed about the horsewhipping, but it wasn't the cabbie he had in mind. He held his peace and was careful about how much brandy he drank.

"Bit bothersome that injury, I'd say. Still that man of yours saved you from anything worse, I heard."

How the devil does the man know about that? Wayland felt helpless, like a rabbit under the hypnotic spell of a stoat as it moved in for the kill.

"Spade? Spode? No, Spray that's it, Sergeant Samuel Spray. That's the fellow."

Wayland waited, silent, for the next pass.

"Got himself in a bit of a pickle, your man, don't y' know. Bit out of his depth, meddling in matters best left to sort themselves out. Catch my drift, old man?"

So that was it. He? they? whoever they were, had somehow got Spray at their mercy. This was intolerable. Wayland finally responded, parrying the final thrust.

"I think I should point out, my Lord, that Sergeant Spray is a policeman, of high repute I might add, who is investigating a murder committed within the jurisdiction of my department. Any impediment that is put in his way is a breach of the law of the land."

"Oh, come now, Charles old chap, we all know these things

aren't set in stone when the security of the realm is at stake."

"I should need rather more evidence of that than so far has come my way."

A pained look crossed the Noble Lord's face, much as a parent might display when a much-loved child misbehaved.

"Oh dear, Charles, you aren't going to make difficulties, are you? I mean to say, old comrades in arms and all that. Not enough for you? No, I see not."

The mood changed.

"My department..." He waved a hand languidly in the direction of the door. Wayland, completely without his bearings, couldn't tell whether the gesture was to the south and Whitehall, or to the northwest toward Dublin. "My department won't like it, but if you insist, I'll have to ask for absolute secrecy, on the honour of a gentleman."

The policeman was struck by the incongruity of such an undertaking being demanded by a man who, despite his title, was engaged in such ungentlemanly conduct of his own.

"It's these Fenian fellows, awful bounders to a man, getting above themselves with dynamite and suchlike. We... we're ferreting away on the inside, trying to see what they're about. You know, who's who, what's what; that sort of thing. You understand, it's all a bit delicate."

The superintendent couldn't see anything delicate about the murdered man at Shallcross Yard, but he understood that agents of the Government, whether Whitehall or Dublin, had infiltrated the Fenians.

"Just tell me one thing more," asked Wayland, emboldened by what had been revealed so far. "Was he one of yours, or one of theirs – the dead man?"

It was quickly extinguished, but a look of uncertainty crossed the other man's face.

"Damned unpredictable, the Irish, don't' y'know. Just as bad whichever side they're from. What d'ye make of a man like Parnell, standing up in Parliament and saying those Manchester Fenians weren't murderers at all? I mean t' say the man's a Protestant and a landowner."

"So, you don't know."

The faintest nod of assent gave Wayland his answer, and with it there was a change of subject.

"Now, Wayland." The time for being friends with Charles had passed. "I've got to be certain you can get your man Spray bridled and bitted and under control. I realise he's a handful; we've had terrible trouble with him ourselves."

As Lord Fancourt continued, "But you must—"

There was a minor volcanic eruption from the depth of the other man's armchair. It took considerable effort for Wayland to become upright in one movement, bad leg notwithstanding, but he stood, angrily confronting the still-seated peer.

"If you or your men have hurt Sam Spray, I shall find a way to make you pay."

For a few moments, there was fear in the other man's eyes at the intensity of Wayland's anger.

Chapter 14

Thursday, September 27th, 1876

His sleepless night had done little for Superintendent Wayland's temper. He'd lain in bed, angry, frustrated and worried, even though on his journey down from London the previous evening, he'd managed to extract a few crumbs of comfort from his visit.

It was true, he'd seen fear in Percy Fancourt's face, but there was no obvious way his threat could be carried out. It had felt rather satisfying at the time, though. He'd even managed, as he departed, to work out in which Gentleman's Club he'd been humiliated. The admission that Fancourt's organisation wasn't sure who either the murdered man or his murderer were really working for was perhaps a greater prize, but Wayland couldn't for the life of him see how it could be used.

Of course, most important of all was the undertaking that Sam Spray was being released from detention and would be arriving on the up Irish Mail that morning. But how the devil was the affair to be managed? Whilst Wayland had disagreed with almost everything Fancourt had said, on one issue they were of the same opinion. Persuading the sergeant to drop his murder investigation would not be easy, and the superintendent was not at all sure he wanted it given up anyway. It was this which had occupied the wakeful night time hours.

Much to the surprise of the desk constable, he arrived at work earlier than usual. Too preoccupied to acknowledge the man, Wayland passed into his inner sanctum without a word. By the time he'd hung up his topcoat and hat, he'd begun to regret his promptitude. He'd risen early on account of his restless night, surprised his housekeeper, and rushed through his breakfast, and was now faced with a three-hour wait for the arrival of the Holyhead express. It had been the prospect of his sergeant's return that had occasioned the urgent activity but now, having exhausted all the alternatives, he was obliged to sit quietly and wait.

Wayland was not a man given to rational thought. He was not given to much thought of any sort. The structure in his life was all externally applied. His early days had been ordered by the discipline of school, and then the Army. He did what he was told and passed on orders from above to those below. He'd never questioned anything until the day he'd come across Sam Spray.

That funny business with the accounts had been difficult. As Lt. Colonel, it was beneath him to go round asking questions, and he'd had an uneasy feeling the theft was down to one of his fellow officers. How a lowly corporal, on guard duty at the entrance to the mess, had worked it out he couldn't imagine, but Spray had done it. Not only done it, but kept it nice and quiet; no scandal, just a resolution. When Wayland had appointed Spray to be his batman, it was this discretion that had secured him the position. He wouldn't step out of line and disturb things, or so he'd thought.

Lines of a different sort had been the preoccupation of Wayland's unit. The Grand Crimean Central Railway, running from the port of Balaklava to the army laying siege to Sevastopol on the plateau above, was the responsibility of the Engineers. It had been one long drag for the horses and winding engines to supply the materials of war, and if a truck broke free there was nothing to stop it careering, ever faster, down toward the coast.

Quite why their colonel had stepped into the path of the wagon had been a mystery to everyone in his unit, not least the man himself. Perhaps it was some vain hope that he could prevent the inevitable accident further down the hill. It was his batman who'd saved his life, pulling most of him clear, with only his leg suffering any damage.

Time was moving slowly for the superintendent, and he couldn't stem the memories flowing into this vacuum. They disturbed and excited him in equal measure. Recollections of the past had an independence that stirred up the silt of his life's experience. The disorder was an affront, but he couldn't escape its fascination. He puzzled over what made him care so much about Sam Spray. The man was of no consequence, he had no family connections, and had never risen out of the ranks. And then again, Spray would question the established order, and had an irritating way of finding complications in Wayland's simplicities. And yet... when Spray had finished with them, the world was a better place.

Outside, on the platform, a porter was calling out: "Crewe, this is Crewe Junction." Wayland pulled out his hunter and flipped the lid. The engraving on the inside didn't usually merit a glance. The men had clubbed together when he'd had to retire, and presented it to him before he'd set off for home after the accident. How the devil it'd been done in such a primitive place, he'd no idea, but he was sure he knew who was responsible.

Colonel Charles Wayland
With our respect
Engineers of the Crimea

As the Irish Mail clanked and groaned to a standstill, a watching man stood up. In the crowded compartment, he'd benefitted from a degree of anonymity, but as passengers started to step out onto the platform he found himself in a quandary; more exposed now, whilst his quarry dozed on.

The sleeper was supposed to alight at Crewe, and the watcher's orders were simple. 'Just make sure he gets out at the right station and reports to his superior in the Railway Constabulary.' Perhaps not quite that easy, it wouldn't be difficult to check that he went to the right office, but what if the Officer in question was absent; the possibility of the sleeping man failing to disembark had not been covered at all.

Two things happened at once. One passenger who must have been bound for Euston, as he had remained seated throughout the melee, reached out and tapped the weary traveller on the knee. "I believe I heard you tell the Guard you were for Crewe, sir."

Outside, a porter called loudly, "Crewe, Crewe Junction, change here for…" Before he'd finished his announcement, there was an eruption in the compartment's corner seat. A dishevelled man rose explosively and, without glancing round, stepped into the hustle and bustle of the busy station. His abrupt movement dislodged his hat. It had been pulled low for the whole of the train journey, hiding his face. As he stood, he pushed the battered bowler to its accustomed position, revealing a black eye and damage to his lip.

Once on the platform, he pushed his way through the crowd and the watcher saw him greeting a uniformed man who, despite his limp, retained a military bearing.

"Ah, there you are, sergeant" was loud enough to be heard at a distance. Had the watcher been closer, he might have noted the softer tone of, "My God, Sam, what have they done to you?"

Chapter 15

Friday, September 28th, 1876

The orders were plain enough. For the older man, it was two weeks furlough, and for the other to make sure his companion had what he needed in the pursuit of recuperation. Their simplicity was deceptive. For a start, Superintendent Wayland's instructions had been framed by the sergeant and presented to his superior officer as the logical progression from a discussion that had occupied much of the previous day.

The Irish Mail had brought a dishevelled Sam Spray to Crewe, but it had also brought a problem. The superintendent had no intention of adhering to the 'Gentleman's Agreement' suggested at yesterday's encounter with Lord Fancourt. Had the man been behaving like a gentleman, it might have been different, but the peer was playing a furtive double game that no man of honour would countenance. Anyway, Wayland had made no such undertaking when the matter was aired, and the returning sergeant had certainly been cruelly used.

No, the problem was that Wayland himself was indulging in a little subterfuge. He'd taken the first step without realising it.

"Best thing if we go somewhere quiet and you can take things a bit leisurely." Wayland steered the new arrival toward the station exit. "You go and secure a growler and we'll be along in a moment."

The bruised and weary sergeant was in no position to argue, and did as he was told. Waiting in the cab, he wondered about the 'we', but the matter was resolved when William Archer appeared and climbed in beside him.

"Sergeant." They were on more formal terms back in Crewe. "Good to see you back." If William was surprised by Sam's stubble, not to say his creased and smelly suit, he made no comment.

The third member of the party gave a destination to the cabbie and then joined the others. The superintendent sat in silence as they journeyed. For the third time in two weeks, Archer found himself heading for the Whale's inner sanctum, only this time, Sam would be there as well.

In this manner, Superintendent Wayland had kept the knowledge of his sergeant's return from the rest of his department. 'For reasons of morale,' he told himself, and it was true, the sight of Spray's bruised face and painful movements would not encourage the other men. This understandable deception was just a start.

Their arrival disturbed the even tenor of his housekeeper's day.

"Oh sir, I hadn't expected you back until your usual time. Is everything alright?" She fluttered around until the three of them were settled. "Shall you be wanting something for luncheon for these gentlemen?"

Not very organised in his subterfuge, Wayland hadn't thought beyond keeping Spray and his injuries away from the other men.

"I could do something cold for you all."

"Thank you, that will be fine." With that, she was dismissed, leaving Archer to pour out the tea.

"Now, sergeant, tell us what you've been up to."

———•••••———

When the first interrogator was dismissed, there had been silence. The new man's footsteps may have been audible from the passageway outside, but he seemed able to move round the cell soundlessly. Sam, his head covered in a sack and apprehensive of what would happen next, was straining to hear something of his movements.

Then it started. As the blows were struck, he curled up into a ball. On the floor now, he drew his manacled hands up to protect himself. Whatever else, he mustn't let another head injury take away his memory. The information he'd garnered since his incarceration was too valuable to lose like that. Throughout the ordeal, it was this knowledge that sustained him. By the time the beating was over, his mind seemed to operate outside his body, almost as if he was observing someone else being tortured.

But as the cell door slammed shut, the trance was broken and suddenly pain was everywhere. He tried to get up, but toppled awkwardly back to the floor. Finally, he managed to sit propped against the wall and take stock. He'd told them nothing and he still had his nuggets of information: that he was in Dublin; he'd been arrested by the authorities and imprisoned by soldiery; Bowler Hat worked for them; his name was Slade; and they didn't know whether they could trust him.

———

"Funny thing was, sir, it just stopped. No more questions, no more threats, no more beatings. They gave me my warrant card and wallet then put me in a closed wagon, and the next thing I knew, I was aboard the Holyhead ferry." Sam was still in pain and finding the transfer of tea from cup to mouth an uncertain matter.

"Here, let me help." William got no thanks for his offer.

"The one thing they didn't return was the paper with the Manchester address. That was what they really wanted to know; how we got hold of it, and what we knew about the people to be found there." The cup made another unsteady journey, and Sam took a second sip.

"Tea suit you? I can send for something stronger."

Sam's "No, thank you" was curt. He wasn't used to being mothered by his fellow officers and it unsettled him.

"Hadn't we better decide how to proceed?" It was an effort to sound authoritative; he couldn't face the pity.

William had explained what he had done on his own initiative, and the superintendent finally persuaded himself of the propriety of revealing his trip to London.

"So, what we know is this." Sam went over the investigation step by step. "Dynamite was stolen by Irishmen. Irish nationalism is on the rise. Two sets of investigations – three, if we include ourselves – are involved, and we're all at each other's throats."

"That's not quite right. Inspector Downes seemed pretty reasonable in the end." This from William.

"When they use it to blow something up, the Railway Constabulary will be held responsible for letting the explosive go." It would be Wayland who took the blame.

"I agree, sir. The most important thing is to find the dynamite and who has it."

At a loss about where to begin, Wayland harrumphed. "What do you suggest?"

This was where the journey to Whaley Bridge started.

"The one lead we have is Tommy Cubbin and the *Kingfisher*." Sam had already made appreciative noises about William's investigations on the canals, "Or at least, their disappearance."

Wayland was doubtful. "There are an awful lot of ifs: if the *Kingfisher* really has disappeared; if she was used to transport the explosive; if it's still on board. Oh yes, and even if the dead dog was Cubbin's lurcher." There was silence for a while. "But I can't see any other line to pursue."

"Your orders might include retuning to the Peak Canal tomorrow, sir, and the two of us making further enquiries after the boat and her skipper – oh, and his horse."

"You're in no fit state to work, sergeant, and your lodgings here in Crewe are no place for a man in your condition. I have it in mind to order a few days' recuperation. You look all in."

"I could do that in Whaley Bridge, sir, whilst Constable Archer here could keep an eye on me."

Chapter 16

Saturday, September 29th, 1876

For once, Lizzie was taken aback, and showed it. "Oh William…" Sam's bruising made raising his arm painful, and it was the younger man who had struck the knocker and stood in the doorway as it opened. He stepped aside: "and Sam… Oh Sam, what has happened to you." Tears welled up and, unable to trust her voice further, she gestured them in.

By the time the men were settled in the parlour and tea had arrived, Lizzie was in control of herself.

"Here, Sam, let me hold it for you." Seeing him in difficulties, she had leant forward and held the cup to his lips.

This time his reply was a grateful "thank you".

"Of course you can have your rooms; I've kept them free for you." William's letter on Monday had made no mention of when he and Sam might return, but Lizzie had kept them empty anyway. "But there's something I should tell you. I've engaged a maid to start tomorrow, so we'll be quite a houseful."

Sam caught something in her voice and looked quizzically.

"You'll have to be gentle with her, Mary's very…" Lizzie was about to say fragile, but that seemed too revealing. "Very young." It would have to do.

It was Saturday, and Jimmy had been sent on an errand for his mam. The both of them knew it was to get him out of the house so she could 'get on', and as he sat in a quiet corner, looking at a paper, his conscience was clear. He was a well lettered lad for his age, even if his teacher might not approve of his reading matter. Not that he'd bought the penny dreadful, it had been blowing about the street and he wasn't entirely sure he'd captured all the pages.

But he did have the cover, with its depiction of a man emerging bloodied but triumphant from a fight. It was in colour, too, and Jimmy relished every gory detail. It had been a dull ten days since the excitement of his trip with Mr Archer to Manchester, and this was a substitute of sorts.

He heard a train arriving at the station up the valley side, but barely looked up until its driver acknowledged the guard and his green flag with a peep on the whistle. As the locomotive noisily dragged its load into motion, the passengers for Whaley were walking down into the town. Jimmy was startled to see a man as equally badly used as the one in his picture.

The two policemen passed on without seeing the boy, but something was afoot, Jimmy was sure of it, and it promised more excitement than his book. Those two were worth keeping an eye on.

Later, he found it necessary to call at 37 Mill End. Mrs Oldroyd always wanted to hear about his trumpeting, and he felt she needed to know when he was next playing with the band. If he timed it right, she might have some baking cooling in the scullery, too.

"Jimmy, this is a nice surprise."

"Afternoon, Missus. It's about the band."

"Yes…" Lizzie was wielding her rolling pin. "Just let me get this ready." The pastry was put in place on top of an apple pie. She took a knife and neatly cut round the dish then rolled the excess into a little ball. "Now, what was that?"

Jimmy, unable to contain his curiosity, said, "Saw Mr Archer an' Mr Spray come off the train. S'pose they came here?"

"And what if they did?" Lizzie busied herself crimping the edge of the pastry.

"I were just sayin'. Mr Spray, alright is 'e?"

"It's none of your business." Lizzie picked up a tray of tea things. "You wait here for a minute and then you can tell me about the band."

Seeing his chance, Jimmy opened the kitchen door for her and then, uninvited, went along the hallway and let her into the parlour.

"Thank you. Now go back."

The door remained open and a fragment of conversation escaped.

"As long as you're up to it, Sam, we'll start at the canal basin tomorrow morning." It was enough. The eavesdropper slipped back to the kitchen.

Chapter 17

Sunday, September 30th, 1876

Jimmy had explained where the next band outing was to be, and Lizzie had asked if he was practising regularly.

"Mam won't let me play at home, says it upsets the neighbours."

"That's a pity, so what do you do?" Lizzie was torn. She thought her neighbours might take the same view, but the boy had to play somewhere.

"Oh, it's alright, missus, along the canal an' the boatmen don't complain." She needn't have worried. "They don't stop anyways."

"What about when it's raining, and it's going to start getting cold?" Jimmy hadn't been given the cornet until March and the weather had been kind ever since.

"Don't you worry 'bout that, missus, there's lots of sheds an' things wot nobody uses anymore between here an' Bugsworth."

On Sunday morning, Jimmy set off early. He took his cornet case with him as he normally did; not that practising a musical instrument just after daybreak had normal written all over it. He'd hidden the cornet in his dad's garden shed, and the case was useful for carrying the second slice of cake he'd been given the day before. He'd eaten the first one there and then, and he'd said "Thanks, missus" when Mrs Oldroyd had offered him another. "For later," she'd said, and popped a few gingerbreads in for good measure. *She's alright, that Mrs Oldroyd,* he thought as a couple of cold sausages joined her offering. *Mam won't miss 'em.*

They had to start at the wharf. *Stands t' reason,* he thought, *they won' want t' miss anything.* His plan was follow on the opposite side of the cut and see what they were up to. By the time Sergeant Spray and Constable Archer put in an appearance, Jimmy was bored and about to give up. *Not as much fun as the Manchester trip,* he thought. And all they did was talk to the boat people; he couldn't even hear what they were saying.

When he'd first arrived, there were a few boats – loaded late on Saturday – turning in the basin. Jimmy watched as deftly angled straps were used to drag the unwieldy craft so they headed for the narrow entry to the cut. Here, the horse was hitched up to a long rope attached to the stubby mast halfway along the hull. After straining into its collar to get thirty tons moving, the great animal would plod sedately off into the distance.

The first northbound train from Cromford departed just after seven and Mary was on it. By no means was it the most convenient journey. Indeed, her connection at Miller's Dale would arrive an hour and five minutes later, and she could have boarded it in Cromford for a direct service to Buxton. But the wait was a pleasure.

Not pleasure, she thought, *relief.* But relief was a pleasure: relief at having her notice accepted; at having worked it out without more awfulness; and leaving with a character. She didn't care that it was mean and mealy-mouthed.

Mary Thomas worked as a maid at Ravenshead House for six months in 1876 and left to take up another post.

She was going to work for Lizzie.

Before leaving for Cromford a week ago, Lizzie had said if she gave notice, Mary could come to 37 Mill End, and help out for her keep. She'd hugged the promise to her all through the intervening days, and now she was on her way.

There was still the problem of Ben. At the thought of him she was gripped, but gripped by what? Seeing him would only set off more recrimination. And yet... not seeing him... what would that bring?

In the event, she was swept past the Midland booking office in a crowd of hurrying passengers and barely had sight of the glass window, with its semi-circular aperture, where Ben dispensed his tickets.

———

Ben Pepperell was a very unhappy young man.

Till now, the worst thing he could remember was when his dad had killed the rabbit that Ben considered a pet, but at the age of nine it passed soon enough. In fact, it had passed by the time he'd finished his plateful of stew a couple of days later. But the misery was showing no sign of going this time, and it had been several weeks.

He'd been so sure she liked him. They had laughed at the same things, and told each other little secrets, and even held hands. Above all, she had looked so happy when they were together. And then, that awful day. He knew there was something wrong before she spoke; she'd been crying by the time they met, her eyes were all bleary. She'd certainly cried afterwards. Not whilst he was with her. He'd done as he was bid and walked away, but as soon as the next corner was turned, he'd stopped and looked back. She was weeping then, and wept all the way onto her train.

That was as far as he'd gone that day, but he was determined to find out more. Ben knew she worked in a big house near Cromford, Ravens… something; she'd mentioned the name once. He knew she came from Whaley Bridge, but that was all. He spent his spare time at the weekends watching passengers on and off the Cromford connections. *She must come through Buxton Midland sometime soon,* he thought. And indeed she had only a week ago, but he'd been working and that pompous bugger had ordered him back into the office. Today, despite being off duty, he was watching the booking hall as soon as it opened.

It was all he could do to stop himself rushing forward to help her with the little case she carried. *Strange that, she'd never had luggage before*; *she only went home for the day.* He held back as she went into the LNW station, and made a rushed purchase himself, of a return to Whaley Bridge, as the train was preparing for the off.

It was his lucky day. Catching sight of a porter handing her case through an open carriage door, he was able to avoid getting into the same compartment. Being Sunday, business was thin and he had no doubt, despite not seeing Mary during the journey, she was still on the train as it drew into their destination. He watched anxiously as a few others stepped off, and was getting desperate by the time she finally disembarked. *Must have got her case stuck on the overhead rack,* he thought.

His door handle had been awkward and the train was moving by the time he got it open. He'd tumbled out, to a glare from the guard as he passed and angry words from a porter who had to run to close the door. What he'd done was risky, both to himself and others, but Ben was driven by something stronger.

Where now? Disorientated by his fall, he found himself staring after the departing train and an empty platform. Across the track, there was some movement. New arrivals started to file out through the barrier. Behind him, the planks of a foot-bridge rattled and he saw Mary's head – her case, along with the rest of her, hidden by the balustrade – bobbing across to the station exit.

By the time he, too, was leaving the station, there was no sign of her, and he ran, desperate, down the slope to a busier road at the bottom. In the main drag, shops were trading and their customers crowding the pavements. *But where was Mary?* Ben scanned the melee in panic. He'd never visited the town, and if he couldn't find her here he'd no idea where else to look. Relief; a familiar figure, trim and carrying her small case, ventured into the roadway and made it safely to the other side.

Ben followed as she turned and set of up the hill. Mill End was steep and straight with terraced houses. He was hanging well back when Mary disappeared at a point where the first detached villa marked the start of greater respectability. As he ran, he kept his eye fixed on its painted railings and arrived, panting, at No 37.

Jimmy watched, fascinated. Low, horse-drawn trucks were being dragged along a tramway. One by one, they would come to rest above a narrowboat moored in the basin, and with a rattle another load of limestone dropped into its hold. The only interruption came with the hauling away of the deeply laden boat, its freeboard barely sufficient to keep it afloat, to be replaced with one riding high in the water, ready to receive the next cargo.

He was so engrossed that he'd lost sight of Constable Archer and his companion. Up till then, the only problem he'd had with them was their slow rate of progress. Whatever Mrs Oldroyd had said, the sergeant wasn't getting about too good. They'd stopped often enough to speak to the boatmen, but they stopped in between as well; for nothing more than a rest, as far as Jimmy could see. But now the hive of activity that was Buggie Basin had swallowed them up.

He'd never been here before, but he'd been taught about it at school. 'Bugsworth had the biggest inland port in the country,' the teacher had said, and she'd told the class they should be proud it was in Derbyshire. The class hadn't been too impressed. The power and speed of the railway was more to their taste.

Jimmy ventured into the basin but it was confusing, and a man shouted at him to 'get out or get hurt'. He retreated to the narrow neck where it connected with the canal, but found himself on the opposite side to the towpath. He waited, not daring to go back and face the wrath of the watching man. He reckoned – with the slow progress made by the two police-men – he could keep up, if they ever reappeared, despite the obstructions in his way.

Don't look very 'appy, was Jimmy's verdict when they did finally emerge.

P'raps cos Mr Spray's not quite right, he thought. He could stay closer now with not much more than the width of the cut between them, but the hedges and overgrown bushes that gave him cover also hid his quarry. Then he lost them and could go no further. A stone wall and some impenetrable thorn was more than he could cope with. It was time for dinner.

The bit of greaseproof wrapping had protected his pocket, but done nothing to separate the contents from each other.

Sitting with his back to the wall, he started with the sausage-flavoured cake. As he daydreamed, something pushed up his elbow and a wet, black nose came to rest dangerously close to his food. It belonged to a shaggy head with floppy ears. Jimmy grabbed his victuals and the dog sat back on its haunches, gazing at him with big, mournful eyes. A wispy tail wagged hopefully in the grass. Unable to resist, a piece of sausage was offered, accepted, and friendship confirmed.

Dinner over, the dog took hold of the boy's sleeve and made to pull him to his feet. The lean, grey animal with, long slim legs, skinny body and straggly coat, was built for running. Jimmy knew about dogs like this; their propensity for catching other people's rabbits rendered them not quite respectable, and it made him love his new friend all the more. He was required to follow. The dog ran back and forth and nudged him toward a place where some stones had fallen out of the wall. It slipped through the gap like a grey shadow disappearing into the dense undergrowth on the other side.

Jimmy was acutely aware of what he could get away with. Arriving home with his jacket in shreds was not a good idea. The thorn was a step too far. He waited, listening to the dog whining, out of sight, until he could hear it no longer. Perhaps he hadn't made a friend for life after all. It was time to go home.

The way back was tedious. Scrambling over walls, detours round impenetrable spinneys, jumping over streams; it had all been exciting when he was on a mission, but now, with nothing achieved, it was hard work. And the dog: he'd even thought up a name, but that, too, had come to nothing. He'd have to cross the canal to get home, and the footbridge at the point where the Whaley arm split was in view when Jimmy's day brightened.

Out of nowhere, a grey streak came from behind, brushing

his leg as it shot past and then, turning as if on a farthing, the lurcher sat, tail wagging, his big brown eyes seeking forgiveness from the boy he had forsaken. The dog could have his name after all. Jimmy and Benjy crossed the bridge, content in each other's company.

———

Sunday was proving busier than usual for Lizzie. No sooner had she seen the two detectives out of the door than she had to think about accommodating Mary. But the physical work was nothing compared with her anxiety about Sam. Her only comfort was that William was with him, but it was obvious that the older man was in pain. Nothing had been said, but his face was bruised and he had a limp. But most worrying of all was his pallor. Her late husband had looked like that in the weeks before he died, and despite telling herself that Sam was injured rather than consumptive, the image of his corpse haunted her.

Also troubling was Mary's predicament. Awful as her ordeal had been, it was clear to Lizzie that worse was to come if she turned out to be with child. It made it even more difficult that the girl had seemed quite oblivious to the possibility, despite conceding that she had missed several monthlies.

"Mary, my love, come in and sit down. You must be tired from your journey."

As the two embraced, the youngster's relief at being safe at last only deepened Lizzie's reservations. Mary was up again almost immediately, excitedly talking about nothing very much as she helped in the kitchen, and only settled when she had a full teacup in her hand.

"Have you told Stephen you've left Cromford?" The look on Mary's face said she had not.

"I don't know what to say to him. He was so pleased for me when they took me on."

The moment had come. "You see, Mary, you might be carrying a child. From what you've told me, I think it's very likely, and it will start to show and..." Lizzie's resolve was weakening, but it was too late.

"You mean, what happened to me could get a child?" Mary was incredulous. "You have to be married to have babies."

The older woman knelt beside the distraught girl's chair and put an arm round her. For an awful moment, it seemed that the advance was to be rejected, but then Mary dissolved into tears and drew Lizzie closer.

The day was punctuated by tears and long silences, but somehow they got through it.

Mary wrote a little note:

Dear Stephen,
I called today but you were at work.
I'll call again and hope to find you back home.
Mary

She and Lizzie took a turn in the town, and Mary used her key to leave it on Stephen's kitchen table. The place looked an even worse mess than on her last visit.

"Do you think... you've been so kind I don't like to ask, but do you think I could have a little time some days to do something about this?" Mary gestured at the mess. The thought of familiar tasks undertaken beneath the protective roof of her childhood was, for a moment, comforting. Then the chilling reality of talking to her brother about... about her circumstances returned. She wept again.

By the time Sam and William found their way back to No 37, Mary had distributed her meagre belongings about her attic room and was helping in the kitchen. She had washed and peeled and chopped to good effect, and the results of her labour were sharing a stew pot, along with a piece of scrag end. They had been simmering for a good three hours when the men arrived.

"Just put those dumplings in and keep an eye on the kettle for me." Lizzie had prepared the suet balls. Tea would be ready in thirty minutes.

Hurrying through to the hallway, she could see things were not right. Sam's heavy topcoat was being dragged off his shoulders by William, and the process was causing a lot of pain. Lizzie rushed forward and elbowed him away.

"Let me help. Whatever you two have been up to, you shouldn't have. You can see he's not well. Really, William, I blame you."

With a deft flick of the wrist and a delicacy usually seen when handling the new born, Sam was divested of his coat and ushered into the most comfortable chair in the parlour. Much was made of arranging cushions, and a footstool was strategically placed for the comfort of his painful leg. Sam did not protest.

"Now, Sam Spray, this has got to stop. You've not said a thing about your injuries since you got back, and today you look all in. Tell me what has happened to you."

By the time he'd finished, even a watered-down version of the previous week's events, left Lizzie in no doubt. "You've broken a rib, perhaps more than one. You aren't going to mend in a few days. A few weeks more like." Sam said nothing.

William, sensing that this was a crucial moment in the connection between the two of them, made a diplomatic withdrawal to the kitchen.

"Let me lift that for you." Mary was struggling with a heavy kettle. She had flinched when he'd entered, but the offer was reassuring and he was allowed to take charge of tea-making. "I'd let it brew for a bit longer."

Fear showed in her eyes and William, whilst not understanding, sat down on the opposite side of the table from the girl.

"You're Mary, aren't you?"

With her fears allayed, she answered, "Yes, sir. Mary Thomas."

"Lizzie said…" Unsure of how things stood, he corrected himself. "Mrs Oldroyd said you were coming. "Stopping here in the attic, aren't you?"

The fear returned. Enquiries about where she might be sleeping, however kindly meant, were not welcome.

"I'm Constable Archer and I'm with Sergeant Spray." He nodded toward the door. We stay here when we're investigating crimes in the area." It was kindly meant, but the revelation was too much for the girl and, crying, she scrambled up the back stairs.

The tea would wait no longer, and William took it through.

"Mary should be doing that, William. I'll have to speak—"

"I'm afraid I upset her, she went upstairs crying. I only explained who Sam and I were, and that we stayed here when we were chasing criminals."

By the time tea was over, Mary was downstairs again helping clear up, cajoled back into the household. The two men, Lizzie assured the timid girl, were not only paying guests but friends, and could be trusted. She was still coming to terms with Sam's story and she could have done without the diversion. He'd told her about his trip to Dublin and getting shut up for a few days, but the breaking of ribs had been glossed over with. "The guards were a bit heavy-handed and free with their boots."

Much had been held back, and Lizzie knew it. Putting flesh on the meagre tale herself distressed her even more than being told the gruesome details straight out, and when a knock on the back door intruded she was in two minds about answering. Rat-a-tat-tat: the caller was in earnest and she couldn't ignore whoever it was.

"Evenin', missus Oldroyd." Jimmy Allcroft was at his most engaging. "I, er… I was hopin' you could help." Two big appealing eyes gazed up at the open door from somewhere near the boy's knee. "It's me dog." Lizzie looked down and, despite her other preoccupations – or perhaps because of them – her heart melted.

"Me mam says there's no room in the house, an' me dad won't have him in the yard cos of upsettin' the pig."

Lizzie had little time for the elder Allcroft's point of view. Her father had kept a pig back home when she was a child. As a little girl, she'd be sent out for a walk when the day came. Except one time, when the men were a bit late starting, and she returned to find the squealing animal lying on its side, two of them sitting astride and her father standing over it brandishing a carving knife.

"He's called Benjy." The grey wispy tail wagged. Lizzie bent down to stroke his head. If anything, she felt the dog needed protection from upset, not the pig. Seeing that Lizzie was softening, Jimmy pushed a bit harder.

"He ain't 'ad much grub t'day, just a bit of sausage I gev him fer 'is dinner."

She could see it happening: the boy sharing his food with the stray, and cementing a bond in the instant. Benjy won the day.

"That was young Jimmy at the door." Lizzie, back in the parlour, was fussing with the cushions and making conversation. "You can't imagine what he's done." She could have added 'what I've done' since not only had she agreed to Benjy living in her yard, she'd given him the remains of the stew, scrag end and all. Whilst they watched the dog at his tea, Jimmy had turned to other matters.

"I see'd them out on the cut today." He nodded toward the other room. "I were there when it were all happening, y'know."

"You mean when you went to Manchester?" Lizzie, just in time, bit her tongue. It would have been tactless to describe the trip as 'running away and playing truant'.

"S'right, I were helpin'." By now, Benjy was licking up the last morsels of his meal, and rattling his bowl. They ignored the intrusion.

"They were follerin' each other. The man at the front 'ad a bowler, bit like Mr Spray's. I knew who he were. See him get 'is pocket picked in Buxton Road day of the gala." Lizzie felt that her curiosity was in some way a betrayal, yet she sat silent and unmoving.

"Don't think Mr Archer saw 'im proper. 'E were still in the whorehouse when Mr Spray set off after 'im."

"Jimmy, do you know what that word means?" Lizzie, shocked, couldn't let it go unchallenged on the lips of a child.

"No, missus, it's what a lad in the street called it."

"I think it would be best if you didn't use it in front of your mum and dad, or anyone else."

"Yes, missus, if you say so. It's our little secret." Lizzie wasn't convinced she wanted to share a secret about a house of ill repute with the boy, and didn't find the gleam in his eye reassuring. She tried to bring the conversation to an end, but Jimmy kept talking.

"Then a man set off after Mr Spray, and Mr Archer followed him. Mr Spray disappeared and Mr Archer ended up at a Police House."

Lizzie had finally managed to silence Jimmy with a piece of cake.

"He's adopted a dog." In the presence of two policemen, she thought it prudent to make no mention of the breed. Lurchers weren't entirely respectable. "Found it loose on the cut."

"I caught a glimpse of him heading that way this morning." William was curious. "What's it like, this dog?"

"Big adorable eyes, and a kind nature."

He waited expectantly and, pressurised by the silence, Lizzie had to continue. "Lean, with a grey wispy coat, stands about this high." She bent down, her hand at the level of its head.

Benjy, having finally laid the enamel of his bowl quite bare, and finding Jimmy reluctant to share his cake, had set off to explore. He'd slid through the half-closed door into the parlour and, finding a friendly hand at head height, pushed his cold black nose into it.

"A lurcher." William saw the animal. "Is the boy still here?"

Chapter 18

Monday, October 1st, 1876

It was still dark when they set off, but by the time they'd reached their destination there was light enough to see. They'd made better time than the previous day with Constable Archer, unencumbered by his injured sergeant, and Jimmy Allcroft now on the towpath side of the canal.

Lizzie had been insistent. "You can't encourage the boy to play truant. I've got my reputation to consider. His mother thinks it's your fault over that trip to Manchester. She told me so."

It had been agreed that Jimmy would get up early and meet 'Mr Archer' at the canal basin at half past five. In return 'Mrs Oldroyd' would make sure there was some breakfast for them both to take on the expedition. William was honour-bound to make sure the boy arrived back in time for the school bell. There had been disagreement over Benjy. In the end, he stayed where he was in a hut in the yard at No 37. The prospect of him slinking off into the thicket as he'd done on Sunday, after swimming across the filthy water of the cut, had persuaded the reluctant boy.

"I were there when Benjy caught up wi' me." In Jimmy's eyes, the trip was framed by his meeting his new friend. "That's where I was 'avin me dinner." They'd walked on further and now stood opposite the end of a stone wall, at right angles to the cut. On one side, open ground; on the other, a thicket of brambles out of which grew mature trees. At the water's edge, willows draped their branches out into the water, and behind ash and oak stood tall.

"Nipped through the wall 'e did an' into that lot." Jimmy gestured toward the trees. "There, y' can see where the gap is." Even in their foreshortened view, stones could be seen tumbling out into the open ground. Beyond, the wall continued over the skyline. They walked on, the tangle of trees continuing for a while, finally giving way to open ground again, bounded by another wall.

"And that's as far as you came?" They were returning now. The sky was lighter and William, mindful of his promise, hurried. He had more than the school bell on his mind. *It could just be a half-eaten rabbit, but what if there was something from the lurcher's past behind the wall?* He didn't share his thoughts with the boy trotting along beside him. "Oh well, nothing very interesting there."

If that was the case, Jimmy couldn't see why he'd been escorted out onto the cut at such short notice. He didn't believe a word of it.

———————

"So you see, Sam, if Jimmy's dog is Tom Cubbin's other lurcher, and it's interested in that area of waste ground, we ought to know what's in there."

It was mid-morning and the two detectives were in the parlour. Sam had surfaced from the first full night's sleep he'd had since before his journey to Dublin. The sizeable dose of laudanum Lizzie had insisted on the night before had done its best, and he had only just had his breakfast. William sensed a shift in the relationship between the other two. He doubted if anything had been said, but there was a tacit acceptance on Sam's part that Lizzie was there in her own right; and on her part, that she had a position of her own in the little group.

"What you need is Alice Crawt. She can help with that."

Alice Crawt had been a school mistress in Whaley Bridge. She was unable to help in person, having been dead for many a long year, but in life she had laboured over a book.

"There's a copy of it in the new library. With a title like *A Historical Survey of Mining, Quarrying, Lime Burning and the Cotton Industry in Whaley Bridge and its Environs, and their Dependence on the Canal and Railway Systems of the Area*, that's where it belongs. Someone donated it for the opening."

Lizzie accompanied the men to the Reading Room and found the book for them. It was handsomely bound and must have reflected civic pride when it was published. No commercial enterprise could have expected to turn a profit on it. The volume had led a charmed life, and important though its subject matter may have seemed to whomever financed it, their interest had not extended to opening the pages. Several of the crisp leaves required cutting.

"Right, William, the section on canals first." Although the pain in his chest made turning the pages difficult, Sergeant Spray was in charge again. His constable leafed through the pages. They were at work.

"There, 'The Peak Forest Canal and Lime burning' that's what we want." It emerged that many sites predated the canal and, insofar as the geography allowed it, it did its best to serve them. In some cases the canal, by advantaging their competitors, rendered enterprises unprofitable. "That's the one, it's about the right distance from Whaley Basin." William was excited by his find '*Lime Kiln. Abandoned by 1831 leaving a redundant canal arm. Will soon be difficult to find its connection with the main waterway, such is the encroachment of nature.*'

"Look at the publication date." William did as he was told. "1856. The entrance would be completely obliterated by now, and the whole site gone back to the wild."

He'd insisted on coming, despite two restraining voices. They had different motives, the voices: Lizzie's was that of a nurse-maid, worrying about the wellbeing of her charge. William felt he would make faster progress on his own. Neither had prevailed, and the two detectives were making their way along Holly Lane.

Alice Crawt had mapped the area showing how, before the canal was built, the kiln had been supplied. Pack horses in long trains must have traversed the route, their wicker panniers laden with limestone. Even by the time the kiln was abandoned, the track would have been little used, and now – forty-five years later – it would be almost impossible to find. And yet...

"What do you make of that?" Much to William's surprise, Sam was keeping up a good pace. He wondered if Lizzie had insisted on a second dose of Laudanum with breakfast. If so, it hadn't been enough to make him sleepy. Sam was striking out ahead. "Come on, it's worth a look."

The rutted and muddy track had seen used well after the closure of the kiln, and before long they saw the reason why.

"Something down there." As they walked on, a stone roof had started to appear from behind a rise in the ground. Ahead, the route petered out, although a stone wall marched on into the distance to disappear over the brow. To the right was access to the farmstead. A mean-looking place, one building designed to house the farmer and the farmed, it stood dilapidated and unloved. A weathered stone, bigger than the rest in the wall, bore the barely discernible name, 'Jagger's Farm'. Had it not been for a figure walking toward them, they might well have assumed it to be derelict.

"What's tha up to?" Belligerence seeped into his every word. "This is my land, and you two," he gestured with a gun resting over his arm, "can bugger off back to where you came from." It wasn't actually aimed at the interlopers, but his meaning was clear.

"We're just looking for old packhorse trails. They've all but disappeared, haven't they?"

"Nosey sods – there ain't bin no pack horses down here in my time, an' I've lived 'ere man an' boy."

"No horses at all?"

"No soddin' horses at all." His manner had turned to menace, and the detectives set off in the direction indicated by the gun.

Safely out of range, they were able to relax.

"Not much to be said for that as an exercise in detective work. Sorry I brought you out here." William was trying to clean his dirty boots as he spoke.

"Your boots, don't they tell you something?"

"Only that I prefer the town to the country."

"That's horse shit you're scraping away at." William was too taken aback by the vulgarity of his companion's language to appreciate Sam's point. "Where there's horse droppings, there's got to be a horse."

"And the man said there weren't any horses at Jagger's Farm."

"And what's more, William, if you'd paid more attention to the good Miss Crawt, you'd realise the significance of the farm's name."

He was beat, all ends up. "Go on, Sam, what have I missed?"

"Miss Crawt explained that in the days of packhorse trains,

the man in charge was a Jagger."

"So, we were on an old packhorse route… and it wouldn't stop in the middle of nowhere, it would have followed that wall straight on to some other destination… a limekiln possibly." William thought he'd redeemed himself.

"Then there was the matter of hoof prints." Afterwards, William realised Sam was having a bit of fun. *And goodness knows he'd earned it, after what he'd been through,* he thought. At the time, he was mortified. "The sort of thing a heavy horse with shoes on would make."

"Tommy Cubbin's horse, you mean, being kept by an impoverished hill farmer for the people who stole it?"

"I think you've got the hang of everything now, William."

———•◦•———

By Monday morning, Superintendent Wayland was doubting the wisdom of Friday's decision. *What had he been thinking of, letting those two go off together with orders about recupera-tion, and taking care… and doing nothing very much, in all probability.* What had possessed him was a mystery now; the man Spray was back in one piece, and a day or two should set him right. Anyway, he had this letter to deal with.

It had lain in wait for him as he arrived. "G'mornin', sir, early post for you in your office." The desk sergeant wasn't usually so interested in what was in his mail but, as he sat down, he saw why. Embossed on the flap was 'Scotland Yard Police Dept.' and it had been franked at a sorting office in Whitehall. It informed the addressee that an Inspector Downes would be arriving on Tuesday, at Crewe on the 11.15 down express and, *would value the opportunity to discuss matters of joint interest concerning an issue of national importance.*

Wayland had heard the name Downes recently, and spent several fruitless minutes searching his mind. A knock on his door distracted him, and by the time he'd taken his first sip of tea, he had it. Archer's escapade in Manchester... that was it. The man couldn't be coming all that way to remonstrate about his men straying into another force's territory... could he? No, it was a matter of national importance, and Archer had said the man was quite a reasonable sort. Completely ignoring his dismissal of Archer's assessment two days ago, he embraced the judgement today.

The superintendent had no qualms about the interview; the man was of lower rank, and probably not a gentleman. He'd heard that some pretty rough sorts had been recruited once the Detective service had got into its stride. No, it was the matter of the dynamite. He had made no report to his superior about its loss and, as far as he knew, no complaint had been received from the goods office, but it was only time. But an issue of national importance? That reeked of explosives and mayhem and, ultimately, dismissal if he put a foot wrong.

There was one man he knew who could ensure everyone's feet ended up in the right place, but Spray was recuperating in the hills. Saying nothing to the sergeant in the outer office, and taking care to replace the letter in its envelope before enclosing it in his pocket book, Wayland took himself off to the station telegraph office. He turned words over in his mind as he walked. Not too explicit... certainly not. There was no knowing who might see them as the telegram found its way to No 37 Mill End; but, enticing enough to induce a man to disobey orders if his duty called. Not a frontal approach, of course.

"Afternoon, Mrs Oldroyd."

Lizzie was on her way to town. "Afternoon to you. Turned out fine. Tell me, have you seen Mrs Maida?" Apart from a few things for tea, she was on a quest for information.

"Not round the shops. Allus says Monday's when they get rid of last week leftovers, she does."

"I'll catch her at home." The casual encounter had run its course and the two women went their separate ways.

Mary had been given the task of peeling potatoes ready for tea. 'The men will want something hot when they get in,' Lizzie had told the girl. It would take her a little while and give Lizzie a chance to complete her own errand with discretion. Two days had passed since Mary had arrived, and nothing more had been said about the need to talk to Stephen. Lizzie would have to force the issue, but first she needed to know when he might be found at home.

"Lizzie Oldroyd, I'll be bound. Come in and I'll make some tea." Lizzie and Elsie Maida were old friends, and it was difficult to refuse.

"I'm sorry I can't, Elsie. I've got some paying guests who'll be wanting their tea. But I need a word with Fred; something to do with the railway. Could you ask him to pop round when it's convenient?"

With that, Lizzie set off for home. As she walked up Mill End, a uniformed youth, perhaps fourteen or fifteen years old, came running down the hill and, after they'd crossed, came to an abrupt halt and set off back in the direction he'd come from.

"Please, missus," he doffed his cap in the manner they'd taught him at the telegraph office. "You're Mrs Oldroyd, aren't you?" Lizzie nodded. "I got to deliver this t' your house, but the girl there said she didn't know nothing 'bout telegrams and wouldn't sign."

Lizzie took the proffered pencil stub and wrote her name. The envelope was addressed to Constable William Archer. *No expense spared,* she thought. Archer would have done and every word costs.

Chapter 19

Tuesday, October 2nd, 1876

Of course, there'd been an exchange of views on the matter. It had been a rerun of the previous day's skirmish, but only one of the combatant's hearts was really in it. Lizzie could see Sam's strength returning day by day, and she knew well enough that whatever there was between the two of them – and she was sure there was something – it would never separate him from his work. William's position was even weaker. The Whale's orders had been clear about Sam, but vague concerning himself. In any case, the material they had was largely down to the sergeant, and he deserved to present it in person.

The telegram that awaited their return the previous evening had been carefully phrased, mentioning as it did, 'all available material', but it had only confirmed the course of action on which they had already agreed, and were now embarked.

The 9.50 all stations to London Road would allow them to catch a connection at Edgeley for Crewe, and arrive at the appointed time. They could not be held responsible for the engine failure which required a change of locomotive at Stockport and left their connection stranded in the platform at Edgeley Station for twenty minutes.

Meanwhile, Superintendent Wayland had met Inspector Downes off the London train, and the two men were sizing each other up across the former's desk.

"Your Constable Archer, good man, is he?"

"One of my two best detectives." Wayland might have said my two only detectives.

"Seemed very steady under fire. Came across him in Manchester last week, 'spect he told you."

"He said you'd arrested him, yes."

"A little misunderstanding; we sorted it out in the end. It was after talking to him that I realised that both of us were hunting the same fox."

"You mean you forced information out of him." Wayland resisted the bonhomie.

"Not at all; tight as a clam he was, that's what I meant about 'steady under fire'. No, he didn't tell me anything, but he and the other chap did blunder into our operation, and it had to be because we were after the same miscreants." Wayland nodded.

"Now, look here, superintendent, do you think we might co-operate? It's going to be awkward if we don't, because I've got a big problem on my hands and it involves the railway."

At this, Wayland could find no way of refusing.

"We've come by information that a very important personage, a member of the royal family, will shortly be travelling incognito from Hathersage to Manchester."

"But that's impossible. I would have been told. I'm always told."

"Both of us should have been told, but we weren't." Downes gave a knowing look. "A private matter we commoners are not supposed to know about."

Wayland was scandalised by the man's casual appraisal of the behaviour of his betters.

"I only found out unofficially, and when I approached His Royal Highness's household, I got pretty short shrift. They'd have had me off the premises until I mentioned the plot we'd got wind of."

It began to dawn on the superintendent that the conversation was getting perilously close to explosives.

"The intention is to blow a bridge in the path of the Prince's train."

A knock on the door interrupted the inspector. The look of relief on Wayland's face passed unnoticed. Downes and the new arrivals were too busy hiding their surprise at the other's presence. The matter of missing dynamite would be much better explained by Sergeant Spray, he thought.

The two women were on their way into the town. Lizzie's quest for information had borne fruit, and she knew that Mary's brother would be at home until mid-morning. Her plan was to apprise Stephen of the girl's changed domicile, and let the two of them get used to the new arrangements. As they walked, she took a sidelong glance at Mary. It wouldn't be long before any casual observer would know; soon she'd have to move on to the difficult business of encouraging the girl to explain things to Stephen. But for now, one step at a time.

It was a startled Stephen who opened the door.

"Hello, Mrs Oldroyd... and Mary, what are you doing here?" He ushered them in, rather shamefaced about the mess. "They didn't sack you, did they?"

Lizzie answered, "Not at all, Mr Thomas. I've offered her a position here in Whaley, and she left Ravenhead with a character."

Happy to let the other two talk, Mary set about tidying up. She produced tea for them all and, before setting it on the table, had to make a space.

"Stephen, tell me about this." In her hand was the print of Sladen Castle. "It's what Father gave you before he died, isn't it?

Mary had never thought about her father's past, any more than Stephen had before the old man's deathbed revelations, but the unfolding tale caught her interest. Even so, she said nothing about there being the same print of Sladen Castle at Ravenhead House. Somehow it seemed too close to the awfulness that had been visited on her, and she wasn't ready to talk to her brother about it.

Stephen, whilst talking freely of starving peasantry and the desperate need that led to the attempt to steal food, said nothing about the cousin who had appeared from nowhere at the funeral.

"Mary has said she'd like a little time off each week to help you manage here, Mr Thomas. I'm quite agreeable if you would find that convenient."

In the general satisfaction at this arrangement, Stephen made no enquiry as to his sister's wages. Lizzie was disposed to help her young friend where she could, but financing a maid was beyond the resources of her modest business. Mary had bed and board, but nothing more.

———

"So, there we have it, the plot laid bare, almost in its entirety." Inspector Downes, much to Wayland's surprise, was in good spirits. Far from looking askance at the mislaying of two boxes of dynamite, he positively revelled in what he had learned. "All we need now is to work out where they intended to explode the stuff."

The little office was crowded. With only two chairs, Archer and Downes were standing. If the protocol of seniority had been adhered to, it would have been the inspector in the second chair, but he had declined.

"My, they gave you a beating over the water there, didn't they?" Downes had made sure that Sam should sit. "Any idea of who they were?" Sam's incarceration was treated as a hoard of treasure to be savoured one item at a time. As his story unfolded, the inspector relished each detail, to the extent that he felt the need to apologise.

"I'm sorry, sergeant, I would not have wished these travails on you, but what you've told us has confirmed long-held suspicions."

He explained that he had thought for a while that a semi-official secret operation was being mounted by the Dublin administration, and Sam's intelligence was the final confirmation.

"You've nailed that man you were following. We could see his finger in and out of the pie, but we never knew who he was. A Mr Slade, you say one of the soldiers called him Slade?"

"That's right; it just slipped out during the interrogation."

"Y'did bloody well to remember it all, in amongst the torture."

"It made it easier, sir, gave me something to fix my mind on. The biggest worry was getting hit over the head again and losing my memory."

At this, Superintendent Wayland would have been squirming in his chair, had his military code not prohibited such a thing. As it was, he allowed himself to warm to the interloper from Scotland Yard for his appreciation of Sam's endurance.

"Y'see, this Slade's playing a double game. We got onto him because of his little Fenian friends, and now we find him drinking at the high table."

Into a short silence the superintendent inserted a solemn pronouncement. "Last week I was summoned to London." The moment had come. Wayland had to dispense with the peer and throw in his lot with these commoners. "There was a lot of gentlemanly discourse, but the heart of it was that Sergeant Spray here was getting too close for comfort and I was to restrain him. It wasn't explained what it was he was close to. The man was an Irish peer who I had known from my early days in the cavalry, and he attempted to play on the connection. An unprincipled bounder then and, it seems, now."

"And his name, sir?"

"Lord Percy Fancourt." As he said it, Charles Wayland felt an encumbrance that had weighed him down for a lifetime slide from his shoulders. At last he could view the world from the high ground on which his sergeant stood.

"That clears up one thing." Sam straightened in his chair. Somehow, in the midst of the discussion, his pain had seemed to recede. "I was blindfold, you understand, and at the time I couldn't remember who I was. This man must have been looking at my warrant card, because he read out my name. You've no idea how much better I felt for knowing that. Anyway, he read down and finally came to the place where you'd signed it, sir." Sam turned to his superior. "And as he read it out, his voice went quiet and then he disappeared."

"So, you think he recognised the superintendent's name?"

"Not at the time, no. I didn't know what to think then, but now? Yes, I'm sure of it."

"So, the remaining question is where?" Downes was very persistent.

"Does it matter, sir, if we can retrieve the dynamite? No bang, no problem."

Downes gave a weary smile at Archer's question. "That's only half the problem solved, constable, and we haven't got hold of the stuff yet. I need to nail the men responsible. It's treason, y'know. A good hanging works wonders."

Sam wasn't so sure that the creation of a martyr or two would help much, but he held his peace. William, unabashed by Downes's rebuke, said, "If we assume the plan is to moor the boat somewhere and blow it up, I know just the place. I walked along there the day I found the dead lurcher. The canal goes under an arch of the Marple viaduct."

Wayland blustered. "But that's the Midland main line, and we're LNW personnel."

"It was the LNW who lost the explosive in the first place," riposted Downes. Wayland was about to revise his view of Scotland Yard man. "Your men here have cracked this business wide open. I should very much value their assistance, if you would be so good as to allow it."

***

Lizzie arrived home on her own. Stephen had gone to work and Mary had stayed to bring order to the chaos of his cottage. It had been a success, Lizzie thought. The change in the girl's circumstances had been accepted; brother and sister were on good terms; and Lizzie herself had received a friendly welcome. It was a good start, although how the news of Mary's pregnancy would be greeted was another matter altogether.

Lizzie was inclined to put it down to spending too much time in the company of detectives and their suspicious minds, but try as she may she couldn't ignore it. Mary hadn't mentioned the print of Sladen Castle at Ravenhead House to Stephen. A week ago, when she'd first seen her father's copy, she had been full of it and it would have made an interesting addition to Stephen's rendition of old Patrick's deathbed revelations. Perhaps Mary couldn't face talking about the place to Stephen and it was entirely innocent, but Lizzie couldn't get the coincidence of the two pictures out of her mind.

Later, such thoughts were overtaken by the men's arrival. They were in remarkably good spirits, and Sam refused any more laudanum, saying it clouded his mind. Lizzie busied herself with a tray of tea and then the preparation of a meal. While she was peeling the potatoes, young Jimmy arrived.

"Afternoon, missus. Just come to take Benjy for his walk." It hadn't occurred to her, when she made the offer, that the lad would be round every day after school. He never asked, not for himself anyway, but she felt compelled to find him a little something.

"You can have what's left from the tray when you've taken Benjy."

"Constable Archer and the sergeant back then, are they?"

That boy knows more than is good for him, Lizzie thought.

"Saw them going up the station earlier. D'ye know where they been?"

"Be off with you, you ask too many questions."

Questions weren't the only problem. He'd turned up with a rabbit, 'fer Benjy's keep'. Nothing was said about it, but she was certain the lurcher had poached it, and she'd ended up feeding it to two policemen.

The tray was back in the kitchen and the cooking well advanced by the time Jimmy returned. With the door ajar, fragments of conversation crept through to the kitchen. As he sat with a rock bun and a glass of milk, he heard the words, 'reinforcements' and 'first thing'. Something was being planned for tomorrow.

Chapter 20

Wednesday, October 3rd, 1876

It all depends on the company you keep, Constable Archer concluded. Having provoked contempt a few days ago for his ignorance from lock keepers both at the Bosley flight and the Peak Forest stop lock, he found himself talking authoritatively to a group of men as they walked together in the dawning day along Holly Lane.

"You've got to keep feeding water in at the summit. It's the locks that use it, every time you pass a boat through." William was getting to the limit of his knowledge, but Inspector Downes and his officers didn't know that. The five of them had arrived on the Parliamentary before first light, and had been met from the train by William and led to Whaley Basin.

"We're in your hands," Downes had said. "Right off our ground we are."

William, who had explored the route only once before, was glad to share the responsibility with his sergeant, who'd gone straight to the basin.

"Ah, sergeant." Downes extended his hand. "Bearing up, are you? Very glad to see you and Archer here." This, to the astonishment of his squad, who were used to much more peremptory treatment on their home turf in Manchester.

As they walked, plans were discussed. "You sure 'bout that?" Downes was querying Sam's assessment that the farmer with the gun wasn't part of the conspiracy.

"You've no idea how hard the living is up here in the Peak, sir. In my opinion, the man was offered money to look after the horse and keep his mouth shut. He'd have been mad not to take it."

"So, what do you suggest, sergeant?"

"We've got to prise him away from the money, sir, that's for sure."

Spray and Archer set off along the track to Jagger's Farm. The rest of the party hung back, their uniforms rather conspicuous for what was afoot. As before, they were confronted by an aggressive farmer with a gun over his arm.

"Told you two buggers to clear off, didn't I?" The gun pointed back along the track in the direction of Holly Lane. "If you aren't along there sharpish, I'll have to use this." He patted the stock.

"We'd got one or two questions to…"

The gun was raised in earnest and pointed straight at Sam. "Get going."

Concentrating on intimidating the intruders, the uniformed men went unnoticed by the farmer. They had approached within earshot when Inspector Downes shouted. The man finally noticed four officers of the law, uniformed and purposeful, bearing down on him. The weapon clattered to ground.

"You'll forgive us if we take charge of that?" Downes spoke whilst one of his men retrieved the piece. "Serious matter, threatening a policeman with a loaded firearm." The uniformed constable broke the gun, and extracted a cartridge. "Not the first time; you did the same thing two days ago."

"But they 'adn't no uniform, 'ow was I to know they was policemen?"

Downes went on. "And then there's the matter of the horse. You said there hadn't been one on the farm for as long as you could remember, but we both of us know that's not true." Downes turned to one of his men. "Why don't you and

Constable Archer here go and find it? Better still, we'll all come, and Mr…" He turned back to the farmer, in handcuffs now. "Mr?"

"Tombs, sir, Nathaniel Tombs."

"Mr Tombs can show us where it is."

Walking down to the farm, the group split into two. Sam was finding the uneven ground difficult and Downes hung back with him.

"That went well."

"Only because you and Archer had the right of it."

"Kind of you to say so, sir."

"Bright lad that Archer; hope some of it rubs off on my lot."

"Yes, sir."

"And you, sergeant, you were pretty steady back there… with a gun at your chest."

"It wasn't cocked, sir. It pays to notice these things."

The vanguard arrived at the yard and hardly needed their guide. Hearing footsteps, the horse whinnied and was traced to a ramshackle stable, no more than a cattle hovel hastily boarded up.

"Belongs to someone else, I'll be bound." Archer took up the interrogation. "Either you stole it, or someone else did." He turned to one of the uniformed men. "What can you get for horse stealing?"

"Used to be transportation; more like 10 years hard now."

There was doubt on Tombs' face. "But I ain't done nuthin'. These two men came 'ere wi' money an' said they'd pay if I looked after th'oss."

"There must have been more to it than that."

"If you know so much about it, work it out for y'self." For a moment, Tombs became truculent.

"You realise this is a treasonable conspiracy you're

involved with?" Archer let the words sink in. "There's a noose just waiting for your neck unless you co-operate."

"An' what if I do?"

"We'll have to see. Now, you were going to tell us a bit more. First question, have there only been the same two men, or have there been others?"

By now the two senior officers had caught up and were inspecting the stable. Inside was a heavy horse, well-muscled and cared for. Just the sort of animal a successful skipper would have to haul his narrowboat. When they'd finished, they turned their attention to the interrogation.

"He says he's only had contact with two men, but there was at least one other, perhaps more. They made him stay in the stable but he heard voices. The two who approached him first didn't say much; one did all the talking and he 'spoke funny'. A couple of rough types, he says. Told him to shoot a grey lurcher if he saw it."

Spray walked over to the prisoner. His bruised face served to create the impression of a man who was free with his fists. "Now, Tombs, you've given us some crumbs, but we want the whole loaf. I don't believe you just stood in the stable. You had a look." He raised his hands to mimic peering through a crack. Tombs, mistaking his intention, flinched.

"How many others, and where did they go?

"I saw nuthin'. Said there'd be trouble if I didn't do what they said."

"What sort of trouble?"

"One of 'em had a revolver."

"So, you knew whatever they were up to was illegal. It had to be: legitimate business isn't done with a gun." Spray looked round at the men. "You see, we're legitimate and we don't have a gun, 'cept yours, of course, but we represent the law, and you're close to being on the wrong side of it. Now! What else did you see?"

"There were only two of them the first time, like I said, when they brought th'oss. Next day, same ones came an' made me stay in the stable. There were others, an' when I looked there were four of 'em goin' down the packhorse track to th'owd limekiln."

Spray nodded. "That's better. I don't suppose one of them wore a bowler hat?"

———•┄•———

Benjy needed a daily walk. A routine had developed. Jimmy came round after school with whatever scraps he'd managed to scrounge, and leave them in the scullery whilst he and the dog set out. Often enough, the cornet came, too, and Benjy would be allowed to roam the towpath whilst the disjointed notes of the third trumpet part of the band's latest piece rang out across the cut.

Today it would be different. The disgruntled Benjy was on the end of a piece of rope. He pulled and jerked at the restraint, but he was needed close by as an alibi. Perhaps, too, he didn't think much to being dragged from his kennel so early in the morning.

Re-inforcements had to be arriving at the station, so boy and dog watched for the Parliamentary to arrive. The back view of Constable Archer had been disappearing down Mill End as the pair had emerged from No 37's back yard, and that had clinched it. They watched as four men in uniform and another man were shown down to the wharf. Jimmy didn't dare follow them closely, but for some distance the road ran parallel to the canal. With a wall between the two offering cover, he

210

was able keep level with the posse and hear snatches of their conversation.

Where the Whaley arm joined the Peak Forest canal, a bridge gave access to the other side and the group of policemen disappeared. Jimmy, still on the wrong side of the wall, couldn't follow. He trotted along the road and finally got onto the towpath. He'd lost his quarry, but Benjy might catch a rabbit, so he let the dog loose and set off toward the place where he'd taken Constable Archer two days before. There was early traffic on the cut. Boats, loaded the night before at Buggie and Whaley basins, were on the move and he met them on his way back. As he dodged the horses, he had to put up with the jeers of the lads leading them.

"Nowt better to do than walk thy dog." And "Watch it, we'll have y'in t' cut ."

Neither boy nor dog noticed another walker overhauling them. He was almost up with the pair when Benjy, who had not uttered a sound since Jimmy had known him, started barking. As the man passed, the dog growled. Jimmy watched his silhouette disappearing into the morning gloom and wondered why it looked familiar.

<hr />

"He claims he never comes down here. Not been since he was a young man, he said."

"D'ye believe him?" Downes had heard the farmer's assertion and was after Spray's opinion.

"It's possible. If this is someone else's land, like he says, he might not be welcome, even if this is an historic right of way. But no, Tombs has only a passing acquaintanceship with the truth."

They were walking on, along the old packhorse track. As before, Archer and the uniformed men were up ahead, with the two senior officers following at a more leisurely pace.

"That constable of yours will have the others scouting around for anything suspicious, I'll be bound. No need to hurry."

By the time they arrived at a crumbling wall, the posse were already through and into the undergrowth. Young ash and birch were already growing up to replace dead and fallen trees. A carpet of dead leaves lay on the ground. Around the edge of the woodland, eager for the light, brambles spread, smothering the old wall. What berries were left had become brown and shrivelled. At one point they had been cut back, and it was through the gap that Downes and Spray followed their men.

"Tombs may not come down here, but someone's cut this back, sir."

Downes, town born and bred, hadn't realised that their path into the wood had been eased by human hand.

"The rogues who threatened Tombs, and the other two, you mean?"

"I doubt Bowler Hat did much of it. If it is Slade, I didn't get the impression he'd have calloused hands."

Downes agreed. "Dirt of a different sort, I don't doubt."

Inside the wood there were further signs of man's intervention – branches recently snapped off and the odd tree trunk dragged aside, the teeming mass of life sheltering beneath now dispersed, but the indentation remaining. Weathered stonework appeared through the trees; the old limekiln, looking so decayed that its covering of ivy seemed to be the only thing keeping it standing. Deeper in now, the ground became waterlogged. They were approaching the head of the canal arm where what had been the end of the wharf had collapsed, allowing precious canal company water to seep out into the bank. The boundary between boggy ground and canal was ill-defined, but out toward the cut, the bank was intact and the arm had remained just about navigable. And there she was.

It must have been a close-run thing, thought Sam. The *Kingfisher*, unladen with freeboard showing, drew a couple of feet for most of her length, but here must have been sufficient depth of water, because she rocked gently as the party boarded. A faint aroma of putrefaction had permeated the wood. At the outset, Sam had thought it came from dead branches, festooned with fungus, decaying along with the leaf mould on the ground. The nearer they came to the *Kingfisher*, the stronger the stink, until, with the hatch over her little cabin in the stern slid open, it became overwhelming.

Inside it was like a butcher's slaughterhouse. On the floor, blood had seeped from beneath a dead man. It was now congealed, but when Sam accidentally put his foot in it, the sole of his boot adhered slightly. It was crowded in the tiny space with the two policemen and two bodies. True, one of them was only that of a terrier, the side of its head crushed by something heavy, but even so, the living were glad to regain the bank, but not before Sam had prised a spent bullet from the woodwork.

"So, Archer had the right of it. The boat was taken, presumably by threatening Cubbin and then shooting him when he was no more use to them." Downes talked as the junior men clambered into the hold.

"Hard to see down here, sir." A muffled voice emerged from beneath the cloth, draped like a tent over planks that ran from the cabin top at the stern to the cratch board at the bow. Downes lifted the canvas at its free corner and, unhooking it as he went, threw it up onto the ridge. "Nothing much in the hold, sir," the voice clearer now, "except for a few empty sacks."

A flicker of uncertainty passed between the two on the bank. "Have a look underneath."

———•·•·•———

His granny was ill, very ill with her chest. That was the story and, grudgingly, he'd been allowed a day off. "Without pay, you understand." The head clerk, pompous to the last added, "The Midland Railway is a generous employer. Just remember that."

By catching a Derby train after work, he'd arrived in Cromford the night before, much to the surprise of old Mrs Pepperell.

"Ben, it's not Sunday, is it?"

"No, Gran, but I've got a day off tomorrow so I thought I'd come and see you. I'm not really off work; I've got an errand to do in Cromford for the office early tomorrow. So, I thought I could spend the evening with you and go out early in the morning.

"But, Ben, what about y're tea? I've got nothing in."

"Don't worry about me, Gran," he lied. "I brought something to eat on the train."

He'd eaten nothing since his mother had stood over him at breakfast time and insisted. Even then, he'd done his best to confound her. He wasn't hungry; food was an irrelevance. It had been for well over a week since he'd last spoken to Mary. For the life of him, he couldn't work out what had gone wrong. But he needed to find out.

It was a dank, misty morning. Whilst in his passion, his mind had been rejecting food, but now his body was missing it and his undernourished frame shivered in the cold. Even the effort of walking up Cromford Hill didn't warm him. Higher, the dampness turned to a persistent mizzle, and he was glad for a rest in the shelter of a bridge. Overhead, a train passed – first the wheezy puffs of a locomotive, then the quarrelsome chatter of a line of trucks. Standing out of the rain, waiting for it to ease, Ben at last came face to face with reality. So far, he'd followed his heart, and it was still telling him what it wanted, but it had failed to deliver the means.

After a while, the mizzle eased and he set off again. The name Ravenhead House had slipped out in conversation, but Mary had never explained exactly where it was. He'd once seen her coming down the hill, and on another occasion she'd said she knew she was almost back there as she went under a bridge. With this meagre information, he resumed his quest.

Finding the place proved simple. Ben asked a postman. His round finished, he was heading back into the village.

"Oh ay, ah knows Ravenhead. Don't know owt about them as live there. No-one does; keeps 'emselves to 'emselves, they do. Some say th'owd man's a Lord, but there's nivver been any mail fer one o' they, an' he ain't been seen fer years. I seen some fer an Hon, though."

"And the servants?"

"Don't see much o' them either. Must be a housekeeper, an' I see a young maid a time or two. She was alright, the little lass. Allus gave a body the time o' day." Ben picked up on the 'was'.

"'Aven't spoke to 'er for a bit. Last time must be a few months ago. Must be keeping 'er 'ead down."

The postman went off down the hill and Ben, following his directions, found himself outside a pair of stout gates. On the other side, a drive climbed, curving slightly, so that only the corner of Ravenhead House showed itself through the railings. He waited.

He waited until the mizzle started again, he waited until

his coat dragged at him with the weight of soaked up rain, and he waited until the light began to fail. No-one had emerged and only one man had entered. In desperation, he tried the gates. As he walked, more of the house appeared. The corner was attached to a self-important, double-fronted, stone built residence, with glass-panelled double doors between. A heavy porch protected the entrance, supported with robust pillars.

Tradesmen followed a well-worn path, taking them round the side away from the imposing portico. Ben followed. It was a relief to have the intimidating frontage out of his sight. The place may have been bereft of the comings and goings common to a house of such substance, but it had eyes. By the time he arrived at the servant's entrance, the door was open and framed a formidable personage.

"What are you doing here, young man?"

"If you please, missus, I would like to have a word with the maid."

"During working hours? I've never heard of such a thing. The staff are here to do their chores, not to bill and coo with young men. Anyway, if it's Mary you're after, she doesn't work here anymore."

"But…"

"No buts, young man, she left last Sunday, and good riddance. No better than she ought to—"

"Who's that at the back?" A man's voice boomed out of the lobby from behind the housekeeper.

The woman turned. "A young man wanting the maid."

"Oh her, she's of no consequence. Send him away."

Ben returned the way he'd come. He glimpsed, through an un-curtained window, the only person to arrive at the house during his long watch. The man who thought Mary was of no consequence. He wouldn't forget the face.

———

"Gently now." Sergeant Spray was in charge. With his service in the Crimea, he'd turned out to be the only one amongst them with any experience of explosives, far in the past though it was, and only with military black powder at that.

"This stuff's safe enough as long as it's kept dry and cool." The uniformed men were carefully lifting two boxes, one at a time, out of the hold. On the side of each was stamped

British Dynamite Company
Ardeer, Scotland

Archer peered down into the boat. The sacking had been thrown aside. "The men who stole it didn't seem to know about that; not the 'keeping it dry' bit, anyway. There's water just below the floorboards."

"Anything that floats must leak a bit." This from Downes. "With Cubbin dead, the only man who understood boats is gone."

"We're only assuming the dead man is Cubbin. They've shot up each other back at the rail yard. It might be one of them." Spray resumed his earlier conversation with Downes.

"We'll have to check, but not yet. This is a tricky business. I want to catch them in the act, but my hands are tied."

Spray looked surprised.

"I only had any co-operation at all by promising the utmost discretion. No mention of royal journeys in this part of the world." There was resignation on Downes's face at Spray's questioning look. "You're better not knowing."

"So, no treason then?"

"No, but they'd have to kill him for treason. I'm not sure that trying is quite enough. As it is, we've got two murders and the theft of explosives and a narrowboat, not to mention assaulting a signalman. You must have something special in the railway regulations for that one."

"We've got to catch them first."

"You got any ideas?" asked Downes. If he was only enquiring out of politeness, he seemed very intent on an answer. "You've as much interest in this affair as I have."

"Superintendent Wayland," the sergeant thought it unwise to call his superior 'the Whale' in the presence of a senior officer, no matter how friendly. "Superintendent Wayland would be most relieved to see the return of the dynamite, and since it was me that lost it, so would I."

Downes agreed.

"But we could let the Fenians run? I take it you have a date for this non-journey, sir?"

"There's a day or two in hand." For a moment, Downes's discretion got in the way of common sense, then, "Saturday. An early express from Sheffield; it's going to make an unscheduled stop to couple up an extra coach."

Spray forbore to ask where.

By now the dynamite was safely on the quay. Archer and one of the inspector's men had been despatched to Jagger's Farm.

"He ought to manage a couple of boxes," the senior officer had said. "Don't you tell him what they're for. When he's made them, keep him out of the way until we're done."

It was a very different Tombs when the two constables arrived. Without a gun, and the word treason still hanging in the air, his truculence had evaporated.

"Yes, officer, I can do that. How big d'ye wants 'em?"

It was a matter of some importance, the size. The dynamite was in the form of sticks, wrapped in brown greaseproof paper, an inch or so in diameter and roughly eight inches long. "Look a bit like a fat cigar," one man had said. Archer had thought they were more like large dog turds, but held his tongue.

"This long, this wide, and this deep." He'd produced three pieces of a hazel wand that he'd snapped at the right lengths. In the absence of a measure, it was the best he could do. "That's for the inside, and we want handles at each end."

"Whad'ye want these—"

"Shut up, and get on with it." The man in uniform had brought muscle to the party. Archer left them and went to look for Tombs' woodpile. To one side of it, he found what he was looking for.

"When you've finished, cut these to just fit inside, lying across."

"Y' has my kindling there. How 'm I going to light my fire?"

"You'll have to find some more. There's plenty down in the wood."

"But it'll all be wet. I collect mine in the summer an' I keep it…" It began to dawn on Tombs that he was saying too much.

He was not a practised liar. Serving two masters was turning out to be an uncomfortable business for a man with a preference for honesty.

"We've had a complaint from one of the quarries. Two boxes of dynamite short on their last delivery. Know anything about it, Maida?"

"We had the loaded explosive wagon in the yard just over

two weeks ago, Mr Oxspring." That bit was true. "The weekend of the gala, when that body was found in the yard."

"Those detectives from Crewe were nosing around; did they say anything about explosives?"

This was the moment. Sergeant Spray had been most insistent. If they were to catch the killer, nothing must be said about the explosive. He'd found it quick enough, and he'd promised to have it back in the yard in time to replace it in the gunpowder van. Fred had hung onto the wagon for as long as he dared, but in the end it had to go. He'd been surprised the matter hadn't surfaced sooner, and now if he trusted the sergeant he must lie.

"No, sir."

"S'pose, I'll 'ave t' report it to Goods at Crewe." The words were laced with reluctance. The amount of paperwork demanded by the Goods Dept. in the normal course of events was notorious. Goods lost or stolen were much worse.

"Sergeant Spray and his constable are in the town at present. You could report it to them, Mr Oxspring." Afterwards, Fred Maida felt shame at his own duplicity, but on the spur of the moment it seemed perfectly natural.

"You know where t' find 'em?" Oxspring sounded happier.

"Yes, sir. They're lodging with a friend of Mrs Maida."

"Give 'em this." The yard master was writing as he spoke. "Tell 'em I'll have t' let Goods know in a day or two. The quarry wants to know what's up."

———•••••———

"Thank you, Mr Tombs. Just put those shavings in as well." The boxes were finished. Inside were two neat rows of brown sticks, each about an inch in diameter. "Now, this officer," Archer nodded in the direction of his uniformed companion, "is going to accompany you to the farmhouse. It would be a good investment for the future if you were to make him comfortable, because you are going to stay together until I return."

"Whad'ye mean? Stay in the farmhouse. I've got stock t' see to."

Archer looked around. Dirty white sheep with mottled black faces were grazing rough grass on the hill, whilst a few chickens pecked away at muddy ground in the untidy yard. From the smell, there were swine somewhere close, but the only sound was that of a barking dog, chained up to its kennel. "Not much needing your attention that I can see. Just do as we say."

They weren't so much heavy as awkward. Earlier, William had declined more than one uniformed man to accompany him, and was regretting it now. He could have done with an extra hand to help with the two boxes, but Tombs needed an eye keeping on him, so he was carrying them on his own.

Down at the old wharf, the men – with nothing better to do – had been exploring the wood. One man had made his way westward from the limekiln.

"You'd better look at this, sir." Downes was summoned. He and Spray stood looking across open moorland towards Marple. In the middle distance, a bridge crossed the cut.

"What you might call an escape route." Downes was voicing his thoughts.

"Or a private entrance." Spray saw a different possibility. "Constable, tell us how you found it."

"Tripped, sir, grabbed the nearest branch and fell over when it came away in me hand. When I stood up, there was this track in front of me."

"I think," Spray turned to Downes, "I think one member of this gang is playing a different game to the others."

Archer had struggled as far as the opening in the wall and called for help. The two boxes had become heavier the nearer to the *Kingfisher* he got. Two uniformed men came to his aid and they were whisked off to the wharf.

"Good, you remembered the extra packing." Downes and his men were standing well back, but Sam was busy. "Right, William, get that kindling out of Tombs' boxes and put in the shaving from here." Engaged in the dangerous job of handling explosives, the two lapsed into their customary familiarity. "Now put them next to each other." One by one, Sam gently lifted the sticks of dynamite in their brown paper wrapping and placed them in the new boxes. As each layer was transferred, he took packing from the old box and placed it on top, making a bed for the next.

"Inspector," Sam called across to Downes, "would you be good enough to get your men to collect small rocks to fill this one to within three inches of the top?" The first box, with British Dynamite Company stamped on the side, was empty of explosive and ready for the deception. "And then the same amount for the second one when we've finished."

No-one was happy at leaving the body where it was. Apart from the implied disrespect, it went against 'procedure' and the uniformed men in particular found it difficult to accept. But orders are orders and they had done their best to restore the *Kingfisher* to the state in which they'd found her. The only difference being the boxes. Back under the sacking in the hold, they were without their dynamite.

"It's the best I can do." The single row of kindling just about passed muster as dynamite sticks under a layer of shavings. "You'll have to hope they don't look too close until you've got them all together."

Downes decided that now the stolen property had been

retrieved, he and his men would be responsible for apprehending the Fenian plotters. Their last co-operative act would be to carry it back to Shallcross and restore it to the care of the yard staff. There was, of course, the unresolved matter of the corpse of Cathal Thomas which had undoubtedly been deprived of life on railway property. Spray couldn't quite let things go at that.

"He was involved with them, Inspector, either for or against. But whichever, I'd like to ask a few questions when you have them under lock and key."

———

Fortunately, it was dark by the time the group of policemen wended their way through Whaley Bridge to the rail yard. They'd done their best to shield the boxes and look as if they were just proceeding normally. Only a boy with a dog took any notice.

As they had passed Jagger's Farm, there was no sign of Tombs, and Inspector Downes had gone in 'for a word', as he'd put to the others.

"Now see here, Tombs, you've got one chance of saving your neck, and one chance only."

The man was still indignant at his house arrest. "This ain't legal. Your officer—"

"Mr Tombs, consider this. You admitted to Constable Archer that you go into the wood to collect firewood, having previously lied about it."

"So, what's that to you?"

"Floating there in the disused canal arm is a stolen narrow-boat. At the very least, a court would assume you knew about it. Particularly if evidence was presented that you had helped the men who stole it."

"But I didn't know…"

"They would further find it difficult to believe that you knew nothing of the dead man on board, and in the absence of any other defendants, might well conclude that you'd murdered him."

"Me? Me, a murderer?" The shocked surprise on Tombs' face suggested innocence, but Downes affected not to notice.

"So, what you are going to do is accommodate one of my men whilst going about your business as if nothing has happened."

"You mean feed him an' all?"

"I do. Then, when those men come back, as come back they will, you bring me a message to Bugsworth. Were you to give the men any inkling that you've had a lodger, you will be in danger. Firstly, from them, because after trying to kill the officer, they'll kill you. You'd know too much. Secondly, if by any mischance you were to escape from them with your life, you will have me to face."

The constable was armed. "Give him all the cartridges you've got," Downes had instructed Tombs. "When we've done, and if you've behaved yourself, we might consider giving the gun back to you." With that, he'd caught up with the others, by now well on their way to Shallcross Yard.

In the gloom, the posse was almost at Henry Oxspring's hut before any notice was taken of them. From inside, the yard-master heard the tramp of boots and emerged, startled, from his doorway to see them bearing down on his refuge.

"Mr Oxspring," Sergeant Spray was on home territory now. "During the course of my investigation into the murder that occurred here twelve days ago…" the man began to feel somehow responsible "…we have uncovered a theft, we believe from your yard."

Two men in uniform stepped forward with a box of dynamite. "Dangerous stuff this, best if you keep a closer eye on it."

"But I only discovered it was missing this morning." Oxspring was confused. "Maida's been in the yard all day."

"What's Fred Maida got to do with this?"

"He has a letter to give you after work, reporting the loss, but he hasn't left yet."

"Ah well, that leaves him right out of it." If Oxpring hadn't been knocked off balance by this exchange, he might have noticed the satisfaction in Spray's voice.

The routine was for a load of explosive destined for several quarries to be delivered in one gunpowder van. It was then moved from yard to yard along the line, where it was held a day at a time for each customer to collect their consignment.

"You see, sergeant, it wasn't until the van arrived at the last quarry that it was realized some was missing."

"Sounds a bit haphazard to me."

Oxspring wished the policeman didn't sound so disapproving. "It's the way we've always done it, sir."

"Hmm... Where's the gunpowder van now?"

"In the yard, empty, waiting for dispatch back to Scotland."

"Right, these men will load the dynamite and you can deliver it in the morning."

The little group had already set off when, rather casually, the sergeant said, "The original boxes went missing; explain to the customer, would you? We might get them back later, but I don't suppose it matters."

Benjy was having a treat. On school days, he only had one walk. Not that he knew anything about school, but he had a grasp of routine, and being taken out a second time midweek was not the usual run of things. Not that it was much fun. Trips along the towpath were best, where he could chase down anything that moved. Here in the town, on the end of a bit of rope, stray cats ignored him.

Jimmy felt the dog tugging on his lead, and hung on all the tighter. He was on a mission and Benjy was his cover. So far as it went, things had gone to plan. The group who'd evaded him in the gloom of early morning had returned. He'd seen them come off the cut and head for Shallcross. Following at a distance, he couldn't work out what was odd about them until they filed into the yard. *There's one missing*, he thought, *and they're carrying things*. He waited.

———

With the dynamite stowed away, Downes and his men departed for the Jodrell. It had been a busy day and the inspector offered to indulge them. "Better here than Bugsworth," he'd said. "The less we're seen over there the better."

"No thanks." Spray had declined an invitation to join them. "I've got one last job here. Take Constable Archer."

Oxspring saw the others leaving and was disappointed to find the sergeant had not gone with them.

"See here, the lock, it's been tampered with." The yard-master's discomfort was extreme. "Must be how the boxes disappeared in the first place. I'm surprised no-one noticed.

"Could have been at one of the quarries."

Spray let this go without comment. *The man's on the defensive,* he thought. *That's enough. He won't ask any awkward questions now.*

On the road down to the town, Archer walked alone. The uniformed officers had formed a little group, and Downes went with them. They disappeared amongst men in caps and grimy mufflers filling the street, as workers poured out of the mills. In amongst them, girls and older women, their hair done up in scarves to keep it from being caught up in the machines they'd been minding all day. Jimmy almost missed his chance as William Archer, too, was swallowed up in the throng.

Down amongst the forest of legs, Benjy stayed close to the one pair he knew. In his past life, some legs had been less friendly than others and he'd learned to be wary. So determined was he to stay by his protector that he tripped Jimmy up, and it was the disturbance caused by his fall that achieved the boy's objective.

"Hello, Jimmy." Archer pulled him to his feet. "You alright? Not the best place to take a dog for a walk. You usually go down by the canal, don't you? More rabbits down there, I'd have thought."

"Been down there earlier, Mr Archer. Saw you and them peelers go off this morning."

"You been following us again?" Archer had done his best to sound as if he disapproved.

"Saw you go off down the other side, that's all. Benjy an' me were on the towpath."

"I see. You got stuck on the wrong side of the cut and lost us." It was no good; Jimmy sensed the suppressed amusement in Archer's voice.

"Saw that man."

"What man?"

"Didn't realise at first, cos he came up behind. In a right dash he were. Knocked into me an' upset Benjy.

"How'd he do that?"

"Nearly tripped over 'im. Barked 'e did, Benjy that is. He don't never bark. Not since he's been wi' me."

"The man?"

"You know, the one what had that bit of paper I' gev you, an' then Mr Spray follered him in Manchester."

"You sure about this? You only saw his back."

"I weren't at first, but in school our teacher started on about dressing respectable, an' I thought of bowler hats, an' that man had one, and I caught on who it were. Saw 'is back when Mr Spray were after 'im."

Chapter 21

Thursday, October 4th, 1876

Constable William Archer presented himself at the door of his superintendent's office and knocked.

"You're the one on duty," Sam had said. "You must go." They'd written the report together, but it bore William's signature.

"You had the right of so much of the case, Sam, it must mention you." In the end, Sam had his way and his name was left out.

"Come in."

The rustle of newspaper being hastily folded crept through the opening door, but as Archer stepped inside, *The Times* lay – neatly quartered – at one end of the desk. Looking up, The Whale nodded and went back to a document in front of him. Archer waited.

"Ah, constable! How is Sergeant Spray?"

"Progressing well, sir; getting about a bit and the bruises are fading." He would have said more, but Wayland was reaching out for the report.

"Just give me the gist."

William couldn't help himself. "It was the sergeant who extracted the information from Tombs, and it was his idea to replace the dynamite, sir. He wouldn't let me put his name in the report. Said he was on leave." It wasn't entirely clear whether or not The Whale's cough was to suppress a chuckle.

"So," the superintendent, having cleared his throat, was unable to keep the satisfaction from his voice, "this is the position. The dynamite is on its way with no-one the wiser, Downes and his men are anticipating arrests tomorrow, and we…" it was left hanging as to which member of the Railway Constabulary it would be, "…are to have an opportunity to question the prisoners."

"There's still the matter of Cathal Lynch, sir." The discovery of a murdered man on railway property had got a bit lost in the general euphoria. "And if Inspector Downes doesn't sweep him up in his operation, there's the man Slade."

"H'mm, Slade…" Wayland sounded pensive. "I suppose he was in Whaley the day Lynch was murdered."

"And he was certainly mixed up with the business of Sam… that is, Sergeant Spray, being so badly treated, sir." William, sensing the reluctance in the other's voice, felt a little encouragement was needed. He and Sam had both concluded some time ago that Slade was involved in the shooting despite a lack of hard evidence to date.

"Yes… yes, constable, Slade must be investigated." William hid his relief at the decision. "You and Sergeant Spray will have to be careful. He has dangerous friends, even if they are over in Dublin."

It seemed that Sam's recuperation was over and he was officially back at work. William realised he'd misinterpreted the superintendent's hesitation. It was born of risks to his men rather than to himself.

Chapter 22

Saturday, October 6th, 1876

Yesterday had been frustrating, with Downes insisting only his officers were to be involved in the operation. The two men from the Railway Constabulary had to spend Friday in enforced idleness. There was sense in the arrangement, as they knew; Downes had armed his constables, but could not do the same for Sam and William. With two murders down to the conspirators, and the prospect of an attempted bombing the next day, it was a decision that brooked no argument.

Not that the time was entirely wasted, even if it moved at a more leisurely pace than was usual.

"More tea, sir?" Mary was helping serve breakfast. Sam accepted the offer. "And you, constable?" On most occasions, when a young man of William's age found himself in close proximity to a young lady, their eyes would meet and a discreet, mutual appraisal would ensue. Not here. The girl gazed fixedly at the floor when not attending to her teapot, despite his trying to catch her eye.

"Young Mary's uncommonly shy," the maid had poured William's second cup and returned to the kitchen, "but bonny for all that."

Sam grunted.

Later, the two men, discretely ensconced in a corner of the White Hart, had talked business. Hanging over their discussion was the goings on at the deserted limekiln, and it was all that either could do to avoid suggesting a stroll along the towpath.

"You sure you can believe what that lad told you?" They were discussing the possible sighting of Slade on the towpath. Sam sounded sceptical. "I mean, how old is he? What does he know about anything?"

It was time for the truth. "That day we went to Manchester…" It all came out: Jimmy in the luggage rack; the instruction to return home forthwith; the ball game in the street; and the recognition of Bowler Hat as the man at Whaley Bridge on the day of the murder. "Thing is, sir, he managed to warn me that you were being followed, and then he was outside the police station when I parted from Downes."

Sam's "Harrumph" could have been one of The Whale's. "I see, so we can rely on what he says? Is that what you're telling me?"

Silence.

"A young scamp who travels without a ticket, disobeys instructions, follows officers of the law…" It was no good. The corners of Sam's mouth had been twitching as he spoke, and he could suppress it no longer. It was the first time he'd laughed since returning from Dublin and his ribs hurt, but it was worth it. He was his old self again.

"Alright, William, let us for one moment suppose that the Allcroft boy is right. Slade was on the towpath on Wednesday. Why was he there?"

"He'd been to check on the *Kingfisher*?"

"He could certainly have done it without going past Jagger's Farm. There's that bridge further along the cut, and he could have crossed and doubled back through the fields and in through the bolthole Downes's man uncovered. Question is, did he see us all there, or did he leave before we arrived?"

"If he didn't see us, then whatever plan there is will go ahead…" William was thinking as he spoke. "Trouble is, we don't know which side he's on. Even if it's Dublin Castle, he wouldn't want Downes to nab the Fenians red-handed."

"I agree, the rivalry between them would get in the way." Sam had seen at first hand the casual brutality of the Dublin operation. "They'd just shoot the plotters and leave it at that. Slade's quite capable of it. I feel pretty sure he was responsible for Cathal Lynch's death, but was it because Lynch had rumbled his connection with the authorities? Or the other way round, and Lynch had let slip he was about to betray the conspiracy himself?"

After the White Hart, they walked a bit and then found somewhere for a bite of lunch and walked again. Talk as they may, the discussion went round in circles, reaching no conclusion, but it served to fill in the time.

It had been getting dark by the time Downes arrived back at the Jodrell. He'd promised to recount the day's events as recompense for their exclusion.

"If there hadn't been murder and violence behind it all, it would have done as a comedy turn on the Halls."

"So, what happened?" It had been William's turn to get the ale, and he was handing round glasses.

"We waited for them to get the *Kingfisher* out into the cut. That way they'd all be together on the boat, except for the one with the horse, and he'd have to be alongside on the towpath."

"What about Tombs?"

"Quiet as a lamb. Helped one of the Fenians with the horse and the man went off none the wiser."

"So, what about the Music Hall turn?" Sam put his glass back on the table.

"Nothing happened until the man and horse turned up on the towpath. He shouted across the cut, and the men on the boat tried to throw him a line. They'd cleared the branches hiding the *Kingfisher*, but still managed to catch the rope in a tree. Then it fell in the water, and of course that made it heavier. They never did manage to get it over."

"So they had to manhandle the boat out?"

"And that's where the fun started, Sam." Warm conviviality had permeated the quiet corner where the three men sat; confidences were shared, and rank had become blurred.

"She was aground. The water level must have been higher when they took her in."

"If the traffic's heavy enough, it defeats the water supply and the level drops." William, keen to show off his new-found knowledge, had recalled his conversation at the stop lock,

"One of them fell in before they had her afloat. He was a real mess; the cells are going to reek tonight."

"If we're right about their target, they'd have to get her bow pointing back the way they'd come in the first place." William pictured the problem

"S'right, and that's where the fun started. In its heyday, the canal arm had a mouth wide enough to allow entry from either direction, but they'd only cleared enough trees to let them in from the west. When they tried to drag *Kingfisher*'s stern toward Buggie Basin, they got her stuck across the canal."

"That'd cause a right shenanigan. There'd be a lot of boats stopped in no time." William had experienced the sort of language their skippers would use. "Rough lot, those boatmen."

"Tommy Cubbin must have been there to sort things out when they moored up. I'm thinking they intended he'd be around to help getting it out. Killing him was a mistake."

Downes went on to describe how, in the end, a couple of skippers left their own boats and sorted the *Kingfisher* out. "Foul-mouthed lot they were. We could hear quite well from where we were hiding. Treated the Fenians like they were idiots. They didn't ask about Cubbin, but they must have known it was his boat – ironic really, with his body still in the cabin."

"Did you have any trouble?" Sam, trying hard to mask his disappointment at being left behind, wanted the details.

"No, the only escape was across the cut and they didn't fancy that. I'd brought up some reinforcements so we had men along the towpath in both directions, and some in a shed near where they had the boat moored." Downes explained that the *Kingfisher* had been penned to the bank by the huge number of boats released from the jam when it was finally cleared. "We just waited till they tried to hitch up the horse, then we stepped out and pointed the guns at them."

"No sign of Slade, I suppose?"

It was off to Manchester in the morning. With no need to get there first thing, they had a comfortable ride on the 8:15 SO stopper. Last time they'd made the journey, Sam and William had been separated and spent their time standing, tight up against other passengers, on the workman's special. Only Jimmy, lifted overhead onto a luggage rack, had escaped the crush. Today, they seemed to have escaped his curiosity.

"You know the way to Minshull Street, William?" Half statement, half question. "That was where they arrested you, wasn't it?"

They'd left the station and, after crossing London Road, were almost there. Sam's jocularity reflected the mood of them both.

"Just follow me and we might get Downes's men to arrest you, too." William dived into a side road, and in a moment they were opposite the Police Station.

There was no mistaking who they were. The desk sergeant had been primed.

"Good morning, gentlemen. Sergeant Spray and Constable Archer, I'll be bound." They were invited to follow. The establishment was certainly more commodious than their own back on Crewe Station, but it had the same dingy gloom that accompanied the preservation of law and order wherever it was undertaken. "In here, if you please."

Inspector Downes, on his home patch, was very much the senior officer. Not that he was difficult, but gone was the easy camaraderie of the previous evening. "Sergeant, constable, come in." Chairs were drawn up and he gestured to his visitors to sit. "Now, about these prisoners." Downes pulled a sheet of paper from a pile on his desk. "This is a list of names: all Irish. Funny thing is, there's only one with an Irish accent."

Spray had the list now. "So, there are five of 'em; would have been six if someone hadn't done for Cathal Lynch."

Archer asked, "How'd you get the names? Are they talking?"

"Not so you'd notice, not even with a bit of encourage-ment." Sam winced at Downes's casual reference to the brutal-ity involved. "We got a start on the names by just listening. We had to put 'em two and three to a cell, and they were calling to each other. There are three Finns, and they use surnames to distinguish one from the other."

"Any idea who's in charge?"

Downes had a scowling man brought in. "This is Finn Lawless." He was bruised around the face, and Sam recognised his reluctance to cough. He'd been given a kicking.

"Somewhere private, sir?" It was Downes's territory, but his methods, or perhaps those of his officers, had failed. Their presence wouldn't do much for the approach that Sam had in mind. For a moment, the inspector hesitated at this erosion of his authority but, relenting, he left Sam and William alone with the prisoner in a room reeking of unwashed bodies and tobacco smoke.

Sam, watching the handcuffed Lawless, recognised the fear in his eyes. A week ago it had been in his own. "Bit of a kicking?"

Lawless grunted from across the table. They were seated; the room was otherwise bare and windowless.

"There's not much you can tell us. You were caught red-handed in possession of a stolen narrowboat with its murdered skipper on board, and believed you had two boxes of stolen dynamite in the hold."

"What d'ye mean, believed?" Lawless had been jolted out of his silence.

"Those two boxes in the hold, you remember them? With British Dynamite Co on the outside? They didn't have dynamite inside; just brown sticks on top of rocks, and covered in packing."

Had he not been shackled, Lawless might well have overcome the two detectives. He rose from his chair, and had the table over. "The lying bastard said he'd checked everything…"

Order had been restored by the time a uniformed man, stationed outside for just such an eventuality, put his head round the door and asked, "You alright, sergeant?"

Angry, as only a man believing himself betrayed can be, Lawless had a corrosive resentment about him.

"It would be him that gave you the information about where and when."

Lawless nodded imperceptibly.

"And told you about where dynamite could be found."

Another nod

"And went with Cathal Lynch to steal it, I expect. So, it was him that killed Lynch."

"He said Cathal was going to betray us." Wilting now, the shackles only accentuating his defeat, the man continued. "I didn't know what to believe then. It was Fl... it was him that put it all together. We were just a bunch of hard-drinking Irishmen with a grievance."

"So, he put you up you it? And here you are facing hanging for murder whilst he's disappeared."

"But we haven't done for anyone." Lawless, revitalised by indignation, sat up straight.

"What about Tommy Cubbin? He looked pretty dead to me."

"That was bloody Flood. We didn't want him dead. He knew about working the boat."

"Unless we can find this man – Flood, you say? – all we've got is you and your mates. The law will have its way." Sam risked a guess at the target. "So, what did he tell you about the Marple viaduct?"

For a time, there was silence. Sam wondered if he'd pushed too far and too fast, or possibly the reverse. He and William waited in silence.

"If we blew the viaduct at a certain time with a train on it, we'd strike a blow for Ireland."

"Why that train?"

Again silence. This time it lasted long enough to discomfort the detectives, but they waited.

A muttered response. "Flood said there'd be royalty on it, and that if we pulled it off, the bloody government would have to take notice."

"So you didn't kill Cubbin, but you were going to kill a

large number of other people, including, you believe, a royal personage 'For Ireland'."

'For Ireland' had a dramatic effect on Lawless. He stood up again, this time without disturbing the table, and adopted – as best he could whilst in handcuffs – a ceremonial pose 'For Ireland'. With this, he clearly felt he'd justified himself and his co-conspirators.

"You born in Ireland?" He was sitting again, and William took up the questioning. "Because you don't sound like it."

"No. Manchester."

"And your father, where was he brought up?"

"Manchester. His father brought the family from Co Cavan."

"You were born in England and fathered by a man who was raised in England..." William was curious. "So where did all this 'For Ireland' business come from?"

"You bloody English, you'll never understand Ireland. Where I was born don't matter, it's what I am that matters. My grandfather taught me that. He watched wagon loads of grain shipped over here while his family died of starvation around him."

The bar on London Road Station hadn't much to recommend it, but at least it was close enough to leave catching their train to the last minute.

"What d'ye make of all that, Sam?"

When they had finished with Lawless, the others had been brought in one by one. They all gave the same story, more or less. Another Finn and a man called Sheehan had held up the train, whilst Lawless and the third Finn had taken control of the *Kingfisher*. Lynch had gone with Flood to Shallcross to move the dynamite. "Cathal told me he didn't trust Flood, when he was told go with him," one man had said.

"By the time we'd finished with 'em, no-one trusted Flood. But Flood or Slade, we're no nearer finding out who he really is."

"One man said they'd seen him head for a Midland service out of this station." This bit of information had been gleaned by William, and he was proud of it. "And he was sure of the time, on account of heading for his own train."

"We're missing something." Sam was on his feet. "Come on, you've no time to finish that." William put down his half empty glass. "We know the time, so we can check with the timetable and see what train he was catching."

Later, on their own train, they wondered if knowing that Slade had caught a Derby stopper, moved things on very much. "He could have left at any of fifteen or so stations." William was mourning the loss of his beer. "So, what we've done is confirm a lot of suspicions, established that Slade put them up to it in the name of Flood, and he once caught a train towards Derby. What I really want to know is why the man was working for both sides?"

"Politics, William, it's a cesspit and if you go near it you get dirtied. One lot is scared, the other lot's too soft on the Irish. They think that by persuading a bunch of labourers to blow a bridge and kill someone important, they can stop the soft lot giving anything away. So, they put a man in to set it running. This time he's called Slade or Flood, but there'll be others, no doubt."

Chapter 23

December, 1876

The craggy upland of the White Peak drops down to a gentler plain along its western edge, and for the most part, the county boundary follows this dramatic change in terrain. But at its northern end, Cheshire projects like a searching finger into what is otherwise Derbyshire's preserve. Here, the Peak Forest Canal crosses the unmarked county boundary on its route from Bugsworth Basin to Marple.

The *Derbyshire Times*, a copy of which lay open on Superintendent Wayland's desk, was quite clear, despite the lack of evidence, as to which side of the boundary the detention of five militant Fenians had taken place. It had reported their arrest in the county some time ago, but a guilty verdict at the Old Bailey occasioned an altogether more expansive piece. Those convicted were 'dastardly, violent and savage, and the disgraceful product of a turbulent society', according to its leading article. It omitted to mention that only one of the men was born in Ireland, or that two of them were of the Protestant faith, but 'grave doubts' were cast on the integrity of the Irish Nationalists' demand for greater autonomy. All in all, Wayland found much to agree with.

Dynamite figured, but as an example of the ingenuity of the constabulary in the pursuit of their duties; nothing was said in court or in the reports of the negligent manner in which the genuine material had been lost, and little of the late Cathal Lynch, whose murder remained unsolved.

Excerpts were read out loud with gusto that his audience

found unappealing.

"This reflects well; see here, much is made of the invaluable assistance rendered by the Railway Constabulary." Wayland looked hopefully for some sign of pleasure at the praise. "That's you and Archer."

All that Sam could see was a murder within his jurisdiction, and his failure to solve it.

Part 3

Chapter 24

December, 1876

A copy of the *Derbyshire Times* had also arrived at 37 Mill End. Lizzie, reading the same reports, tended more toward the superintendent's elation than his sergeant's downbeat assessment, though her reasons were more to do with Sam's success and his safe return to health. The Fenian conspiracy meant nothing to Mary when she, too, glanced at the open page as it lay on the kitchen table, but something, tucked away at the bottom of that week's litany of wrongdoing and retribution, caught her attention.

Lizzie, engrossed in her needlework, barely noticed Mary's departure, although the girl had clattered up the stairs in a hurry. It was only when the button was securely reattached, and what might just have been a sob floated down from the attic, that she got to wondering about her disappearance. A year ago, she might have followed straight away, but in the meantime she had given houseroom to members of the detective fraternity and, seeing the world through their eyes – if only fleetingly – led her back to the newspaper.

A short piece concerned disorder in a street close to Buxton Station. A young man, believed to be an employee of the railway, had been assaulted. The reporter had not been present and all his information was hearsay, so he couched the matter in general terms, but he understood drink had been taken, and the attack had petered out into shouted accusations. Of two things he was sure, the victim's name – Pepperell – and the matter had concerned the honour of a lady.

Mary's condition was apparent for all to see by the time she chanced on the newspaper report, but earlier, despite her reluctance, she had been persuaded that her brother should be told.

"He's going to find out one day, Mary, and wouldn't it be better if you volunteer the news than he finds out for himself?"

The weather had been chilly and a loose coat had not been out of place on Mary's trips to tidy up Stephen's cottage, but she could hardly wear it indoors. One day he was going to come home whilst she was still there.

"Will you be there with me, Lizzie?" Mary had wept, and her friend could only agree. Lizzie had thought apprehensively of this moment right from when the distressed girl had first come to her but, despite the accusation of deceit which Stephen would undoubtedly throw at her, she was resolved to see it through.

"Of course, my love, we'll go to him together."

And so they had done. Stephen, home from work early one day, was surprised to find Lizzie helping his sister with the housework. In the odd moments when he and Mary had met over the past weeks, the bloom of youth – enhanced by being with child – had entirely escaped him, perhaps obscured by her misery. He was certainly confused by her tears before she blurted out, "I am to have a baby. Lizzie says so."

Drawing her friend into the center of things at the outset had deflected her brother's opening salvo.

"What the devil do you mean by this?" He'd glared at Lizzie. "She's only a girl and I'm her family. I should have been told."

"We are telling you. We're telling you now, Stephen."

Lizzie had done her best to draw his fire, but it couldn't last. He had turned on his sister.

"How could you do this?" he shouted. "You'll be an outcast. The Church won't have you; your mother's family will disown you; no-one will marry you…" There had to be more awfulness, but for the moment Stephen couldn't think of any. Lizzie had venture into the silence.

"I'm looking after Mary; she is living at Mill End with me."

"You can't do this, you interfering busybody, you're not family, you have no right to…" Stephen ran out of words, and as he did so, he began to realise how ridiculous he was sounding. Silence followed; in it, tears were shed by the distraught girl, stunned by the outburst.

"Who was it?" Another outlet for Stephen's ire had presented itself. "Who was the man who…" What had been done was left hanging in the air. Stephen couldn't find words to use in the presence of two women to describe the act. "It's that boy you've been keeping company with, that booking clerk, Pepperell…" Too late, Stephen had realized he'd said too much. "That booking clerk at Buxton Midland."

———

Lizzie had met a flat refusal when she and Mary discussed telling Stephen of the girl's predicament.

"No, Lizzie, you can't ask me that. What happened is a secret; you promised to keep it." At this point, she had burst into tears, and Lizzie abandoned any hope of mitigating the girl's condition on account of her violation. Even when Stephen had allowed Ben's name to slip out, still Mary had remained silent on the matter.

The piece in the newspaper had changed everything. Lizzie

climbed the stairs and, by the time she entered the attic, Mary's tears had dried up. She was sitting on her bed staring straight ahead with a sense of purpose about her that Lizzie had not seen in the girl for months.

"It's Stephen, it has to be. He thinks Ben is the father of this baby so he went and hit him."

Lizzie, although rather agreeing, pointed out, "It makes no mention of the attacker's name."

"It doesn't matter, it's him. I know it is. He thinks Ben would do this to me." Mary stood up. "I must tell him. I can't let him harm Ben. Will you come with me, now?"

Lizzie marvelled at the girl's determination to protect Ben whilst being so careless of herself. Not that Mary could do anything about her situation. Lizzie's respectability was the only thing that stood in the way of the complete destruction of the girl's reputation.

<hr />

A regular two pints of ale a week is not adequate preparation for a drinking spree, and Stephen had become very drunk the day Mary had broken her news. The urge to talk about it was overwhelming but, at least whilst he was still sober enough to reason, he'd known it could only make things worse. Drunken incoherence had taken over later, but his slurred speech and muddled thoughts failed to attract an audience as he sat, on his own, in a corner of The Railway Inn. For a while, he was allowed to close his eyes and rest his head against the wall, sinking into a stupor as the alcohol became too much for him. However, when he slid somnolent to the floor, it became too much for the landlord. He shook Stephen awake and sent on his way.

The one thing remaining, as he'd struggled with a monumental headache the next day, was a name. It had shone clear through the fog of his hangover and became a focus for his anger. For the next few days, work got in the way, but as soon as it allowed, he'd set off to do something about his fixation.

He couldn't manage without help. Before he boarded a Buxton train, he'd revisited the Railway Inn. His journey had a sobering effect, and as he needed more help at his destination, he'd spent some time in the station bar. The enterprise could have ended there, had it not been for the name. It wouldn't go away, and it drove him forward. Whilst he could still walk, Stephen had dragged himself out into the cold December air in search of Ben Pepperell.

Much railway work goes unseen by the travelling public. A ganger, out in all weathers working on the track, or a signalman behind his row of polished levers, is barely noticed in the onward rush of modern travel. Booking tickets is a different matter, and the clerk is on show to every traveller. Protected behind his glass with a half-moon cut out at the bottom, Ben had been safe from the kind of confrontation Stephen had in mind, but the ticket clerk would have to come out sometime.

As Stephen waited, this time in the rather more salubrious Midland station, he carried on drinking. It was nearly his downfall, but slipping out of the bar before refilling his glass he'd just caught sight of his quarry setting off for home.

The bare bones of what happened next appeared in the *Derbyshire Times*, but the passerby who thought it worthwhile contacting the paper's reporter was a distance away and missed some detail.

"Hey you!" Stephen's slurred voice carried. "It was you; it must have been you; you've ruined her." He'd swung a punch and staggered when it missed. "You're Ben Pev... Pever... ell."

"Yes, I am." Not wanting things to escalate, Ben had spoken quietly as he dodged another drunken lunge.

"She's my sister, y' know, an' I'm supposed to stop this sort of thing." By now, the pantomime had edged round a corner, and the report in the public press ended at that point.

"What sort of thing?"

Although drunk and angry enough to fuel his flying fists, Stephen hadn't quite been able to state Mary's condition. "She's... she's... having a... she's got herself in trouble."

"Who are you talking about?" In the heat of the moment, fending off the other man's attack, Ben hadn't understood.

"My sister. I told you." The alcohol, having impaired Stephen's mind and released his anger, had started to impair his physique and he was finding it difficult to keep up his assault. "My sister, Mary. Mary Thomas."

The aggressor had stood unsteady and exhausted, all his fight gone, but Ben had been hit by a killer blow nonetheless.

"You mean Mary? My Mary is with child and you think it's mine?" The news revealed all Ben had needed to know. "You think I've taken advantage of a sweet girl, barely out of childhood, and then abandoned her?"

Now Ben understood Mary's problem. She couldn't face him with the truth and that was why she wouldn't see him.

As Stephen's anger had subsided into the inertia of exhaustion, the other man's had taken hold. Ben had been sober and what he felt grew out of a cold disappointment that overwhelmed him, but he'd been unable to determine what or who he was angry with. In his confusion, he'd walked off uncertainly, not even attempting to defend his innocence.

The two women walked through the December gloom. It was dark and Whaley Bridge was quiet, waiting for the mills and pits to release their tired employees onto the streets at the end of a day's work.

As the evidence of her shame had developed, so had Mary's reluctance to be seen. She would venture out when absolutely obliged to, and then only as it grew dark. Pools of light spilling onto the road from shops still open to catch some late trade, were a particular problem and she would dart with relief into the shadows between. Not on this occasion. Lizzie watched as she walked, back straight and head held high. Boldly, she ignored the exposure of the shop fronts and scorned the shadows as she and her friend made for the Thomas family home.

Stephen was there by the time they arrived, and it seemed to Lizzie her companion was far from needing support. Since the initial revelation, Mary had sheltered from her brother's ire by avoiding him. Now she stood, her condition plain to see, and looked him in the eye.

"You've no reason to attack Ben. He's nothing to do with this baby." She caressed her rounded belly.

"Whad'ye mean... I didn't... how do you know?" Stephen hadn't seen the newspaper.

"I was rap...raped by a man at Ravenhead." What to say had been much discussed, and Lizzie had overcome her reluctance about the use of so unseemly a word in the interest of clarity when advising Mary about her speaking out.

"It was Mr Henry. He attacked me on the landing by the back stairs. I didn't know what was happening, but it hurt and Lizzie says it's why I'm like... like this."

With her mission accomplished, Mary wilted and would have fallen had Lizzie not caught the frail girl and helped her onto a chair. Tears flowed and fell to the table where she had laid her head.

Stephen, silent and confused, stood watching, helpless in the face of such desperate unhappiness. It wasn't until his sister had recovered enough to be gently led back to Mill End that his own resolve began to harden.

The next day, a late departing freight train caused havoc with the timings of a Manchester-bound express. By the time it set out from Whaley Bridge, the goods had missed its slot, and as it made its ponderous way towards Stockport it held up the faster trains. Perhaps the signalman who let it out onto the mainline was at fault, too, but he so arranged his report that traffic control were in no doubt about the culprit.

Its departure had been delayed for want of a guard. A distracted Stephen had been unable to get off to sleep and had failed to wake at the appointed hour. The reprimand he received some days later was as nothing compared with the turmoil he was suffering at Mary's disclosures. His shame at being unable to defend his sister's honour was exacerbated by the unfairness of the accusations he'd hurled at Pepperell.

In this last regard, at least, he could do something to put things right, and a few days later he'd set off for Buxton. Sober this time, he caught up with an understandably defensive Ben.

"No, please, Pepperell. I've come to make amends for… I had quite the wrong of it." Unable to recall much from the alcoholic haze of their last encounter, Stephen was unsure of what he was apologizing for. "When Mary told me about the child, she couldn't bring herself to say what had really happened. I just assumed…"

"You thought I'd dishonour your sister and then abandon

her?" Ben's voice rose with indignation. He clenched his fists; it looked as if he was about to start another brawl.

"No, no, hear me out. There's more. We can fight then if we must…" This time Stephen knew it would be more serious with both men sober, and more fisticuffs would settle nothing.

"She was… she was raped." There. The word was out. To Stephen's surprise, a look of relief spread over the other man's face.

"I thought she'd…" He stood silent as Ben searched for words. In that moment, it dawned on Stephen that the other man truly cared for Mary, and he'd harboured the belief that she'd betrayed him. "I thought she'd…" Tears welled up and, embarrassed, Ben turned away to wipe his eyes.

Later, with matters explained and hands shaken, a sense of common purpose developed between the two men.

Ben was insistent. "I must see Mary and tell her how I still feel about her." Stephen was unsure as to whether that included caring for another man's child, but held his tongue. "I'm coming back with you now."

Other matters were discussed. They parted in Whaley Bridge, by which time they both knew what had to be done.

Ben made his way to Mill End. As a result of his reconciliation with her brother, he knew Mary was living with a Mrs Oldroyd, and that No 37 was a refuge for her. The way Stephen had spoken, he understood her to be kind and reasonable. He knocked.

"May I see Mary, please? I'm Ben Pepperell."

"Mary's resting. I'll see if she's awake."

Ben was left fretting in the hall. The guardian angel, who in Ben's mind had become a demon as he waited, descended the stairs.

"You've seen Stephen?" Lizzie made a guess. "And he's

told you what has happened to Mary?"

"Yes, and I'm here to tell her that I love her, come what may." In his agitation, Ben missed the soft footsteps on the landing above.

"And are you ready to take on another man's child?"

Whatever his answer would have been, it was his slight hesitation that did for Ben's hopes. Upstairs, a door banged.

"I'm sorry, young man." Lizzie's voice was full of regret. "Mary feels unable to see you."

Chapter 25

Thursday, February 1st, 1877

It rankled still. No-one else had seemed to consider the unsolved murder of Cathal Lynch as a failure. Superintendent Wayland appeared content with the reports in the press and the praise for his department sent down the line from Euston. Scotland Yard had sent him a formal note of thanks, and Inspector Downes had let it be known he was anticipating promotion for his part in confounding the Fenian plot. If Lynch hadn't been shot in Whaley Bridge, then so far as Downes was concerned he'd have been hanged in Strangeways with the others. 'Saved us the job' he'd been heard to say.

It appeared to Sergeant Spray that only he felt his professional integrity impugned by it.

To be sure, he had other more congenial things to occupy his mind. Visits to Whaley Bridge of a social nature had culminated in sharing Christmas dinner for a second year with Lizzie and her father. This time, there was no interruption by a desperate man with a knife. Mary was there, too, and whilst Sam was ignorant of matters pertaining to childbirth, even he could see her time was nearly come as she waddled to and fro helping Lizzie with the meal.

He and Lizzie had developed an easy, informal relationship. When he visited, they talked and walked and ate together, and in some respects it was the detective who was the more confiding. Certainly, there was no discussion of Mary's predicament. Lizzie, honouring her promise, volunteered nothing, and Sam – sensing the delicacy of the matter – made no enquiry.

When a uniformed boy arrived at the constabulary headquarters on Crewe station, everything changed.

"Superintendent Wayland. Telegram for Superintendent Wayland." The lad marched into the outer office without knocking. There was only one constable present, guarding access to his superior, and he was in the process of roundly castigating the lad for his impertinence when Superintendent Wayland emerged.

"Here, give me that. You sign, constable."

The boy protested as The Whale retired. "He's supposed to sign if it's his." After an attempt to complete his reprimand, the desk officer told the lad to wait for a reply. He started whistling.

Back in his inner sanctum, Wayland stared at the telegram. *What is it about the uplands?* he wondered. *It had been the same in the Crimea; down at sea level it was quiet and orderly, all the killing went up in the hills at Sevastopol.*

BODY FOUND SHALLCROSS YARD STOP PLEASE ADVISE STOP OXPRING

"Find Spray." The voice was loud enough to pass through the door.

To shout back would amount to insubordination. The constable knocked.

"Will there be a reply, sir? The lad's still here."

"Get rid of him and find the sergeant."

The door was closed again.

"Stop that bloody whistling and bugger off." The telegraph boy was sent on his way.

A little bit of the superintendent had always been uneasy. True, he'd basked in whatever praise came his way and he'd been punctilious in passing it on, but Spray's reserve – never stated, but obvious enough – had unsettled him, and now he was to find out why.

"It was too easy, sir." Spray was standing in The Whale's office. "There's always been more to this than those poor benighted Irishmen." He ignored his superior's disapproving look. "They didn't plan the affair; a bunch of unlettered labourers, mostly from Little Ireland in Manchester. No, there was always a whiff of political intrigue behind it and the stench hasn't gone away."

Wayland bristled. *What does the man know about political intrigue?* The thought wilted as it crossed his mind when he recalled it was Spray who had exposed Fancourt, and Fancourt was into politics good and deep.

"When we find out whose body it is, perhaps we can get a bit closer to the centre of this putrefying mess of deceit."

The disgust in the sergeant's voice was clear enough.

"Right, sergeant, you'd best get over there," a fragment of his long lost classical education came to Wayland, "and start shovelling like Heracles."

——•◦•◦•——

Shallcross yard was busy. The only concession to the investigation had been to shunt the wagon, which had brought the body into the yard, to the remote siding which months earlier had held the explosives van.

"You take long time to arrive." Fred shrugged, palms facing upward. "We have keep things moving."

Sam looked despairingly at the solitary mineral wagon.

"That how we found him." A frayed end of rope hung loose from a corner of the canvas cover. It flapped in the breeze.

"Young Roy try to tie it down, but rope too short so he climb up; and soon climb down again."

"So, the rope had snapped." In his mind's eye, Sam visualised a heavy object falling onto the canvas, held up tent-like on a central ridge, and the rotten lash parting under the strain. "I'd better have a look." He climbed up onto the buffer and peered over the side into the wagon. Much as he expected, the body lay cradled in the sagging canvas, aligned parallel with the ridge, for all the world like a mariner in his hammock.

What grated, on this otherwise tranquil scene, was the blood. Face down, the dead man's hair was matted with it, and copious quantities had found its way down to his collar. Rolling him onto his side, Spray could see rather less had run down his forehead and face. *Must have been upright when he was assaulted from behind,* he thought. With so little on the canvas, it suggested he was dead by the time he'd arrived on the truck. *Probably bludgeoned to death and then dropped from a bridge.*

"The question is, where?" Spray had jumped down. "Come on, you must know where it's been."

Fred looked at the label attached to the planking. "Come from Killers at Middleton Quarry. They have a branch at Steeplehouse."

"That's almost at Cromford." Sam, thinking back to his previous encounter with the line, added, "A good distance. How long to get here?"

"It take about day and a half."

"Big question, Fred: when did it arrive?" Simple to ask, but surprisingly difficult to answer. Wagons could be in the yard a day or two, waiting for others destined for the same destination.

"Hey, Roy, you come here and help Mr Spray." Royston and his gaffer conferred.

"This one's not regular, Mr Spray." It was young Roy who spoke. "Something's broke and it's going for repair. That's why it's empty."

"But why the cover?" Only loaded trucks had covers, to keep the wet out of the limestone. With nothing supporting it, this one had sagged to form a litter for the corpse.

"They can stand idle for weeks in the repair yard." Fred provided the explanation, "This time of year they fill up wi' snow."

"So, you don't know when it arrived?" It mattered to Sam, and the urgency came through in his voice.

"Only been here two days." Roy had scavenged the titbit from his memory. "Load from Steeplehouse came through last thing Tuesday." By now, they were looking at a ledger in the office. "This is it, see – Killers at Steeplehouse."

"So it set off Monday morning?"

"First thing."

In the end, they undid the lashings and lifted the body and its sling out of the wagon and lowered it to the ground with as much reverence for the dead as circumstances allowed. In the process, it disappeared into folds of canvas. When the coarse fabric was pulled aside, it revealed the dead man still face down. A plank was laid alongside. Between them, Sam, Fred, and Roy rolled the cadaver so that it came to lie supine on the plank.

All three stood in silence, looking at the dead man. For Roy, it must have been the novelty of death that held his attention. Fred, for his part, found himself contemplating something more familiar.

"I see this man before." The silence resumed as the little Italian searched his memory. "He make me think of celebration... Sam, Sam, you remember the day of the gala? Me and young Jimmy see a boy try to pick his pocket. He grab the boy and hurt him bad."

And young Jimmy picked up what was dropped in the fracas. Sam, too, was considering why the face was familiar. The bit of paper dropped by the dip had only been the beginning. It had led him through Manchester and onto Dublin on the tail of a man in a bowler hat. *He's not wearing his bowler today.*

—•••—

By the time Sam arrived, unannounced, at 37 Mill End, it had been a long day. The body had been taken care of and an autopsy arranged. To his surprise, a new institution had sprung up which made his job both easier and less convenient. A public mortuary now offered the dead a resting place on their journey from last breath to last rites. For those unlucky enough to die at the hand of another, an official doctor had been appointed to temporarily impede their passing with a postmortem.

The victim had died in Derbyshire. Arrangements had to be made for the cadaver to be transported to the county morgue. The coroner, a new man appointed in the aftermath of the unfortunate affair the previous year, agreed to undertake the examination. But as the corpse was to lie in Buxton, Sergeant Spray had made his own examination before it left on its journey.

A pleasantly surprised Lizzie admitted him. Although there was always a bed for him, even at a moment's notice, matters had not proceeded to the point of him having his own key. They shook hands and he was shown into the parlour. It was true that they had indulged in a brief embrace on occasion, and once a peck on the cheek, but the surprise of his late arrival precluded such dangerous intimacy.

"There's been a body found at Shallcross, and I'm investigating." Lizzie showed no surprise. The eventful life of a policeman had become commonplace for her. "At least we know his name."

"That must help no end." Supper was arriving on the table. Not for the first time, Sam marvelled at her ability to produce a meal at a moment's notice. She spoke over her shoulder. "Are you on your own, or should I make up a bed for William?"

"Not tonight. The Whale didn't say anything about him joining the investigation. A pity, really; he'd be interested in the case. Do you know, the dead man was in Whaley Bridge on the day of the gala, and Fred Maida saw him at a funeral last spring?" The little Italian had dredged the final titbit from the depths of his memory before they parted.

"You mean he's something to do with that awful Irish business?" It was too late, even if Sam wanted to, he couldn't shut her out of the discussion now.

With some difficulty, Mary had washed up after Sam's meal. She was very near her time and the sink was a long reach beyond her swollen belly, but she insisted on doing what she could to assist her benefactor.

"I can't stop her." Lizzie said, after the pregnant girl had made a painfully slow ascent to her room. "It must help to keep her mind off the birth."

Now she had gone, the discussion resumed. "You mean he was the man that led you to Dublin?" Little had been said about what had happened in Ireland, but Sam's injuries had been plain to see and Lizzie knew just enough to apportion the blame. "Well, I'm not sorry. You said you'd found out who he was?"

"A man called Henry Slade. The Hon—"

A teacup fell, the bone china tinkling as it cracked, spilling

Lizzie's tea on the polished floor. In the silence that followed, both of them waited… for what? Sam had never seen Lizzie do anything so clumsy, and she was so taken aback as to be speechless. But not for long.

"From Ravenhead House by Cromford?" For a moment, she could put her conundrum aside whilst she scavenged for every last detail.

"Yes, that's right, but how do you know where he's from?"

Later, in a more rational frame of mind, Lizzie could justify what she did next, but at the time she was torn between her promise of silence to Mary and her desire to tell Sam all she knew. Although the rape was the least important part of Sam's investigation, it proved impossible to tell the story without the parentage of Mary's baby and the manner of its conception, being part of it.

"So you see why it was impossible for her to stay at Ravenhead House. Oh, and then there are the pictures." The secret picture of Sladen Castle stolen by Mary's father; and its twin that was to be found at Ravenhead House; and the elderly man who no-one ever saw unless he lost his way in his own house. It all spilled out in a jumble.

Sam listened, not moving, as if any disturbance might interrupt the flow.

Chapter 26

Friday, February 2nd, 1877

Snow was in the air on Friday morning and Sam was lucky to find a seat on an early train. It was busy, but judging from the crowd on platform one opposite, Manchester was the more popular destination. Seated, buttock to buttock, he created his own little island amongst the rustling newspapers of his fellow Buxton-bound passengers and considered what he knew.

The fates had seemed to be smiling when he'd found the letter addressed to 'The Hon. Henry Slade' in the dead man's pocket. Had he achieved no more on the first day of the investigation, he'd have made a good start. But now, sifting through the information Lizzie had given him the evening before, a disturbing prospect was beginning to emerge.

It would have been a convenience to pay the doctor doing the autopsy a visit since he was changing trains in Buxton, but he'd been told very firmly that there would be no report before Monday at the earliest. Anyway, it had been pretty obvious from all the blood that Slade had died from a blow to the head; several blows, given that he'd bled so.

This time, as he entered Buxton Midland station, he remembered to buy a Cromford ticket. The young man who sold it to him jogged his memory. *Lizzie said something about a ticket clerk last night.* He'd written the man's name down in his notebook. *Someone would have to talk to him,* but not now. Sam had other things on his mind.

"Is Ravenhead House somewhere near?"

"Down into Cromford, then up the hill on t'other side," was

the ticket collector's reply.

He'd been climbing since he left the village. Now near the top, Sam was seeking further guidance from a postman.

"S'right, just beyond the bridge, then up to the left."

"Deliver there, do you?"

"Nah, last time were some weeks ago. Here, you're a bit nosey?"

"Just trying to find my way."

"It'll be good riddance when y' get there. They ain't got no time for no-one." This last came from over the man's shoulder as he set off downhill.

Now, facing an unfriendly housekeeper across the threshold, he could only agree.

"Be off. It's tradesmen round the back, and we've no truck with the likes of you anyway."

She could have been handsome in her earlier days, with blue eyes and black hair, now flecked with grey. *But she would have had to lose the pinched mouth of perpetual disapproval*, thought Sam.

"I've come with news of the Hon. Henry Slade. He lives here, I understand."

The woman glared. "What if he does?"

"I'm a policeman of the detective sort, and I'd like to speak to his closest relative."

"There's no other family here." Still defiant.

"I have it on good authority that there is an elderly, infirm man under this roof." Your roof, he might have said, since only the woman was beneath it: Sam was still standing outside. "If, as I believe him to be, he is the Hon. Henry Slade's father, I think he has the right to be the first to hear what I have to say."

"But he... but you... but..." the woman wilted.

"Perhaps if I were to come inside, we could clarify things." There was no further resistance to his entry, and she led him to a morning room. Outside, a cold February sun was barely winning its battle with some grey, angry clouds. The weather matched Sam's situation.

"My warrant card."

"Sergeant S. Spray, LNWR Constabulary." The woman mouthed the words, as if she couldn't quite trust herself to speak. "Why the railway? Is this something to do with the line just by Ravenhead?"

"It is, but I really must speak to Henry Slade's father... or his mother," he added as an afterthought, "if she lives here."

The sudden collapse into tears took Sam by surprise, and interrupted proceedings. Sam could hardly stop her from withdrawing to compose herself. She returned with dry eyes and a tray of tea.

"Now, Mr Spray, since you seem to have found out more about this household than we care to have known, I had better explain how things stand. I take it we can rely on your discretion." The policeman wondered about the 'we' and gave no such undertaking, but she continued. "I am Mrs Small, housekeeper at Ravenhead House, and it is true Mr Henry's father lives here; in body, at least. His wife died a long time ago, and he's been... he's... for a while he's..." Sam waited in the silence. "He's not been himself."

"I still need to speak to him. What I have to say should be said to one of Mr Slade's kin."

"But I'm... I'm... I'm sure you're right." Were the tears about to return? Sam couldn't be sure. "I'll take you to him."

Whether the doors were locked to keep the invalid 'out' or 'in' wasn't clear, but there was much jangling of keys as the two of them went deeper into the house. A maid of some sort waited in the shadows as they passed on a first floor landing. Before he left, he must have a word with the staff, Sam reminded himself.

They were at the end of a top floor passage, gloomy and unlit, when the last lock was turned. A waft of warm air making its way past Mrs Small, as she stood in the doorway, was redolent of a life nearing its end. It was the aroma of bedclothes in need of airing, mingled with that of a pisspot in need of emptying, and breakfast, some of which had found its way onto the coverlet. Even more adhered to a wispy beard, whose owner looked apprehensively at the visitors.

"Who's that?"

"It's a man come to visit you, sir, he's Mr—"

"No, not him, that woman." A skinny hand, blue veins prominent in its pallor, waved toward empty space across the room. "There… now she's gone."

His frightening moment having passed, the old man turned to the solid flesh of reality.

"A Mr who d'ye say?" He glared at the stranger.

"Mr Spray. He's a policeman of the detective sort, he says."

"Stuff and nonsense. He hasn't got a gun. They always have guns."

"No, sir, that was back… that was somewhere else."

In a moment of enlightenment, Sam realised he was listening to Irish accents. Not the brogue of the common man – he'd have caught that in a moment – but the refined tones of the gentry. It was much smoothed over by a long sojourn in England, and occasionally local tones of Derbyshire could be heard in the woman's speech, but he'd placed them both.

"Just to be clear on the matter, sir, is Henry Slade your son?"

"Yes, I suppose so." Uncertainty crept into the old man's voice, and he looked to the housekeeper for reassurance.

"He is, isn't he?" Then to Sam, "What's the little bastard done now?"

"I'm afraid he's dead, sir. His body was found in a rail wagon at Whaley Bridge that had started its journey at Steeplehouse, and it's likely he died near here."

"I see; a train ride." The old man's mind wandered off down a byway. "They built a railway at home when I was young. I can't remember now where it went, but I had a ride."

Sam, keen to get him back into the real world, said, "He was murdered."

"How'd he die?" The question was clear enough.

"It looks like he was beaten to death with a cudgel."

"Oh! That's alright." The old man was wandering again. "It wouldn't be Perky Boy then. Percy would have used a gun."

"Who's Percy?"

"They were good times, until they weren't. Blighted, that's what happened; blighted we were."

"And Percy?"

"Who's Percy?"

"You mentioned Percy who might have used a gun."

The old man's gaze wandered, perhaps looking for help from the housekeeper. Sam looked round, too. Mrs Small, slumped in a chair, was beyond assisting anyone. Immobile, she was staring at the wall opposite, silent tears running down her cheeks and her knuckles showing white as she clasped her hands together.

"Mrs Small, pull yourself together, woman." The voice came from long ago. It belonged to someone used to having his own way and who no longer existed, and having flickered back to life, died as the old man lay back, exhausted.

Chapter 27

It was impossible do the whole thing in one day; that much was certain. Even two would depend on the ferry timetable. Bradshaw had been uninformative, merely saying that the GWR services to Neyland connected with an Irish ferry. His pass would get him as far as Birmingham, then it was the Midland to Gloucester and a GWR ticket to the coast. Sam was looking forward to that part of the journey; it was changing at Crewe that worried him.

He couldn't recall The Whale's exact words, but even if he hadn't categorically forbidden it, he'd made it clear that Sam wasn't to go back to Dublin. Overhearing the conversation, a casual listener might well have assumed the whole of Ireland was included, but Sam interpreted things differently; Waterford hadn't been mentioned, and Waterford was where he was bound.

In the event, it wasn't just his superintendent he had to dodge.

The Bakery was an easy walk from Crewe Station, and as a family the Archers were early risers. It could hardly be otherwise in the household of a master baker, and William was rarely late to work. Saturdays were no exception, despite there being little chance of a lost minute or two being noticed, what with the sergeant away somewhere. The Whale usually put in an appearance, but he was never early; except today.

"There you are, constable." To William's surprise, Superintendent Wayland was on the platform outside the office. "I was hoping to catch you before you disappeared on other duties."

"There's nothing that won't wait, sir." A mystified William followed into the inner sanctum. It took a while for his superior officer to settle, what with easing into his chair and shuffling papers on the desk. William stood, wondering when he was going to come to the point.

"Sent Sergeant Spray to Whaley Bridge on Thursday. Another body in the rail yard."

This was news; nothing had been said to the men about another murder. "Yes, sir."

"Said he thought the Fenian business wasn't over. Didn't believe him at first; didn't want to. Dangerous, those Irishmen, glad to be rid of them. Been giving it some thought."

It seemed to William that the Whale was still thinking. He'd never seen him so uncertain.

"Two days now, haven't heard anything." There was a pause. "Best if you go, make sure all's well, that sort of thing."

William recalled his mother bidding him, "Look out for the little ones, William, whilst they're out in the street." As the eldest, it was to be expected. Sam Spray, twice his age and senior in rank, was different.

"Yes, sir. Do you think there's a problem?" In his experience, Sam was quite capable of going off for a week at a time without reporting back.

"He might need some assistance. Worked with him a lot so you know how it goes."

"Yes, sir."

"And bloody well let me know what's happening!" With

this, Superintendent Wayland heaved himself out of his chair. "There's a train for Stockport in a few minutes. I'll see you onto it."

———•·••·•———

To Sam's dismay, his train was routed into the platform on which the constabulary office was situated. Hat pulled low, he hesitantly looked out of the window.

"Come on, man, if you're not getting out here, there's some that are. It is Crewe, don't y' know."

Despite his caution, his fellow passengers propelled him, willy-nilly, into the open. To his relief, the coast was clear. Very soon, carriage doors were slammed shut, and with a whistle, a flash of green and a peep from the engine, the train eased slowly away. By the time the guards van passed Sam, it had accelerated and suddenly the opposite platform came into view across two sets of empty track. He glanced at the scattering of waiting passengers. Their train must be due, as several of them were lining the platform edge. Some were looking impatiently along the line towards London and, fortunately for Sam, Superintendent Wayland and Constable Archer were amongst them.

He hurried, head bowed, toward safety. *If those two are waiting for a train, they can't be on the footbridge*, he reasoned, as he made his way to his platform. There'd be a couple of changes before Gloucester but, once in his seat, Sam gave himself up to the pleasure of anticipation. True, he would have to pay for it out of his own pocket.

Once he changed at Birmingham, his LNWR pass wouldn't cut any ice, but for the first time in his life he was to travel on the broad gauge. He'd never even seen it quite apart from riding it.

There'd been time enough to consider more serious matters earlier, during the first two legs of his journey. He'd questioned the indoor staff at Ravenhead, without any demur from the housekeeper, but how their answers had borne on the case wasn't clear. The monosyllabic kitchen maid said as much without speaking as with. "Yes" she knew Mary; "No" she didn't know why she'd left, but her smirk betrayed her. She had become positively verbose when asked how long had she been at Ravenhead: "'Bout five year."

"Had any trouble like Mary's?" There was no reply, and Sam had spent time trying to decipher the maid's expression. In the end, he was still unsure as to whether she was envious of the attention Mary had attracted, or jealous that Mary had been dragged onto the less desirable girl's territory. Either way, there was no sympathy for the ill use that had gone the younger girl's way.

"Ever do anything for Lord Sladen?" By that time, Sam had established that the helpless old man held an Irish Peerage. Lizzie had proved right about the picture of Sladen Castle, and he'd been shown a print of what had once been the family seat.

"See to his dinner sometime."

"Ever say anything about his family?" Sam made it sound like an aside.

"Don't listen. Talks rubbish, 'cept when he don't. Told me off clear enough when I forgot the salt fer 'is eggs. Went back to some nonsense about a fan after. Said it'd rule the world, or summat."

By the time he'd spoken to them all, Sam had sorted the staff into two groups. The locals consisted of the cook, the kitchen maid and Mary's replacement. The youngster seemed happy enough; The Hon Henry must have died before meting out the same treatment as he had to her predecessor. The two others were older and were both Irish, but the outside man's brogue was quite unlike Mrs Small's genteel tones.

Tobacco smoke, seeping out from a garden shed, had given the grizzled old man away. He sat staring into space, a mug of cold tea by his elbow, at home in his own world. *Not hiding exactly, just keeping out of the way*, Sam thought. *There couldn't be much to do outside in February, could there?* Sam regretted his ignorance of gardening.

"Good day to you. You're Mr …?"

"Who's askin'?"

"Sergeant Spray, Railway Police." Sam showed his warrant card, but the man hardly glanced at it.

"Police." With accent on the first syllable, the man wasn't a local. "You'll be askin' questions, an' I'll not be answerin' them."

"Did you know Henry Slade was dead?"

There was no more staring into space. "Is he now? An' how did that come about?"

Sam had caught his attention. "We'll talk about that when you tell me who you are."

Curiosity won over obduracy. "Tobin. James Tobin."

"He was bludgeoned over the head and sent on a journey to Whaley Bridge. That journey started round here."

"A crack on the head, y'say?" Sam had puzzled over Tobin's reply – not the content; the tone. Satisfaction? Relief, perhaps?

He'd heard the same in Lord Sladen's reaction. "So, it's not Percy's doing?" queried Sam.

"Don't seem like it…" Only as he spoke did the import of his reply strike Tobin. "Like it was an accident then," he ended lamely.

"Percy would have shot him, if he was going to do him in?" Sam knew he was taking a risk. The peer had wandered in and out of his mind as they'd talked earlier. It was unclear as to which side of the dividing line had delivered up the name Percy.

"I got no more to say." *Not truculent now, more rattled*, thought Sam. Tobin looked round the shed, as if for a line of escape, but to Sam's surprise, he reached into a large watering can. "Y'know more'n is good for ye."

No doubt the revolver was intended to emphasise his words. Cobwebs had lessened its sense of menace, as had a dead leaf dangling from the barrel; the watering can had done it no favours, but guns could be lethal. Sam knew it only too well, nonetheless he lunged forward and, grasping the barrel, wrenched it from the Irishman.

"Should have cocked it." He broke it open. "And loaded it."

There'd been no further resistance. "It was Mr Henry's."

Sam noted the RIC imprint on the body of the revolver, just in front of the chamber. "Do you know where he got it?"

"No. He asked me to keep it for him. Came for it when he wanted it."

Sam looked again. Behind the cobwebs, oil glistened. It had been kept in working order and, if his nose didn't deceive him, fired recently.

<hr />

"William. Hello, I wasn't expecting you. Sam said you weren't coming."

Having been 'seen off' by his superintendent, Constable Archer had spent his journey to Whaley Bridge in contemplation. He couldn't get The Whale's strange manner out of his mind. He knew the two of them went back as far as the Crimea, but his concern for Sam had gone well beyond a leader's care for those he commanded. *Must be the Irish threat,* he concluded. *Strange, though.*

"The Whale, that is, Superintendent Wayland, sent me to…" William settled for "assist."

"There's no-one to assist just now. Sam went off this morning saying he'd be away for a day of two." Where he'd gone, Lizzie couldn't say. "But he did leave a message of sorts."

Tea was brewed and the conversation resumed in the parlour. "Sam said, 'if William turns up before I'm back tell him we're looking for anyone with a stick, heavy enough to bludgeon a man to death, between Ravenhead and Steeplehouse quarry earlier this week.' Oh, and I'm to tell you everything I told him."

With Lizzie about her chores, William was left with his thoughts for the second time that morning. Before she'd taken the dirty crocks, he'd watched her put away a rather untidy brown volume and, idly, he wondered what it was. Books stared back at him from behind the glass of a display cabinet, along with some china pieces. An out-of-date Bradshaw rested at an angle in the space at the end of an otherwise tightly packed row. When he retrieved it, he found bookmarks, in the form of several slips of paper, peeping out.

Studying each marked page, a journey emerged which, had it started that morning, could take a traveller the next two days. Its destination became clear, and William began to share some of The Whale's apprehension.

Anticipation would have to be its own reward.

Gloucester GWR station was a busy place, but not with portly locomotives, hauling corpulent carriages, in which passengers luxuriated with extra elbow room. True, evidence was still to be found in the extravagantly long sleepers and a space between sets of track well in excess of the six foot of Sam's experience. Holes were to be seen drilled in the redundant ends of the timbers where chairs had been removed, along with the rails they'd supported, but progress was rampant, the broad gauge had gone, and his journey to Neyland would be as mundane as the one to Gloucester. *I really must get hold of an up-to-date Bradshaw,* he thought.

The rest of Sam's day became a blur. Once past Chepstow, he was in a mysterious country of outlandish spelling and smoke. His journey would run for a while alongside the majestic Severn and then dodge inland. Pitheads and furnaces were punctuated by snatched scenes of rural tranquillity. Later, after a succession of river crossings, he came upon the Bristol Channel, only to turn inland along an estuary so beautiful Sam was constrained to ask the guard its name. At least Towy was short, and wasn't made up of too many 'l's and too few vowels. Beyond Carmarthen, place names became more readable where he could see them in the twilight, and then, Neyland.

Porters abounded on the arrival platform, and there were plenty of pickings. Copious numbers of trunks and hatboxes were transferred from the guards van to trolleys and hand carts. Their owners supervised, 'careful with that, porter' and 'will you just put this on top' as a piece of hand luggage joined a precarious stack. There was, it seemed, no need for the passengers to give instructions as to where they and their impedimenta were heading.

When the rush was over, Sam enquired, "The South Wales Hotel?" The porter, who knew a poor tipper at a glance, only just managed a "sir".

Sam's hand luggage hadn't attracted much respect, but the man was more helpful about a cheap bed for the night.

"The missus'll put you up, sir. For tomorrow morning's sailing, are y'?"

"If that's the Waterford service?"

It was off to Cromford for William. "No," Lizzie didn't know where Steeplehouse was, but, "it must be near High Peak Junction, from what Sam said." He'd have to ask, when he arrived, but Ravenhead House would be his starting point.

At a distance, the postman was easy to miss. By the time William arrived in the village, it was early afternoon and the man was descending Cromford Hill, swinging his empty bag. As he came closer, red piping could be seen on his dark-blue cap, but that was as near as he got to a uniform. The official blue frock coat was spreading to the provinces, William had seen it on the streets of Crewe, but up in the Peak they were slow to adopt the fancy London ways and only the cap had arrived.

"Excuse me, sir, but do you deliver to Ravenhead House?"

"Who wants to know?"

"Just trying to get my bearings..." William was hesitant in his reply.

"Second rumman in two days askin' the same. Nobody goes there as can 'elpit."

"I'm a policeman..."

"Are y' now." A look of recognition came over the postman's face. "And t'other one yesterday, 'e were a bobby, too, I suppose? Summat's up. So, what is it?"

"We're investigating the death of a man called Henry Slade. He's been murdered."

"The Honourable; and that's why you want Ravenhead?"

Truculence had been transformed into curiosity.

"So, you know who he is?"

"Whatever mail goes to Ravenhead goes to the Hon. Henry Slade, but there's nowt much. A man came out once an' snatched a letter from me, and I 'spect it were 'im, but he never said."

William tried to ask more questions.

"Sorry, mister, I've got another round. A drink in the Greyhound later might mek talkin' a bit easier?"

One last question had elicited directions to Steeplehouse. Not that it was much of a place. A branch from the Cromford & High Peak Railway led off to Killer's quarry. Its point of departure, or perhaps the single house on the opposite side of the track, gave the place its name.

"Up the hill, and turn when y'see the brig." William was given a withering look when he asked for clarification. "Where t' track goes over the road."

He climbed and turned and walked. When he came to a point where the lane went over the branch line, he scrambled down beside the abutment, reasoning that the rails might be the straightest route to the quarry. Loaded trucks stood waiting, the leading one under the bridge.

"Oi, you, y'not allowed." The man was leading a horse dragging another loaded wagon to join the others. "'S private an' it's dangerous an' we don't allow any old rag tag in."

Having established his credentials, William found his way to the foreman's hut. Despite the stove, it wasn't much warmer inside than out in the yard.

"No, nowt's 'appened out of the ordinary in the last week or two. Very steady."

William asked about blasting.

"Aven't had one for a fortnight. Big fall last time."

"How often do you check your explosive store?"

"Check? We gets it out when we need some, if that's what y'mean."

"Anyone nosing around who doesn't belong here?"

"Only you."

They went to look at the dynamite. The magazine was the disused body from a covered rail wagon. The hasp was identical to the one broken open at Shallcross, but this was in one piece.

"Door round the back's been sealed permanent." Despite the reassurance, William had a look. The store stood at the edge of the yard, and in the summer there must have been a luxuriant growth of weeds behind it. Now, deep in winter, there were only brown stalks and dead leaves in a sea of mud. It didn't smell, but William asked anyway.

"Do the men come round here for a jimmy riddle?" He was told that they usually pissed in a stream that passed through the site. Even as William wondered where it ended up, he was looking at the footprints. Inevitably, there had been rain and the prints were blurred, but he made out at least two different prints and possibly three.

What William Cavendish would have made of the hospital created from part of his magnificent stables in Buxton will never be known. The fifth Duke died forty-six years before the Devonshire Royal Infirmary was founded. The body of Henry Slade had been brought to a small, tiled room, set aside there for the reception of corpses in deference to the burgeoning movement toward public mortuaries, and awaited the postmortem examination requested by Sergeant Spray.

It had lain there, undisturbed, since Thursday evening. The winter temperatures of February had kept decomposition to a minimum, and would have to do so for a while longer. Dr Bracegirdle was a foxhunting man and he was enjoying a season following the Wynnstay pack. Indeed, his two hunters were stabled across the other side of Cheshire and his custom was to stay overnight both before and after a day in the field. Nothing would disturb the body's tranquillity until the good doctor returned.

When he finally arrived on Monday, his head still ached from the jolly time he'd had with his hunting friends, and he made a late start. By then, the clerk who'd accepted the body had succumbed to pneumonia, and the man who attended Dr Bracegirdle knew nothing of the case. By the time the man was due to leave for home, the postmortem report had lain, undisturbed, on a small desk in what served as the mortuary office for most of the afternoon. Seeing Sergeant Spray's name and the constabulary address in Crewe, he took it upon himself to enclose the report in an envelope and despatch it, last post, via the Royal Mail who would no doubt deliver it the next day.

Chapter 28

Sunday, February 4th, 1877

Waves buffeted the PS *Vulture* as she worked her way across the Irish Sea. On board passengers, suffering various degrees of apprehension and discomfort, sheltered in the saloon. It was certainly not a day for inhaling invigorating sea air out on deck, but the bar was doing a good trade. Sam sat on his own, nursing a beer. The last time he'd crossed to Ireland it had poured uncertainly from a tap in the head of a barrel, but aboard the *Vulture* it was brandy for the men and sherry for the ladies. His request for beer had drawn a look of disdain from the steward, who reluctantly produced a bottle of India Pale Ale.

All around were voices of the Quality, mostly English, but also genteel Irish accents of the Protestant ascendency. From the conversations he could overhear, the men were destined for the hunting field and the women for an endless round of tea parties and balls. Their sport was hunting, too: not foxes, but eligible young men, suitable catches for their unmarried daughters.

It was a more comfortable crossing than the *Athulmney* had provided. Sam certainly didn't miss the all-pervading stench left behind by its bovine cargo, but then, his passage to Drogheda had cost him four shillings, and The Whale had made sure he was repaid. What he would say to this vastly more expensive voyage to Waterford was more problematical.

After they'd opened up the explosive store, and he'd been reassured that everything was in order, William had set off along the siding. Another loaded wagon had been added at the quarry end of the train, and as he clambered up to the overbridge, he could see the foremost truck still below. The foreman had said it was standard procedure to place the leading wagon under the bridge and draw others up to it as they were loaded. A locomotive would arrive with a rake of empties and take the full ones away. Usually, the exchange took place at two day intervals, and there'd been no hold-ups in the quarry recently.

Leaning over the low parapet, he'd peered down onto an inviting canvas sheet, looking for all the world like a litter waiting to take the next body away. William had pondered 'if', 'how', and 'why'.

Apart from the footprints, he'd found some fabric torn on a splinter and, more importantly, what looked like blood. The dynamite store's rear door had been sealed, just as the foreman said, but the strap and pin hinges were still in place. At just below shoulder height, he could imagine a staggering man falling against the wooden planking and hitting his head on the pin. It was here he'd found some congealed blood.

So, if a man had died there, how did his body get into a wagon? To William, standing on the bridge, dropping it over the edge had looked very attractive, but it would have to have been carried a considerable distance and then manhandled up a steep embankment first; all in the dark. How, would require two people at least. But why? Couldn't two people have lifted a corpse into an empty wagon in the yard? Of course; it might have been found next day when the quarrymen came in to work. That must be the why.

The roaring fire had warmed William whilst he sat waiting in the Greyhound. As it drove the chill of February from his bones, he'd begun to relax. All day he'd felt a presence, as if a watchful Sam Spray was looking on, but by the time he'd ordered his first half, his silent companion had slipped away. By the time the postman had arrived, William was in a comfortable half doze.

"Hey up, mister. Ah thowt we were 'avin a chat ower a drink."

He'd jerked back into wakefulness and fetched the man some ale. It started to disappear at an alarming rate and William's first question had been all but drowned out by a loud belch.

"Come again?"

"I asked whether you'd seen anyone unusual on the hill, or round Ravenhead in the last few weeks?"

"Seen old Ma Pepperell's lad a time or two. I don't know him, but I see 'im come from her house in a Midland rig, and she told me her grandson visits reg'lar."

"Can you remember when?"

"Four or five month back. He asked the way."

"To Ravenhead?"

"Ay, an' he wanted to know who lived there."

"And more recently?"

The postman looked pensively into his beer mug. He upended the pint pot and tapped it on the table.

William took the hint and bought a refill.

"So yer 'oping I seen something suspicious?" Another large gulp of ale interrupted the flow. "Might ha' done. Didn't think anything of at the time, but it were odd." More ale was supped. "Late Monday, I were up Cromford Hill. We don't do a late delivery up there reg'lar, but a telegram came in. Not my business telegrams – we has a lad fer that, but the little bugger were sick, or so his ma said. Anyway, it were getting dark and I saw two men near Ravenhead."

"Could you recognise them?"

"Too far away to be sure of anything, and they disappeared as I got near. Odd tho', I could swear they was in railway rig.

"And the telegram? Where did you deliver it?"

"To Ravenhead, o' course."

"But you said hardly anything goes to Ravenhead."

It was a race. The beer mug was the clear winner, its contents disappearing before William had gathered all the intelligence he needed; he had to pay for another refill. Only then did the postman explain he'd been talking about mail deliveries.

"Telegram boy came back to work t'day. There weren't nothin' wrong wi 'im. Bright as a button he were. I told him, I didn't think much to going up there an extra time on his account. Cheeky little sod offered to change jobs, said he often has to go up to Ravenhead."

"I expect you know what was in the telegram,"

The shocked look on the postman's face was riven with insincerity. "Agi'n reg'lations. Only person to know is the telegraphist, then it's sealed."

"This telegraphist; honest and reliable, I suppose?"

"He'd better be, he's my eldest lad." The beer mug was getting low again. "Only the youngsters can manage these new-fangled machines."

William was losing count of the refills he'd bought, but it must be nearly enough to turn a man's loose tongue into incoherence. He tried to mask his professional persona.

"How about a deal between two mates drinking together?" The other man raised an eyebrow. "I buy you another pint and you tell me, unofficially of course, what you reckon might have been in that envelope."

They must have crossed on the voyage, but *Vulture*'s passengers, tucked up in her saloon with their brandies and sweet sherries, would not have seen her sister ship on its way to Neyland. Sam had made enquiries – there were two crossings a day in each direction, and as the *Vulture* arrived at Waterford the PS *Limerick* would be docking on the Welsh side of the Irish Sea.

Perhaps out of deference to his superintendent, Sam hurried on his journey, as if by doing so he might catch the return sailing that day. It would be impossible, the rational part of his mind knew it, but he made the best speed he could manage on the rough road to Sladen Castle.

"Why d'ye want that old ruin?" He'd asked several people and had a variety of replies, but they had all been unhelpful until this one. "There's no-one lived there since the famine."

"Just curiosity about someone who came from there."

"The parson'll be y're man."

Sam was heading for a parish church. Always uncomfortable with anything so organised – his youthful contact with Quakerism had seen to that – he was apprehensive. Stone built, with tower, it was imposing even at a distance and he found himself joining a trickle of people heading in the same direction.

At the last minute, a brougham passed, with much shouting to clear a passage through the people on foot. As its two passengers dismounted at the church entrance, a jaunting car rattled up from the opposite direction and deposited four more. Two young children scampered eagerly past the earlier arrivals, only to be called, sternly, to join their parents at a respectful distance behind those more exalted than themselves.

Sam's plan had been to find the church that had served Sladen Castle, and then onto the rectory. He hadn't bargained on his arrival coinciding with that of the congregation for a service. He joined the throng. Seated at the back and looking over bald patches and Sunday hats, he could see the back of the front pew, higher than the rest, with millinery of a more sumptuous quality than the rest peeping over the top. *No doubt it had arrived in the brougham*, he mused.

Sam, who enjoyed the Whaley Bridge Brass Band, despite its failings, was disappointed in the droning organ. Things came to a crescendo as the rector arrived and the congregation rose to its feet. The service was an incomprehensible blur of kneeling, sitting and standing, which he followed dutifully. It didn't take much detective work to see that the board with its numbers had a relationship to the hymns, but the Quaker in him had failed to recognise the need to collect a hymn book on the way in.

For the first part of the service, the Reverend Oliver Bloor had been largely hidden from those in the rear pews, although his powerful voice had carried. As he mounted his pulpit, a broad, powerful man with a florid face above a white, starched collar and a black cassock came into view. For Sam, accustomed to making up his own mind about the rightness and wrongness of things, the sermon was an irritating harangue, but thinking it over later, he found little to disagree with.

Then it was done, and the celebrant proceeded down the aisle followed by his congregation. To reach the door and out into a cold February evening, the Reverend Bloor had to turn in front of Sam, standing dutifully by his latecomer's pew. He nodded to the stranger who responded, but Sam was more intrigued by the man's boots: each one, filthy with mud, making a regular appearance from beneath his shabby cassock as he walked.

Standing in the porch, the rector shook hands until his

church was all but empty. "Good evening to you, sir. It's a pleasure to see new faces amongst my flock."

Sam was the last to leave. "Good evening, Mr Bloor. I fear I have the advantage, I saw your name as I arrived. My name is Spray, Samuel Spray, and I'm glad to make your acquaintance."

Shrewd eyes peered out beneath greying brows. "With an accent like yours, you've come across the Irish Sea, and it's not to hear an obscure clergyman like me preach. How can I help you?"

Before Sam had got very far with his explanation, the Reverend Bloor was ushering him out of the church. "Will ye' come with me? I take my tea late of a Sunday on account of the service; there'll be enough for us both."

It was only a step or two to the rectory. Seen in daylight, it had looked tidy enough, but Sam had only seen the front. Now, in the dark, he was led round the back and was met by a distinctly agricultural aroma.

"'Tis always like this in the winter. I keep the cattle in my yard; it saves the pasture for the spring growth."

Sam slipped and almost fell. "Careful there, Mr Spray, or we'll be after dunking you in the trough."

They entered a farmhouse kitchen, large scrubbed table in the middle, a blacked range and open shelves showing their wares.

"Martha... where are you, woman, we've got a guest." An acerbic-looking woman came in from the scullery. "You'll be laying up for three."

"And whose portion will he be havin'?"

"Dammit, woman, there's always enough for cold on Monday. We'll eat that. Bloody servants, y' hire a housekeeper and she does just what she likes." This last was said within her hearing.

Martha stalked out, muttering. "Just cos he's the rector, he thinks he's God."

Sam expected a sulk and a long wait for his meal, but not a bit of it. Stewed mutton appeared, and he found himself with a larger plateful of potatoes, parsnips and dumplings than even Lizzie would serve. A barrel of plain lay propped on a shelf, and foaming glasses of Guinness accompanied the meal. To Sam's surprise, the housekeeper not only ate with them, but drank, too.

"Now, Mr Spray, you've got this corpse on your railway. Does it have a name?" Tea things had been cleared away, and a clattering of plates and cutlery suggested the housekeeper was washing up.

"Yes, sir, he's Henry Slade, or more properly, The Hon. Henry…"

There was a loud snort from the scullery. "That scapegrace, he's not what you think he is."

"Get to y're dishes, woman, this is man's talk." Bloor's attention returned to Sam.

"Lord Sladen has a modest establishment in Derbyshire, and we think our man died near the family home. The problem is, his body was found in a railway wagon some thirty miles away, but we're sure it's him, and his father confirmed where he lived."

"That old reprobate, I'm surprised he's still alive." This from the scullery.

"The dishes, woman, that's what I said."

"Do you think, Mr Bloor, that the good lady might have something helpful to contribute?" Sam spoke in a whisper, not wishing to undermine the rector.

"To be sure, she'll have plenty to say, but not until she's done the dishes." The sound of a saucepan landing heavily on a flagged floor echoed round the kitchen. An eyebrow was raised, but no more, and Sam resumed.

"The housekeeper, a Mrs Small—" This time, indignation won over the pots.

"Aishling Small is no Mrs, she's Miss, an' if she says different she's lying."

The rector shrugged his shoulders as his instructions were ignored and his servant joined them at the table.

"He don't know anything, Mr Spray, the old rector was here then. Now, he was a real gentleman."

The story unfolded in all its unsavoury detail. Sam found it difficult to feel for landowners, but it turned out that many great estates were bankrupted by the potato blight in the forties. Rather, his sympathies lay with the starving peasants.

"I'd been a maid at the castle. They said Lady Sladen died in childbirth, but she never looked as if she was carrying. Now, Aishling Small, her ladies maid, that was different. She did look like she was with child just before I left. When I said something about who the father was, I was dismissed without a character."

"So, what happened then?" The narrative had stopped and Sam wanted more.

"I didn't take the living until a while later, and she was here already." The Reverend Bloor nodded toward the woman. "The castle was empty. I don't gossip, you understand, Mr Spray." Sam nodded politely. "The word was that the estate had been in debt and the loan was called in."

"Did the word have anything to say about who owned the loan?"

"Mr Spray," the clergyman sounded shocked. "I couldn't go about asking questions like that, what with me so new in the parish."

"But?"

"You old hypocrite. You know very well it was Lord Sladen's neighbour. Ever since then, it's been joined with the Fancourt estate." The housekeeper had her second wind. "Everyone knew that Lord Fancourt had ruined Lord Sladen to get his hands on the estate."

———

After her dinner, Mary had gone to rest in her little attic room. It was an effort. Lizzie could see the poor girl's swollen ankles as she dragged herself up the stairs. She was near her time and it would have been a kindness to make one of the other bedrooms available, but William had one of them and Sam would be back soon... wouldn't he?

Lizzie tried not to think of where he had gone. After William had left for Cromford, she fell to wondering why she was returning her old Bradshaw to its shelf for the second time that day. She wondered, too, about the bookmarks, and drew the same conclusion William had done. Sam had journeyed to Ireland.

It was mid-afternoon when Mary's cry found its way down two flights of stairs and into the parlour. Anxiety about Sam vanished, as Lizzie followed it to its source. By the time she arrived, the pain had subsided. A frightened Mary asked, "Is this what it's going to be like, giving birth?"

Lizzie had to agree, despite her lack of personal knowledge. "Yes, my dear, I think you've started to have the baby."

What was needed was experience. There was plenty of that in Mary's big extended family, but it had been disturbingly difficult to get any promises of help when Lizzie had asked around. There'd been pursed lips and raised eyebrows aplenty, but no offers. Elsie Maida, on the other hand, wore her faith lightly, and wasn't inclined to let it get in the way of common humanity. It was the same independence of mind and generosity of spirit that had led her to defy her family and marry a penniless Italian immigrant all those years ago. The love match had resulted in a large family of children, and latterly grandchildren. She knew about childbirth alright and was happy to help out.

Getting hold of her was the problem. Quite why Lizzie didn't want to leave Mary at this early point in her labour, wasn't entirely clear, other than the girl was gripping her hand desperately as another spasm of pain overtook her. No, Lizzie would have to hope she could catch young Jimmy when he came to feed Benjy and send a message that way.

Up in the roof, with its sloping walls, the only light in Mary's room came through a little dormer facing to the back. In the summer it served as ventilation, too, but on a late afternoon in February it provided a cold draught when Lizzie opened it. If she was to stay with the frightened girl, it was the only way she'd hear Jimmy when he arrived.

It was the dog, not Jimmy himself, who alerted her. Benjy was mostly quiet – the present arrangement wouldn't have survived constant barking – but the prospect of food and a run out usually elicited an excited yelp. It was that sound, floating up over the eaves, that led Lizzie to call down, "Jimmy… Jimmy, Benjy's scraps are in the scullery and could you stay a minute whilst I come down."

It was impossible to see the dormer from the yard below, but he obeyed the disembodied voice and waited until Lizzie managed to disengage from Mary's grip and go downstairs.

"Jimmy, could you run round to Mrs Maida's and give her a message?"

"Yes, missus, what'll I say?"

"Tell her 'please could she come and help see to things'."

"Y' mean the bab's comin'?" Jimmy looked knowingly up to where Lizzie's voice had come from. "She alright, is she?"

It wasn't that Mary's condition was secret. There'd been enough gossip around the town, but nothing had been said specifically to Jimmy, and his silence on the matter had lulled Lizzie into believing that such things would pass over the head of an eleven-year-old.

"She's only got you; wi' havin' no man about. I'd best get off an' give that message."

He left, with the dog trotting obediently at his side. Lizzie mused on a changing world that seemed to be leaving her behind.

Chapter 29

Monday, February 5th, 1877

The PS *Milford* looked smarter and newer than the *Vulture* had on yesterday's crossing. Sam was impressed until, commenting on the matter, he'd been told its predecessor of the same name had foundered a year or two back and the present vessel was a replacement. He was not reassured.

To catch the half past nine sailing, he'd had to be up early; no mean feat after an evening with the Reverend Oliver Bloor. His housekeeper had left them early.

"No noise, and I don't want no mess in the mornin'."

"Be off with you, woman. If I want to make a mess in my own kitchen, I will."

She gave a loud disapproving sniff. Sam had thanked her for the meal and she replied pointedly, "Now there's a real gentleman for ye," over her shoulder as she stalked out.

"Now, sir, do you think we could have a look at the parish registers?" It sounded peremptory, he'd known, but it was a matter of some urgency for Sam to get the business done before the Reverend Bloor took any more Guinness.

They'd set off through the yard for the church. It was dark, and this time it was the rector who was stumbling. As he had the lantern, progress was not only slow, but uncertain. The Parish Registers, when they got to the vestry, had been in a dusty pile at the back of a cupboard. Only the top one looked as if it had been disturbed for many years.

Sam wanted the record covering 1846 to '49, and he'd hoped they would be arranged on the basis of one year, one book. Such profligacy was not to be indulged as the entries were continuous, or would have been if one volume had not been removed. It was beyond coincidence that the period in question was just the one in which he'd been interested.

Back in the farmhouse kitchen, more Guinness had been poured. By the end of supper, Sam had already drunk more than usual, but in his disappointment he accepted another pint. For him, drinking was a social activity, but for a man in Holy Orders it would have been unseemly to frequent public houses and Oliver Bloor had taken to drinking in the privacy of his rectory. For him, it had become an end in itself.

Perhaps Sam had been too pressing in his enquiries, later, he couldn't quite recall, but the rector had taken exception to his tone and a lot of shouting ensued. An indignant Martha appeared in her night attire. "I said no noise and no mess, either." The housekeeper had caught sight of a modest spillage.

"Away with you, woman." The Rev Bloor was rising to his feet.

Martha took hold of a chair by its back and raised it so the legs projected outward. Initially, Sam assumed this to be a defensive move, but she had advanced and backed her employer into a corner.

"But, Martha, he accused me of failing in my duty." Cowering would be an overstatement, but the rector spoke apologetically.

"And which duty would that be?" The chair was still held with intent.

"He said I'd been negligent with the parish records." Standing was proving beyond the man and he slid, slowly, down the wall. "Just because he couldn't find the one he wanted."

"It's come to that has it, you old fool? If the drink hadn't addled y'e brain, you'd know just where it is."

The chair was replaced on the floor and Martha, in shapeless flannelette and a night cap, sat down opposite Sam.

"I see you're a serious man, Mr Spray, so I'll tell y' what I know. It can't harm Henry Slade and I suppose it's for the best to expose his killer."

Eerily, it seemed to Sam she knew who would be exposed.

"It's like this, y' see." Martha went on to explain that after she'd been dismissed, the then rector had taken her on at the rectory despite having no character. "He was a cousin of Lady Sladen and he knew all about the 'goings on' up at the castle."

A fraught relationship between the Sladen and Fancourt families had lasted for generations, and the lesser gentry had been obliged to take sides. The old rector, with his ties of kinship, was for Sladen.

"It was just after they left the castle, when the old Lord Fancourt sent word that his man of business was to see the parish records. The old rector knew just what they were after and took one volume out of the vestry and brought it in here."

With no safe, it had been kept on the shelves, hidden amongst other books.

"He treated a servant girl with respect." This aimed at the recumbent figure on the floor. "The poor man was taken mortal ill, and he told me where it was in case the incomer arrived too late."

"So, you know what's in it that's so important?" For the first time since he'd arrived, the housekeeper's self-possession had slipped.

"I'll get the register." Martha bent over the recumbent Bloor, rolled him to one side and fished something from his weskit. Sam was summoned to follow. He surmised that the sermon he'd been obliged to sit through earlier had been written at the desk in the middle of the den. The rector's key opened its central drawer. "Mr Bloor came and I told him about it, so he locked it in here."

"Can you remember when you came here; you said it was shortly before Lady Sladen died?"

"It was the spring of '47. I'd be eighteen."

Sam, sober now, found what he wanted. He shut the register and replaced it.

"So you see, Mr Policeman, the Hon. Henry Slade, isn't the Hon. at all. He's the bastard child of an old goat with a title and a servant girl who couldn't say no."

"But the Sladen family were finished anyway." Sam had wondered why it was so important.

"I seem to be doing all the work for you." Martha had recovered her assertiveness. "You don't know much, do ye?"

They were back in the kitchen, Sam sitting quietly at the table.

"Have y' asked how they're livin' in a big house wi' servants if the family has no money?"

Sam had asked himself the question, but held his tongue.

"It's on account of old Lady Sladen. She weren't proper gentry, but she came from money. New money from the 'cradle of the cotton industry'. I heard her say the name of the place once."

"Cromford?" Sam had risked an interjection.

"That's the place." Martha had glared. "You know more'n you're lettin' on. Anyway, there were a house that went to her children, and no-one else could get at it. Well, by the time she died, she hadn't no children, so Aishling Small's bastard had to serve."

Two hours out from Waterford, Sam sat staring at a porthole in the *Milford*'s saloon. Beyond, a grey winter sea rose and tumbled, the wave crests topped off with white spray, but his mind was elsewhere. *For the sake of argument*, he thought, *I'll accept the story as it was told.* The Register of Births certainly bore it out, but he couldn't imagine that the pretence of Aishling Small's baby being a legitimate Slade hadn't leaked out somehow. Gossip was the lifeblood of small communities and it must have come to the ears of the Fancourt faction.

If Percy Fancourt knew, then he could have been manipulating Henry Slade for years. He could, for instance, have forced him into the Fenian world, to further some devious scheme hatched up in Dublin. But it didn't make sense for the puppet master to kill his puppet. The other way round; yes. Henry Slade must have wished himself free of Fancourt every day of his life.

———⋅•⋅•⋅———

The deal between two mates drinking together had led William further down the road to ruin than he'd been before. When the bargain was finally closed, he was well past going anywhere else and took a room at the Greyhound. Everything was swirling around him and, as he lay down, it got worse. Only in the morning, with a thumping head and unsteady legs, did he appreciate what a pit he'd fallen into. No breakfast either. It was, however, cheap.

Well, that and... and what. Why had he spent the evening getting drunk? Incongruously, his mother's voice pierced his headache. 'William, what have you been up to?' *What had he been up to? If only he could remember. He'd written something down; yes that must be it, his notebook.*

It certainly wasn't in its usual pocket, he felt for it there several times, and it wasn't in any of his other pockets either.

His headache got worse the more he bent down, but it was worth it. *Why, oh why, had he tucked it into the top of a sock?* Straightening up, the giddiness threatened; *shouldn't have moved so quickly*, he thought.

But there it was, the gist of a telegram delivered to Henry Slade on Sunday 28th January, and a bonus, too – old Ma Pepperell's address. She had to be worth talking to, he reasoned later, as the throbbing in his head receded. Her grandson had been asking directions some time ago, and men in railway servants' uniform had been seen near the place the night that the murder must have occurred. When Lizzie followed Sam's instruction and re-told her story, William thought she'd mentioned a disappointed booking clerk. Hadn't she…? Was his name Pepperell? The throbbing started again.

———

"What do you want, young man?" Old Ma Pepperell wasn't going to stand any nonsense. "Paid me rent on Friday. It ain't come round again, 'as it?"

"I'm not the ren—"

"An' the coal man comes of a Thursday, so 'es not due."

William waited.

"An' I took me milk in earlier… so what you doin' knockin' on me door?"

"I'm a policeman, and I just wanted to ask some questions." William got a penetrating stare from bright, beady eyes. She may have lost most of her teeth, but her wits were intact.

"Oh yes, and what'll they be about, these questions?"

"It might be easier if I came inside." The old lady seemed impervious to the cold, but William was feeling very fragile. About to let him in, she turned back.

"If you're a policeman, shouldn't you be showing me a card, or something?"

Panic struck. What if it was in his other sock? He couldn't remember the warrant card's whereabouts from the earlier journey round his person.

"Never mind, you look reet nesh, you'd best set y'sen by the fire."

Now, settled in her parlour. "Well, get on wi' it. I ain't got all day."

Once started on the subject of her grandson, there was no stopping. "He's allus been a grand lad, right from a little 'un. I used t' look after 'im a lot back then, an' 'e looks after me now. Comes of a Sunday mostly. Been a bit moody lately, I think he's sweet on a girl, but he ain't told me 'bout it. Came wi' a friend on Monday. Now that was odd."

"Coming with a friend?"

"Well that, yes, but the Monday really. It's usually a Sunday. Mind you, they looked like they'd been a long time on the journey, the two of 'em."

"How do mean?"

"Their uniforms were soaked through, like they'd been out in the wet all night."

"Uniforms? What sort of uniforms?"

"Y'know… railway uniforms. I don't understand 'em, but they weren't the same."

Indignant now. "I don't know what the world's coming to, I really don't. When I was a girl, if we wanted to go anywhere we walked. All this riding about on trains ain't natural. Never been on one and don't expect to." The old lady had been talking into space but she turned to William. "Do you know, Ben's friend came from Whaley Bridge? It were the other side of the world when I was young." Her mood changed. "Here, you 'aven't said why you're askin' all these questions." Mrs Pepperell glared at a nonplussed William, who'd said almost nothing. "Come on then, what're you askin' about?"

His hangover must have been improving. He had a flash of inspiration. "It's Ben's friend I'm interested in. Did Ben say his name?"

"Stephen, I think … or was it Thomas?"

———

It had started with his sergeant. Reluctantly, Superintendent Wayland had to admit to himself that almost everything of any consequence started with Sergeant Spray. What had he said?

"It was too easy."

Like the woodworm in his old campaign chest, the words had eaten away since Spray had spoken them. What if this last murder wasn't just a body in a rail yard? By Sunday afternoon, he'd made up his mind. He could just get a letter into the last collection.

It grieved him, though. Downes was all well and good, but he wasn't a gentleman, and getting him involved again was irksome. Nonetheless, newly-promoted Detective Chief Inspector Downes suffered the professional slight of a letter on Monday morning, addressed to his previous rank. The mail had been arranged so that the constable who had brought it into Downes's office would escape any backlash from the insult by the simple expedient of putting Wayland's letter at the bottom of the pile.

———

It was well through the morning before Wayland's letter received any attention, but when it did, Downes took notice. It was reading 'Sergeant Spray has been despatched to the scene to investigate any Fenian connection' that made his mind up for him. Had Wayland alone made such an assessment, he might have ignored the suggestion as fanciful, but Spray was a different matter. He assumed it was Spray who thought there was a Fenian connection and if that was the sergeant's judgement, then Downes was certainly interested.

Tomorrow, he would go to Crewe.

If there was a curse on vessels named *Milford*, it didn't strike on the Monday crossing, and Sam watched from her deck as she docked at Neyland in the early afternoon. The melee that had greeted rail passengers arriving on Saturday was repeated on the quayside. Porters touted for business, luggage was manhandled and Sam was ignored.

They weren't all heading for the hotel. A London boat train stood waiting and by Sam's calculation, it should get him to Gloucester in time to catch a Birmingham connection that day. He was hopeful that he might even make Crewe, if all went well. This time the country west of Carmarthen flashed by in daylight, and further on the eastern bank of the Towy, previously seen in the late afternoon gloom, had more delights to offer. The flood tide had filled the estuary and, as he approached Ferryside, a small boat full of passengers struggled to make a landing in time to catch the train. Across the water he could see a castle, still dominant despite being no more than a ruin. Sam made an enquiry, to be told that Llanstephan Castle had been:

"Built by English oppressors to control the Welsh a long

time ago, and nothing has changed in five hundred years." As he spoke, the guard's accent had become more impenetrable, and his words were suffused with a startling venom. The resentment of a respectable middle-aged man in a well-filled uniform, with shiny buttons bearing the crest of the Great Western Railway, was a revelation. Earlier in the investigation, Sam had tried to understand why a group of otherwise unexceptional men had been driven to take up arms and join the Fenian cause. A portly Welshman had revealed all.

"This'll take time. First ones do, y'know." Lizzie didn't know, but she was learning fast. "Have you got a cradle?" No, she hadn't, but to her relief, Elsie Maida had taken charge. "Is that young Jimmy still about?"

Jimmy, having delivered the message and taken Benjy out in the hope of a kill, had been in the yard gutting and deskinning. An unspoken agreement ruled. If the carcass was presented ready for the pot, no questions would be asked as to its provenance. Rabbit stew appeared on the table at least once a week at No 37.

"Send him to tell Fred to bring our old one. It'll be better than your bottom drawer."

Downstairs now, Lizzie had found Jimmy closing her meat safe on the principle ingredient of a meal.

"Just put summat in there fer ye', missus."

He'd seemed happy with another errand, and Benjy with an extra run.

It was next morning, after a night of fitful sleep – and on Mary's part, cramping pains – when Jimmy appeared again on his way to school.

"How's the lass? Has the bab come yet?" *He's a sponge,* Lizzie thought, *picking up anything and everything like a... like a detective.*

"Nothing yet, Jimmy, now be off with you or you'll be late for the bell."

She spoke with a confidence she didn't feel. Upstairs, Elsie was in charge, and to Lizzies's eye, her weariness was tinged with anxiety. How long was normal hadn't been discussed.

———

He couldn't put it off any longer. He'd been ordered to go to Whaley Bridge and assist Sergeant Spray. Nothing had been said about the possibility of Sergeant Spray not being there. So far, William could stretch the instruction to cover his actions, but no more. In the morning, he would have to travel to Crewe and present himself at the office.

He took what comfort he could on the journey back to Whaley Bridge. *It's not as if I'm empty-handed,* he thought. *I've the name of two suspects, a serviceable motive and site for the murder.* Any deductions he might have made about the missing sergeant, he'd keep to himself. The Whale couldn't complain... could he?

———

Gloucester meant changing stations. In the distance, he could see a crowd milling about on the Midland forecourt. Nearer, Sam became aware of raised voices and a lot of jostling. The Birmingham platform was choked, too, forming a continuous mass of unhappy, noisy and disappointed people. With no hope of getting to the ticket office for information, he asked a would-be passenger.

"Trains to Birmingham cancelled, they haven't said why."

Just then, gold braid on a smart peaked hat appeared, rising above the crowd as its owner climbed unsteadily onto a luggage trolley.

"Ladies and gentlemen…" There were cries of "not many of them about" from the unruly element.

"All services to the North are cancelled until tomorrow due to a derailment at…" The location was lost in shouts and boos. Disrespectful words were directed at the Midland Railway, and the Station Master retreated hastily before anything worse came his way. He was prevented by company rivalry from publicising an alternative route to Birmingham via Didcot on the GWR, even if the restive mob were in a mood to listen.

It would have been of no interest to Sam. He had in his pocket a return ticket for the Midland journey, and very little else. Rail travel was an expensive business, and crossing the Irish Sea on board a comfortable passenger ferry was even worse. He'd run out of money.

There was nothing for it but an uncomfortable night on the station, and a seat on the first train out in the morning.

Chapter 30

New life can be very noisy.

After a restless night, during which turns had been taken by Lizzie and Mrs Maida – as Mary insisted on calling Elsie – to sit dozing whilst the girl's labour dragged on, Tuesday's dawning provoked a change. The embarrassed mother found herself lying in a wet bed, and shortly after her waters had broken Mary started labouring in earnest.

She shouted out each time the spasms gripped her, comforted by Lizzie as best she could. In a life usually so well ordered, only Sam's disappearance to Dublin came close to eliciting the sense of helplessness she felt as Mary cried out with increasing frequency. Mopping her forehead with a damp cloth, and holding her hand as she gripped tighter each time her body tensed, seemed wholly inadequate in the face of the girl's need.

But then, after screams of ever greater intensity, it was over. The exhausted mother lay silent and turned her head away. Faced with an uncertain world beyond the womb, the newborn child took her first breath and started to cry.

There was no comforting the noisy infant. Elsie had her hands full attending to the afterbirth, changing bedding, and cleaning up the new mother. It was left to Lizzie, cradling the little scrap of new life, to try and bring her solace.

"Tek 'er downstairs and let 'er suck yer finger after you've dipped it in warm watter wi' a bit of sugar mixed in," had been Elsie's advice.

With the baby on one arm, Lizzie was attempting to mix

sugar into boiling water and then add cold, with the other hand. At least she knew a draught would be bad for the child.

"Don't stand there, come in or go out, but close the door." Jimmy should have been on his way to school. "Pour some of this into the cup so it's just warm." The boy stepped inside, and it was a relief to get him to help.

"The bab's arrived. Is it a boy, missus?"

With a sugary finger to suck on, to Lizzie's relief, the insistent bawling had stopped. "No, Jimmy, she's a little girl."

From Jimmy's tone, he'd have been more impressed by a boy. But he got as far as asking if she had a name and then trotted off to school with his trophy – a nugget of information that only he knew about.

———

"Is there enough for two?" The startled constable looked up to find Superintendent Wayland arriving at the office unexpectedly. Brewing tea so early was usually frowned on when the misdemeanour came to light, but not today.

Quite why The Whale had brushed his housekeeper aside and left without his breakfast wasn't clear, either to the servant or her master. *Certainly, if there was to be any response from Downes, it would be today,* he'd thought. Then, what about Archer? The man really was the limit. He'd had a clear order to report back about what was going on out there. Wayland quite forgot that it was only three days ago he'd issued the instruction, and that the third day was only an hour or two old. And what about his sergeant? Spray really should know better, it's his fault; he's leading the younger man astray. The superintendent peered irritably into the dregs, unwilling to admit his worry.

It was in this fractious state of mind that Constable Archer found his senior officer when he arrived a few minutes later. William had decided to extend his journey the evening before, and instead of staying in Whaley Bridge, to travel on to Stockport and Crewe to spend the night at home with his family. Not that he was greeted with unalloyed joy. His mother was pleased to see him, but his brothers had usurped his accommodation and were none too pleased to be squeezed back into their usual quarters.

If William had to face The Whale's wrath, he'd rather it was early in the day.

"Morning, sir." After knocking, he'd taken the unintelligible grunt as an invitation to proceed.

"Well? Have you made any progress? And where's Sergeant Spray?"

It seemed politic to answer in the order the questions had been asked. William had sketched out a report and started to read. "I proceeded as instructed to Whaley…"

"Good heavens, constable, I don't want all that taradiddle, just give me the meat."

With the essentials spelled out, Wayland was thoughtful. "So, if you're right, this was a local crime. Two young men set out to settle a score with a monster who'd abused a poor servant girl and left her with child. Nothing to do with the Fenians, after all…" A long silence followed. "And I've got that London policeman involved. He's going to think we've wasted his time." Another pause, then an eruption. "And Sergeant Spray, he got us into all this. You haven't told me—"

William was reprieved by a knock on the door. "There's a Detective Chief Inspector to see you, sir." The desk constable did his best, but Downes pushed past him.

"Morning, Wayland." He nodded perfunctorily to Archer.

"You wrote to me about a murder. Said Spray thought the Fenian business wasn't over yet." Carelessness about rank worked both ways. Superintendent Wayland bristled momentarily, but wilted as Downes took the second seat, uninvited.

"Tell the Detective Chief Inspector what you've told me, constable."

———

Enough coal to keep an overnight fire going in the waiting room was the best the Midland could manage for its stranded passengers. Those who were commencing their journey at Gloucester had gone home, but Sam and a small group who were in transit spent a cold night on uncomfortable benches and were stiff and chilled to the core by morning.

They'd been sustained by the promise of an early train for Birmingham and true enough, an elderly Midland locomotive clanked and snuffled its way into the station before daylight. The Parliamentary was boarded by a crowd of rough labouring types who had appeared suddenly minutes before the train, and gave no quarter to the interlopers. There was much pushing and shoving as every mile or two some left and others joined. At three times the journey length he and William had endured on their way to Manchester, the slow stopper took an age to reach New Street.

Finally, dishevelled, hungry and tired, Sam reached Crewe.

"Excuse me, sir." The midday mail had just been delivered and the postman was leaving as Sam tried to enter the office.

"Morning, sergeant, you look a bit..." the desk constable thought better of his comment. "Constable Archer and a detective chief inspector are in there with the superintendent. In a funny mood, 'e is; asked to share my tea with 'im earlier. All sounds a bit serious now, though." As he spoke, he'd been glancing at the recent delivery. "Here, sergeant, this is for you."

Sam, about to knock the door of the inner sanctum, opened the envelope instead.

———•••••———

The man on the visitor's chair was clearly indignant, but there was more. Detective Chief Inspector Downes was finding advantage in the situation, and revelling in the discomfiture of the officer opposite him.

Superintendent Wayland had the more comfortable seat; they were, after all, in his office, but that was his only satisfaction. He sat there, as a physical incarnation of his nickname might, wounded by the whaler's harpoon, but still capable of lashing out dangerously. Standing in a corner, attempting invisibility, was Constable Archer. It was he who had precipitated the standoff, having related the 'meat' of his investigation to each of the two senior men in turn. He had the air of a one who wished he'd kept his mouth shut.

It was this tableau, frozen for a moment, which met Sergeant Spray as he knocked and opened the door. He could recall the scene with great clarity later, but immediately he'd entered there was hubbub.

"Spray! Where the devil have you been?"

As The Whale spoke, so did Downes. "Ah, Spray, at last. You set all this rolling, what have you got to say for yourself?" The two voices clashed in an incomprehensible jumble of words. Had any of the others been looking, they would have seen relief on Constable Archer's face.

An uneasy, spiky order was restored.

"To answer your question first, sir," Sam turned to

The Whale, "I've been to Ireland; Waterf—"

"Ireland, sergeant? I expressly forbade any more journeys in that direction."

"If I remember correctly, sir, it was Dublin that was out of bounds."

"Don't know what you expected to find there," this from Downes. "Your constable has evidence to show this was a local matter. Tell him, Archer."

William's 'meat' was given another airing. At least this time it would be heard by a sympathetic ear.

"So, you've established a place where the man died, constable, and quite some distance away where he was thrown into the rail wagon."

"Yes, sir." The answer was directed to Spray.

"And you've identified a couple of young men with a motive who attacked him?"

"Yes, sir."

"What if they didn't kill him; just knocked him about a bit? Perhaps they thought they'd killed him without meaning to when he hit his head and didn't get up. The journey to the bridge would have been a lot easier if he'd come to his senses and walked there."

"I suppose so, sir."

Spray turned to his superintendent. "I have to admit, sir, I made a mistake right at the outset of this affair."

That any member of the assembled company of combatants could make such an admission brought a moment's stunned silence. As Spray went on, aggression seeped away. "I assumed, and led Constable Archer to believe, that the dead man had been bludgeoned to death. I think we can commend the work he's done on that assumption."

Wayland's harrumph suggested it was his prerogative to

distribute the accolades even though Spray had all the answers.

"But we now have a postmortem report." It was the 'we' that finally settled the peace. Sharing ownership of the intelligence that, 'Henry Slade died from a single bullet wound to the head' with the others, sealed it.

"It was all the blood and a big gash in the side of his head that fooled me." The report that had just arrived in the mail, was circulated.

"Somewhere near the Steeplehouse overbridge, there'll be a .422 calibre round."

"Really, sergeant, how can you know that?" Downes was intrigued.

"I know where the revolver is that it came from."

He had his audience now.

———

A finger dipped in sugar water was never going to satisfy the hungry infant for long, but worn out with the rigours of parturition, the little girl fell asleep. The upsurge of emotion engendered by the nursing of a newborn baby all but overwhelmed Lizzie. Their shared warmth was creating a bond, and she knew it would be hard to break.

Back up the stairs she went, to find an exhausted Elsie ready to go home.

"Goodness knows what Fred's been living on. His stomach'll think his throat's been cut. Give the bab to Mary for a bit, and then put it down in the cot."

There was no movement from Mary as she lay looking away.

"Look, Mary, this is your little girl." Lizzie bent over the recumbent mother. "Would you hold her for a while?"

Reluctantly she took the child, holding her as she might a bag of eggs, delicately but without emotion. The baby stirred at the disturbance, and Mary's first reaction to the baby was a look of panic in her eyes.

Elsie, as she went, said, "I'll be back later and see if she'll latch on."

Left alone with helplessness spread out in front of her, Lizzie could feel the panic spreading, too. *Get a grip on yourself,* she told herself, *this is only the beginning.*

———

"So, Slade was Fancourt's creature, you say, jumping about like a marionette whilst the puppet master played politics in Dublin... and worse." Wayland looked uncomfortable at Downes's analogy.

Sam's investigation was under discussion. "Yes, sir. That's how he must have come by a Royal Irish Constabulary revolver, from Fancourt. The Webley has RIC imprinted on it."

"So, how did it get back into Tobin's shed?" Things had become convivial enough for William to risk a question. The Whale, confidence restored, saw it as an impertinence and asserted his position by repeating the query.

"When Slade got that telegram," Sam turned toward the younger man, "of which Constable Archer obtained the contents, he must have felt the meeting with Fancourt might turn nasty, so he went armed."

"He'd be surprised by the two young railwaymen, but not frightened. After all, they hadn't sent the summons." Downes was getting into his stride. "He must have let them get too close and they put him down before he could get to his gun."

"Fancourt must have known all about Ravenhead. He may

even have being paying Tobin for information." Sam had thought there was something shifty about the handyman's answers at his questioning. "Slade would have been so groggy and couldn't stop Fancourt getting the gun when they finally met. After that, it was to the bridge, and bang. Then the revolver was returned to the shed."

"But why?" The question was on the lips of all three men, but it was The Whale who blurted it out. "Why would Fancourt want his man dead? With the hold he had over the whole Sladen tribe, he could manipulate Henry Slade into anything."

"Fear, sir; Slade's and his own. Slade was so frightened that Cathal Thomas had rumbled him that he killed him in a panic. Why else would he leave a body in Shallcross Yard, drawing attention to what they'd done with the dynamite?"

"How do we know for sure that it was Slade's work?" Downes wanted proof.

"I made a note of the calibre of the round that killed Thomas, and the one that killed Cubbin." Sam flicked the pages of his notebook. "And they match the revolver in Slade's possession."

"Hmm." Downes didn't sound convinced.

"When Slade lost his nerve, I believe Fancourt did, too. It was all very well to pull his strings, but if he couldn't be relied on to do the right dance, he was going to endanger the puppeteer as well as himself."

"He let the conspiracy go on, sergeant. If he was worried, why didn't he cut and run earlier?" Downes again.

"He must have thought things were under control after trying to intimidate the superintendent. But it didn't have the desired effect." It was a delicate matter, commenting on a superior officer's integrity without appearing impertinent. Having nodded in Wayland's direction, Sam continued.

"We missed Slade when the others were arrested. I believe

Fancourt thought we'd get to him in the end; it was safer to kill him."

There was a long silence. Each man with his own thoughts. Happiest of all was William Archer. He'd had a compliment from his sergeant for his part in the investigation, and avoided any tricky questions from The Whale.

For his part, Superintendent Wayland's bacon had been saved by Spray's arrival and his department had produced vital information. That had to show well in the final report, but he was still confused about Fancourt's behaviour. What was a gentleman doing getting mixed up with... with what? Which side was he really on? If only someone would explain, without him having to ask.

Downes, despite his apparent scepticism, believed the story, and was searching it for enough evidence to convict a man in court. He was ignoring the two young railwaymen. They'd done no more than give Slade what he deserved. Fancourt was the problem. They could try breaking down the handyman at Ravenhead, but Tobin might not talk, and they'd need to recover the lethal round from Steeplehouse: easier said than done.

Sam was tired enough not to care. Whatever happened next would be decided well above his head. He could do no more.

———

The summons came a week or two later. It started out from a very grand location at Euston, and had travelled via an office messenger to be put directly into the hand of a guard as he prepared for the departure of his train.

"You stop at Crewe, don't you?"

"Yes, sir. We change engines there."

"Very good. You'll have time to deliver this to Superintendent Wayland in the Constabulary Office."

It was an early train, and the letter was delivered before midday. No doubt its sender had planned it so, for Wayland was bid to be at the office of Mr Richard Moon, Chairman of the London & North Western Railway by half past five that very day.

Such meetings, crossing as they do an enormous gulf of social distinction, could be worrying. And as he travelled south, Charles Wayland recalled the discomfort of them both on their only previous meeting, orchestrated by Fancourt.

He was escorted through the building with the same disdain as on his previous visit, but this time the clerk led him to a door sporting an etched brass plate reading Richard Moon Esq., Chairman.

"Ah, Wayland, you two know each other." The three of them were inside the chairman's office, and Wayland nodded to his own superior officer who had already arrived. "I've been hearing good reports of your work." Moon nodded toward the other man. "And not only from our Chief of Constabulary."

The door opened discretely. "You'll take a drink?" A decanter and three glasses were brought in on a silver tray. "Scotch suit you, gentleman?" The servant poured generous measures and withdrew. "Now, to the matter in hand." There was warmth in Moon's tone and Wayland relaxed a little, allowing himself a sip of scotch.

"I had a meeting with the Home Secretary last evening. The Secretary of State for the Colonies, and the Commissioner of the Metropolitan Police were there. We discussed Fenian unrest and the way their most recent conspiracy was foiled. Praise was heaped on the Railway Constabulary, and your work in particular, Wayland."

As Moon sampled his scotch, Wayland found a gap in the discourse. "I must mention Sergeant Spray, sir. It was his work…"

"Yes, yes, Wayland, but it's your department, along with your Chief here. Where officers lead, the men follow." Moon spoke in a tone belying the pomposity of his words. "Amongst other things, my attention was drawn to this piece." A copy of the previous day's *Times* was proffered. It was folded so as to show a list of overseas appointments by the Colonial Office. Wayland started reading.

> *Lord Percy Fancourt.*
> *Appointed as Resident*
> *Officer to the Crown Colony*
> *of…*

"It's somewhere in the South Atlantic. Not much there. Last man died of drink after six months. Achieving justice not always a straight forward matter, don't 'y'know."

He finished reading and went to return the paper.

"Keep it, Wayland; show it round the office to anyone who's interested." Moon drained his glass and stood up, arm outstretched. "Pleasure to meet you, superintendent."

Pleasantries were over. The Whale dragged himself upright and shook hands with Moon and the Police Chief. As he turned away, the door opened as if by magic. From behind, he heard an exchange.

"Do something about the man Spray, would you."

"As you wish, sir."

End Piece

A thaw set in after heavy snowfalls earlier in February.

Whaley Bridge, deep in the Goyt valley, warmed a little and slowly the snow melted. Once the slush had cleared, optimists of the town held their breath, waiting for spring. Higher ground up in the Peak kept its white blanket for longer, but finally the melt water started careering downhill, giving the river menace as it raced and tumbled through the town.

Lizzie, too, waited and hoped. The days since Mary had given birth had been a worrying time. Her little one had been persuaded to latch on and took to the breast eagerly, but it was never Mary who picked the child up at feed time. And when suckling was over, it was Lizzie who would take the little girl and nurse her back to sleep. Elsie, having brought the confinement to a successful conclusion, was back caring for her family, and on her occasional visits saw only a thriving infant. Mary's listlessness was put down to the glooms. "It's common enough after the baby's born," she'd said. What Elsie didn't see were the times when despair led to bouts of inconsolable weeping, and moments of spite that hurt Lizzie, only for them to subside and leave the young mother withdrawn and torpid.

The cruelty in winter's tail arrived overnight. The temperature dropped, and by morning low grey-black clouds threatened. Sam had promised a visit and Lizzie worried he might get caught in the coming storm. In the event, his train arrived as the snow started, and walking up to No 37 his were the first footprints in its pristine whiteness.

For a while they chatted companionably before Lizzie went

off to see to the tea, leaving Sam to mend the parlour fire. A shovel full all but smothered it, but as he watched, flames came licking over the coals and what had smouldered a moment earlier burst into flames. A faint noise interrupted his reverie, possibly a footstep out in the hallway, and then the click of a latch.

Lizzie bustled in with a tray laid for three.

"I'll slip upstairs and see if I can tempt Mary."

"I heard someone go out." As he spoke, Sam turned to the window to see the snow, heavier now. Lizzie was already out of the room.

"She's gone." By now, a distraught Lizzie was back downstairs. "Sam, she's gone and so has the baby. They're out in this…"

Sipping freshly brewed tea and tending the fire were abandoned on the instant, and Sam was outside before he'd finished buttoning his coat. The imprints he'd made earlier had disappeared, but still visible were Mary's as she had made her way down Old Mill End. The fresh snow blanked out any sound of his footsteps, but lower down he could hear the river in full spate, rushing and tumbling its way along the valley. A forlorn figure standing against the balustrade of a bridge materialised through the blinding snow, and Sam, running and sliding now, called out.

Mary took no notice until he'd almost caught up with her.

"No… leave me alone, I'm not worthy, it's better…" She had turned toward him as she spoke, and he made a desperate lunge to stop the girl as she threw herself backward over the bridge's guard rail. It was done in a moment and, despite Sam having reached her, Mary fell, helpless, into the merciless, tearing, overfull, river Goyt below.

Stunned for a moment by his failure, Sam was surprised to

find he had a little bundle of warmth in his arms. Having slept through the tragedy, the baby opened her eyes and, liking what she saw, gurgled contentedly.

Glossary

Allus	Always
Ascendency (more properly, the Protestant Ascendency)	The landowners, judiciary, clergy and other professional classes who, as the ruling elite, contro..ed an Irish population largely composed of Catholics
Bawdy House	Brothel
Blower	Policeman's informant
Bluebottle	Policeman
Brig	Bridge
Cess	Railway track bed outside the running lines
Character	Testimonial given by an employer
Crow (of an engine's whistle)	A short blast to attract attention
Cut	Canal
Da	Father
Diagram	The planned route and timing of a train
Ducket	Projection on the side of a brake van with slit windows to enable the guard to see along the length of his train
Failed	An engine declared unfit for service by its driver (of an engine)
Four Foot	The gap between the rails of a running line

Ginnell	Passage between houses in a terrace
Growler	Four wheeled cab for hire
Jack	Policeman
Jimmy riddle	urinate
Judy	Prostitute
Knotty	North Staffordshire Railway
Light (of an engine)	An engine running with no train
Mark	Victim of a criminal act
Mugwump Specific	Treatment for Venereal Disease
Nebuchadnezzar	Penis
Nesh	Cold (reet nesh, very cold), of a person
Parliamentary (train)	One cheap train / day imposed on Railway companies in 1844 by Act of Parliament
Plain	Cheapest version of Guinness with the lowest alcohol content
Provost's Man	Military Policeman
P S (before a ships name)	Paddle Steamer
Romish	Catholic (slightly dismissive)
R. U. C.	Royal Ulster Constabulary
Rumman	General term for an odd person
Scally	Bad Lad
Sen	Self (y'sen, yourself)
Shant	Canal side drinking den
Shenanigan	Dishonest and amusing chaos
Six foot	The space between two sets of running lines
Snap	Workman's meal

Sojers	Soldiers
Strapping Post	Timber bollard set into the canal bank to take a rope hauled at an angle
Tubes (boiler)	Tubes running the length of a locomotive's boiler carrying smoke from the fire and heating the water
Weskit	Waistcoat

Historical Notes, Acknowledgements and Disclaimer

In the 1840s, *Phytophthora Infestans* spread throughout Europe. The fungus caused potato blight and its worst effects were felt in Ireland. By the time An Gorta Mór, as the Irish potato famine was called in Gaelic, was over the population had declined by two million, half of whom had starved to death. Failure of the potato crop was the immediate, but not the only cause, coming as it did to a people subjugated by a regime that found the local culture, at best, totally alien and, more commonly, dangerous.

Even as the peasantry were dying, grain was still being exported to England by the big estates. In the end, shortage of labour brought many of them down.

By the time this book opens, Charles Stewart Parnell had just entered parliament. His peaceful movement for land reform and a measure of self-government for Ireland was in its infancy, but gathering momentum. It was seen as a threat by the Fenians, who were prepared to fight for an independent state, and to the Ascendancy who were resistant to any change.

In the 1880s, an agent provocateur of doubtful provenance was involved in a Fenian plot to murder Queen Victoria. Christy Campbell, in his brilliant book *Fenian Fire*, exposes the details of deception and infighting between government departments and the police before it was foiled.

Echoes Down the Line owes much to Campbell's history for its main story, but it is populated by fictitious characters who are involved in imaginary events, bearing no relation to anyone living or dead. The Peak District and North East Cheshire provide much of the book's background, but specific locations are the product of the author's imagination.

About the Author

Educated at a Quaker school and Guys Hospital, the author has used material from his earlier life to inform his writing. A five generation connection with the Peak district provides it with a strong sense of place, and his interest in railways and canals provide its background.

The chance discovery in a second hand shop of a book about a Fenian conspiracy triggered an interest in the movement for Irish independence. *Echoes Down the Line* entwines aspects of this fight with more local matters.

This is his second novel. He has also written a number of unpublished short stories and is preparing a third volume in the Sam Spray series.

Coming up in *Signal Failures*

The man was more genial than he remembered.

Back then, in the company chairman's sumptuous office the two policemen had been a little in awe of their surroundings despite the congratulations being showered on them, and the tumblers of scotch.

Neither would have admitted to being intimidated at the time, and certainly not now when the more senior of the two was on his home turf. As Superintendent Wayland eyed him warily, the chief of the railway constabulary was doing his best to set his junior at ease.

"Good journey Charles?"

It was midday and the morning train had arrived on time.

"Fine, thank you, sir." The inconvenience of arriving at his office on Crewe station moments before a telegraph boy, whose missive instructed near instant embarkation for London, was not mentioned.

"No need for formality today, old chap; Montague, please."

It had been different back in India, thought Wayland. They had been junior officers together where he'd been known as The Whale and the other man as Monty, but Montague had stayed where he was in the regiment, rising to full colonel, whilst The Whale, unable to pay his way in a fashionable cavalry unit, had transferred to the engineers. There, advancement was without purchase, and he'd risen to a lesser rank; a more modest achievement in every way.

"I hear your men have been busy out there."

Wayland knew that 'out there' was anywhere north of Euston; alien territory to the police chief, and was grateful for it.

"Don't get north too often." Whiskey was being offered. Inferior to the chairman's, and in smaller glasses, too.

Wayland endeavoured to make his sip look like a good mouthful.

"We've a couple of investigations that are taking up the men's time."

"And yours, too, I hear."

My visit to the Home Office? thought Wayland. *How the devil had he heard about that?*

"Best if you leave the London stuff to those who know their way round the metropolis, Charles. Just tell us what you're after and we'll see to it… What were you after by the way?"

"Just a few details about official provision for the poor and needy." He'd done his best to avoid the trap, but without a doubt he'd been warned off.

"Good thing if you keep your chaps on routine matters, Charles. Excellent fellow that sergeant of yours, no doubt about it: bit like a ferret don't you know. Gets his teeth into things… most commendable, but best if you prize his jaw open and let this one go."

Previously published

It is December 1875 and the recently established Railway Constabulary is faced with its first murder case. Sergeant Sam Spray is in charge and along with his assistant Constable William Archer they explore the railways, canals and wild country of the White Peak. The many twists and turns of the case are complicated by the reserved sergeant's emotional entanglement with his landlady, the cool Elizabeth (Lizzie) Oldroyd. The case's solution and Sam's relationship with Lizzie turn out to be uncomfortably connected.

Fatal Connections
Published by Melrose Books, 2016
ISBN 978-1-910792-23-0   paperback
     978-1-910792-24-7   epub
     978-1-910792-25-4   mobi